YOUNG PETRELLA

YOUNG PETRELLA

MICHAEL GILBERT

PERENNIAL LIBRARY

Harper & Row, Publishers, New York
Cambridge, Philadelphia, San Francisco, Washington
London, Mexico City, São Paulo, Singapore, Sydney

"The Conspirators" was first published in the *Edgar Wallace Mystery* magazine in August 1966; the remainder in *Argosy* between November 1956 and August 1958.

LIBRARY OF CONGRESS CATALOG CARD NUMBER: 87-46138
ISBN: 0-06-015934-0

88 89 90 91 92 HC 10 9 8 7 6 5 4 3 2 1

Contents

Introduction

I have great affection for Patrick Petrella. My own youth as a
writer and his youth as a policeman started together on the
northern heights of London.

Time jerks by so quickly and so violently that these stories
have become, in a sense, history. They tell of a time when the
picture of the Metropolitan Police, as viewed by the public
and their elected local representatives, differed significantly
from the picture as it is seen today.

To the criminal the policeman has always been a natural
enemy. To the vast majority of the people, who are not
criminals, he used to be, just as naturally, a friend.

The criminal's outlook has not, I think, changed. He and
the policeman are both professionals engaged in a job of
work. When professionals come into opposition there is a
fight. Sometimes one side wins. Sometimes the other. There
is little rancour.

With some sections of the public, however, there has
unquestionably been a change. And whatever side one takes,
no one can deny that it is a change for the worse. There exist
now people, both black and white, who consider themselves
to be oppressed. To them, quite naturally, the police are the
arms of the oppressor. Summing up the opinions of a
selected group of black youths, the researchers of the Policy
Studies Institute recorded: "Everyone in the group held
unfavourable or highly unfavourable attitudes towards the
police force, ranging from deep bitterness and resentment to
feelings of hatred and animosity." This report was written in
1983, some twenty-five years after the period covered by
these stories. Had such a view been generally current at the
time it would, no doubt, have tinged them with darker
colours.

The difficulties which Petrella did encounter have not been
minimised. His superior officers often viewed the young
man with a suspicion which was, I am afraid, sometimes
well founded. "Do you know," Superintendent Barstow
asked him, "why God gave young policemen two feet but

7

only one head?" In two of the stories I introduced Councillor Hayes, who was openly hostile to the police. The editor of the magazine in which the stories were appearing was upset. Surely, she said, I was exaggerating. Members of the Council would support, not oppose, the efforts of their own force. Readers of today's press reports must judge for themselves whether I was exaggerating or understating the case.

So read the stories as history, as annals of a time lighter in some respects, darker in others, and differing in ways both large and small from the present. A time when £50 was a lot of money. A time when there were no such things as riot squads, and police were organised into divisions, not districts; a time when policemen might hope, if they did their job properly, to control the illegal import of cocaine; a time when the blue lamp did not mark the headquarters of a band of oppressors but was a lighthouse, shining hopefully in a dark and frightening street.

Prologue

The Conspirators

EVERY August, whilst Patrick Petrella was a detective constable up at Highside, the circus and funfair appeared on the Heath. If duty took him there, Petrella cut his visit as short as possible. Otherwise, his colleagues noticed, he avoided it altogether. Later, when he was promoted, and married, his wife remarked on the same peculiarity. He had not bothered to explain it to his colleagues at Highside. And he hesitated to do so even to his wife, from whom he had few secrets. In the end, he did tell her about it.

They were motoring in France, and had stopped in a village to buy stores for their midday meal. On the whitewashed wall, outside the *mairie*, a poster, faded by the hot sun of Provence, advertised the Cirque Jacquetti.

"Goodness," said Petrella, "I wonder if Sam Borner still runs it. I don't think he can do. He must be eighty, if he's still alive."

"Please tell me about Sam," said Jane, in her most irresistible voice.

Still Petrella hesitated. For it had all happened a long time ago. And it had been the first time he had grasped the fact that hate can be more compelling than love; and the first time that he had seen, in action, a conspiracy to kill. The passage of time had buried these events deep, but small things – the distant roar of a caged lion, a clockwork clown tumbling about the pavement, a tattered circus poster – still had the power to twitch at his nerves.

"I'll tell you when we stop for lunch," he said. "It was my first murder case. I was eleven years old at the time."

When you are young, each summer hangs on a thread of remembrance. A sight, a sound, a smell. To Patrick Petrella, that pre-war summer at Perpignan hung on a poster. Not faded and fly-blown like the one he had just seen, but eye-catching in its glorious colours. It depicted two white horses, in harness of black leather and trappings of gold, cantering round a sawdust ring, each ridden by a slender, graceful, grave-eyed lemur, dressed in a lady's riding-habit with a tiny crimson cap on one side of its furry head.

Patrick was vague as to why his family were in Perpignan – as vague as to why they had spent the summer before in Cairo or the summer before that in Casablanca. He knew that his father worked for the Spanish Government, and he surmised that it was government business which had brought them to the French side of the Pyrenees. It was something to do with refugees, and every now and then they would go for long drives through the mountains, meeting French and Spanish policemen and shepherds and muleteers on both sides of the frontier. But for the most part his father was closeted with Monsieur le Commissaire Theron, in the police station, and Patrick was free to amuse himself.

As well as his native Spanish he spoke street-boy Arabic and French, and he slipped about the sunlit streets of Perpignan, a thin, dark, friendly shadow, making new acquaintances along the river front, dropping one, picking up another, listening more than he spoke. It did not take him long to discover the Cirque Jacquetti in the Champ des Martyrs, the little plateau on the inland side of the city where the dragoons had shot and sabred more than a hundred unarmed Huguenots during the Repression.

The Champ des Martyrs was the permanent base of the Jacquettis. It was from there that its component parts, the first- and second-ring circuses, and the funfair, sometimes operating with the circus, and sometimes on its own, went out on planned marches, south to the Rock of Gibraltar, north as far as Bruges and Ostend, where they met, but did not trespass on, the territory of the other great European troupe, the German Müller-Hilde. Perpignan was their base. Patrick liked it best when, as now, it was almost empty. August was the peak of the trouping season. All that was left behind, inside the high wire perimeter, was a shed full of old funfair machinery, a row of caravans, most of them empty, the cages where the big cats lived, the stables for the horses, the kennels for the dogs, and a handful of people.

Manfredo and Ramon were called brothers, although, in the complicated in-breeding of circus life, no one quite knew whether they were really brothers, half-brothers, or cousins. Both were swarthy, handsome and attractive, and both were bullies, in the way that men who spend their lives controlling big cats often are.

Domenico Stromboli, who came from Naples, looked after the dogs. Or, to be truthful, the dogs looked after Stromboli. He was a cripple. Polio had reduced his arms and one of his legs to withered sticks. The circus had built him a little padded carriage, which two of the six Alsatians took turns to pull. He had first appeared, to Patrick's fascinated gaze, driving at a hand-canter across the wide and dusty compound, with two Alsatian dogs running escort in front of him and two more behind, surrounded by a tumbling, snapping, skirmishing pack of poodles.

Patrick had got into the closely guarded enclosure by the kindness of his special friend, Auguste. Auguste was a stand-in clown. He looked after the horses. His particular charges were Rosalie and Marguerite, the beautiful white thorough-breds, whose likeness Patrick had so often admired on the poster. They were resting for a few weeks. Sam Borner, who had married, twenty years before, into the Jacquetti family, and had now the controlling voice in the circus, knew the virtue of not overdriving a willing and successful turn.

"That's *his* caravan," said Auguste. "Would you like to have a peep at it?"

"I'd like to very much," said Petrella. "If he wouldn't mind."

"He's in town, with Donna. Nina may be there. She won't tell on us."

They climbed the stairs and opened the door, cut in two halves, heavy as a lock gate, built to last, like everything in that wonderful vehicle.

Patrick thought he had never seen anything so entrancing in his whole life. It was at once snug and spacious, and entirely beautiful.

Everything that could shine, shone. The polished teak-wood tables, and settles and built-in cupboards; the brass fittings of the lamps, and the window and door-fittings, and the ship's chronometer above the stove, itself a gleaming altar of glazed brick and winking steel. In one corner stood the cage where Leopold and Lorenzo, the riding lemurs lived. They sat on a log and stared back at Patrick as he gazed, round-eyed, at them.

Lorenzo wrinkled up his eyes, and lifted his upper lip.

"He's laughing at me," said Patrick.

"Laughing at me," agreed a gruff voice behind him. Patrick swung round.

The largest parrot he had ever seen was sitting on a table behind the door.

He was dark bottle-green all over, except for plum-coloured ruffs around his legs. His head was cocked on one side, and a single round yellow eye was fixed on the boy.

"Oh," said Patrick. "Oh, what a beauty."

"What a beauty," said the bird complacently. It swung down neatly from the rail on top of the cupboard and waddled along the window-seat.

"Stand still," said Auguste. "Quite still. He likes you, I think."

"W-what," said Patrick, "w-wwould he do if he didn't?"

"Bite your ear off," said Auguste. "Just you ask Ramon or Manfredo. It's war to the knife between them and Nestor. They used to tease him – pull his tail feathers out. He bit Manfredo through the thumb. Nearly cut it off."

Patrick watched the parrot, scarcely daring to breathe. It sidled along the table top towards him, still transfixing him with one unwinking yellow eye. Then it dipped its green head suddenly forward, caught the corner of Patrick's handkerchief, and whipped it out of his pocket.

"Hey!" said Patrick.

"Hey!" said the parrot, dropped the handkerchief and broke into a scream of laughter.

"He *does* like you, see," said a long-legged, dark-haired girl. She had come out of the back part of the caravan, where she had been tidying and cleaning the bedroom. "If he takes something of yours, it shows he likes you."

She picked up the parrot without fuss, held it in one hand, and smoothed its head feathers with the other. The parrot preened itself.

"This person is Nina," said Auguste. "She is a wonderful girl. She is loved by all creatures, and fears none."

Although he was only eleven, Patrick was an observant boy, and when Auguste said "creatures" it occurred to him that he might be including two-legged creatures as well. She was a very attractive girl.

The week that followed was a week of unmixed delight. Tolerated by old Stromboli, encouraged by Auguste and

Nina, he explored every corner of the Jacquetti encampment. He avoided Ramon and Manfredo and studied the great Sam Borner, owner and boss of the Jacquettis, and his wife Donna, from a respectful distance. But these were only the humans. It was the animals which entranced him. The six great Alsatian dogs, who were the policemen of the kingdom, and the tumbling crowd of poodles who formed the CID – sharp-eyed, sneaky, ubiquitous. The old circus horses, their working life over, who lived at ease, grazing behind the caravans by day and stabled by night in the shed opposite Sam Borner's caravan. Rosalie and Marguerite, queens of the ring, each with a stall of her own, with a name on a shingle nailed over it; the great cats, in their cages at the far end of the enclosure, to be watched like Ramon and Manfredo but not approached. White doves which lived on the rafters of the pony-shed, and would come to Nina when she whistled. A marmoset which shared Auguste's caravan, and spent its day vainly trying to catch the pigeons. Leopold and Lorenzo the lemurs, who could ride and look after horses as well as any stable boy, who lived in Sam Borner's caravan, and were taken out of their cage by Nina every afternoon for a walk on long leather leads; and Nestor the parrot, said to be more than a hundred years old, and very wise.

It was at the end of that week, on the Sunday morning, that Monsieur Theron came to call on Patrick's father.

Their talk took place in the front sitting-room, a place of French rectitude and gloom. M. Theron was a middle-aged Basque with a short brown beard and a deceptively mild appearance. It was later to deceive the Germans, to their undoing. Patrick sat, unnoticed, in a corner behind a table covered with family photographs. He listened, in growing horror, to what was being recounted.

"Dead," said M. Theron. "The skull fractured by a single blow."

"How long?"

"Discovered at six o'clock this morning. The doctor said that death must have occurred at least five hours before. Not more than seven."

"Died about midnight, then," said Patrick's father.

Patrick had heard only scraps of the earlier conversation.

15

He had thought they were talking about refugees. Now he wished that he had listened. Because it was to do with the circus. Someone had been killed.

"We have held his brother for questioning."

So! It was Manfredo or Ramon. Patrick felt a sense of relief. It would have been terrible if it had been one of his friends: Auguste, or Nina, or Stromboli. Even the majestic Sam Borner, or his kindly little wife. If someone had to be dead, better one of the savage Spaniards.

"It will be difficult to prove anything," said M. Theron. "It is true that the field is surrounded by a barbed-wire fence, but an active man could surmount it almost anywhere."

"Have you any particular reason to suspect Ramon?"

"Spaniards —" said M. Theron, and then stopped. It had occurred to him that what he was about to say might not, in the circumstances, be very tactful.

"Can behave like wild beasts," agreed Patrick's father, smoothly. "But there is usually some particular reason for a killing as cold-blooded as this would seem to have been."

"The brothers were drinking in the Café d'Algerie – it is a riverside drinking place – until close on eleven o'clock. They were excited, and shouting. They left separately. So far that is all we have established."

When M. Theron had departed, Patrick said to his father, "It is *not* true."

"What is not true, Patrick?"

"It is not true that anyone from outside could get over the wire fence and into the field of the circus. By day, it would be difficult. By night, impossible."

"How so?"

"Because of the dogs. Would you like to try?"

Patrick's father looked at him seriously. He said, "I have no official standing here. M. Theron consults me because he is friendly, and, I suspect, a little out of his depth with a case which involves two Spaniards, a Yorkshireman with a Milanese wife, a Neapolitan, a Belgian, and a local girl."

Patrick's mouth opened.

"B-but," he said, "how do you know about these people?"

"You have talked to me about them, many times."

"I talked to you," said Patrick, "but you didn't listen."

"When you grow up and become a policeman," said his father, "as I believe is your intention, you will find that it is a

16

great advantage not to appear too attentive. As I was saying,
I have no status in this matter. But if what you tell me is true,
it is clearly a fact of importance, which should be established
in a proper scientific manner. We will take a walk together,
this evening, after dinner."

They approached the Champ des Martyrs with due
precaution, from the back. It was a soft night, with the moon
half full. Ahead of them loomed the bulk of the machinery
shed, concealing them from view. The corner of the wire
fence was supported here by an upright of iron angle-bar.

"This would be the best place," said Patrick's father. He
spoke in a whisper. "Will you go over, or shall I?"

"I'd better," said Patrick. "They know me."

He gripped the stanchion, and climbed up, easily enough,
using the strands of the wire as steps. He had reached the top,
and was steadying himself, with one hand on the roof of the
shed, when a shrill yap sounded. As Patrick dropped to the
ground, two dark forms materialised at the corner of the
shed.

Patrick moved out from behind the shed, into the
moonlight. The Alsatians were uncertain. The boy looked,
and smelled, like someone they knew, but was behaving
suspiciously. A small black dog ran up. Patrick stopped, and
it jumped into his arms and started licking his face. The
Alsatians lost interest. If Kiki vouched for the stranger, he
was all right. Patrick walked back to his father, put the toy
poodle gently down and climbed out.

"You see?" he said.

"Yes," said his father. "I see."

The processes of the law are never quick. It was nearly a
week later that Sam Borner's wife called on them. Donna
Borner had been fifteen, a promising equestrienne, when
Sam had married her and inherited his slice of the Jacquetti
enterprise. Twenty-five years of married life and the rearing
of three sons had rounded out her figure and engraved some
wrinkles on her face, but, until that black week, life had
treated her kindly.

Now she was frightened.

She said, in an accent in which her north Italian consonants
mixed curiously with broad Yorkshire vowels, "They have

taken Sam for questioning. They took him this morning.
They will not let me see him. It is a terrible mistake."

Patrick's father made her sit down. He talked to her, and
Patrick admired the skill with which he extracted the facts
without seeming to ask any questions at all.

The police, at first, had suspected Ramon. He was a violent
man, he had been drinking, he had been the last person seen
with Manfredo. But he could have had no hand in the killing.
When he left the café he had caused an uproar by trying to
break into the house of a girl he knew. The police had been
called. He had been arrested, and had spent the night in one
of the police lock-ups. As soon as this was established he had,
of course, to be released.

"*I* should not have let him go quite so quickly," said
Patrick's father. "I should like to know exactly at what time
he caused this convenient uproar."

Donna Borner was uncertain. What she did know was that
Ramon, exculpated, had turned inquisitor. He had vowed to
find the killer of his brother. And the possible suspects were
so very few. The killing had occurred just outside the pony-
shed, inside the camp. It was not at all easy for an outsider to
get in undetected, because of the dogs.

Patrick's father nodded. He said that he knew about the
dogs. Who could have been in the camp, legitimately, that
night?

The answer was simple. Stromboli, neither of whose arms
was strong enough to lift a tack-hammer, let alone a sledge
hammer. Auguste, who had a caravan in the middle of the
line of caravans. Donna herself, and her husband. They had
the caravan at the end, nearest to the pony-shed. The other
caravans belonged to people who were out on circuit, and
they were empty. Ramon and Manfredo had a caravan at the
far end, near the cages of the big cats who were in their
charge.

Patrick's father had a pencil in his hand, and was drawing a
little sketch as she spoke, marking in the stables, the dog
kennels, the machine-sheds and the cages, round three sides
of a square, and the line of caravans along the top.

He said, "And Nina?"

"How did you know about Nina?" asked Donna. "Oh, I
see . . . " She had spotted Patrick, in his favourite place in
the corner. "The boy told you. He is friends with all at the

18

camp. It could not have been Nina. She is a local girl. She sleeps at home."

Patrick's father was drawing a series of little arrows on his diagram. One ran from the corner behind the shed to the dog-kennels; a second from the kennels to the pony stables; a third from the stables to the line of caravans.

"So," he said at last. "Auguste – or your husband."

"Certainly, it could have been Auguste," agreed M. Theron. "Although he is thin as a rush, he is tough as a rush, too, and has very strong wrists and forearms. All clowns have. It is their early training in tumbling. Certainly he had a motive also. Not long ago he interfered to defend Nina when Manfredo was being offensive, and received a thrashing for his pains."

"Then — ?" said Patrick's father.

"Fortunately for him – unfortunately for Monsieur Borner – Auguste can show that he was nowhere near the camp that night." He looked out of the corner of his eye at Patrick, and said: "Auguste spent that night with Nina, in her house."

Patrick's father said to him, "I think you'd better buzz off, old boy."

"Oh, nonsense," said Patrick impatiently. "We all knew that Auguste was Nina's lover. That's why he stuck up for her, and got knocked about by Manfredo. Manfredo wanted her himself. I didn't say anything about it because I wasn't sure whether it was a terribly good alibi. After all, if she was fond of him, she'd say he was there, wouldn't she?"

M. Theron smiled, and said, "Very true. But in this case the concierge of the house where Nina lodges confirms it. Auguste arrived at ten o'clock in the evening, and did not leave until six o'clock the following morning."

"A concierge is a zealous watch dog," said Patrick's father. "But even she must sleep sometimes."

"Agreed," said M. Theron. "But this one did not go to bed before one o'clock. Until that time she could hear the man and girl laughing and talking in their room. Manfredo, remember, was dead by one o'clock."

"Did she see Auguste, or simply hear his voice?"

"Heard him," said M. Theron. "What was in your mind?"

"He has a funny high-pitched voice. Easy to imitate."

"That's true enough," said Patrick. "I've heard Nestor – he's the Borners' parrot – imitate him exactly. But then, he can take off all of them."

M. Theron was frowning.

"I am a man of logic," he said. "If it be accepted that no one except its regular inmates could enter the camp after dark without being detected by the dogs, we have the following position. A man is struck down and killed, with a heavy instrument – most probably of metal and circular in shape, according to the autopsy – a sledge hammer, perhaps. The man who is killed was a bully, and a lecher. Any one of his fellows might have had cause to strike the blow. When was the blow struck? Between eleven o'clock and one o'clock, says the doctor. But we can be more precise than that. The man Stromboli heard Manfredo come back to the camp."

Patrick and his father looked up quickly.

"Yes. That is so. We learned it only this morning. The old man sleeps with his dogs. The sharp-eared *caniches!* They woke him at midnight. He heard Manfredo. The inmates, when they come in late, they do not use the gate. There are places at the back where they climb through the wire."

"He knew it must be one of the regulars," said Patrick's father. "But how did he know it was Manfredo?"

"He heard him. Manfredo was intoxicated. And he was talking to himself – loudly."

"Did Stromboli go out to see?"

"He says no. He would not interfere with Manfredo sober. Certainly not when he was intoxicated."

Patrick's father had taken out his sketch plan. Now he marked a spot behind the row of machinery-sheds.

"Manfredo would climb in on the south side, behind the machinery-sheds – here? Emerge by the end of the sheds, pass Stromboli and the dogs – so? And make his way across the open centre of the compound, towards the row of caravans on the north side."

M. Theron nodded. "And these caravans, remember, Senor Petrella, at that precise moment, were all empty save one. The large caravan at the end, occupied by Borner and his wife. Let us suppose that Borner hears this sot approaching. Staggering across the open. He sees his chance.

20

He picks up a heavy, iron tent hammer. He creeps up behind him. One blow, and it is finished."

"But why? Why would he do it?"

"He had a reason. All the circus knew it. I have no doubt your boy knows it, too."

Patrick looked at his father, who said, "Tell me."

"It was about ten days ago," said Patrick unhappily. "Three days before Manfredo was killed. Nina was taking Leopold and Lorenzo for their afternoon walk – they are the lemurs, who live in Sam Borner's caravan and ride the ponies. Lorenzo slipped his leash, got into Manfredo's caravan and stole an orange. They're both terrible thieves. Manfredo chased him out, and Lorenzo got into a tree, and started to eat the orange and throw the peel at Manfredo. Everyone was laughing – except Manfredo. He was mad. He got his long whip, the one he uses on his cats, and flicked Lorenzo with it. It nearly cut his tail off."

"And do you think," said his father, "that that would be sufficient provocation — ?"

"Circus people think of their animals as children," said M. Theron. "If someone flicked your child with a whip — ?"

"They're terribly valuable, too," said Patrick. "They ride Rosalie and Marguerite, you see. It's one of the main attractions of the circus. They're awfully clever with them. Just like real jockeys. It's taken Sam fifteen years to train them."

Patrick broke off. It suddenly occurred to him that he might be talking too much. His father had returned to his sketch plan.

"One thing puzzles me," he said. "Manfredo was found in the entrance of the stable."

"If you are thinking," said M. Theron, with a smile, "that one of the horses may have kicked him, I can assure you that it is impossible. Unless it had legs of elastic! The nearest horse was tethered in its stall a full ten paces from the door."

"I wasn't thinking of that. I was wondering what he was doing there at all. His caravan is at the other end of the line. Crossing the open compound he would go to the right to get to it. Why did he bear left-handed towards the stables?"

"Who knows?" said M. Theron. "He was drunk. He may have lost direction."

"He might," said Patrick's father. "It's curious, all the

same." He was frowning in a way that Patrick recognised. He said, "I, too, am a man of logic. I will concede to you that Borner is the only man who could have done this thing *by himself*. His wife would be a tacit accomplice, but we need not concern ourselves with her. Have you, however, considered that it could have been done, quite easily, by *two* people in concert – a conspiracy?"

It was clear that M. Theron had not thought about it.

"I will suggest two possible combinations. There may well be more. Clearly Auguste and Nina could have worked it. No one *saw* Auguste after eleven o'clock. The concierge heard his high-pitched voice. A voice which, as we have heard, even the parrot could imitate. If a parrot, how much more easily could a clever girl do so?"

M. Theron frowned and said, "Auguste seems to me – somehow – pyschologically an unlikely murderer."

"Agreed. Then let me suggest a second one. Ramon. Who knows what tensions may grow between brothers? Did not Cain kill Abel?"

"But — "

"But Ramon was in a police-station cell by midnight. Agreed. But suppose he followed his brother back to the circus, killed him at half past eleven, and immediately took steps to have himself arrested. That trouble he stirred up – it seemed to me a little obvious even at the time."

"But — "

"But we are told that Manfredo was alive at twelve. Who by? By Stromboli. But who knows that *he* may not be in with Ramon? The two of them together — "

"A conspiracy," said M. Theron. He sounded unhappy; as a man may, who has arrived at what seems to be the unique solution of a problem, and perceived that it may, at best, be one of three.

"I worked out a fourth possibility," said Patrick's father, "involving Ramon, Stromboli *and* Sam Borner."

"No, no," said M. Theron. "Three is enough. You have said quite sufficient to make me doubt my own diagnosis. Possibly I ought to let Mr. Borner go? It is not right to detain a man who might be innocent. On the other hand, it might be wise to detain him for his own protection. That brute, Ramon, has sworn to avenge his brother."

22

He took himself off, a worried frown on his good-natured face. After he had gone, Patrick said to his father, "Did you really believe any of those ideas, or did you make them up to get Sam out of a hole?"

"Didn't they sound convincing?"

"Oh, yes. They were terribly convincing."

Patrick's father looked hard at him. If his son was capable of pulling his leg, he must be growing up.

"But I gather that they didn't convince you."

"They were quite all right," said Patrick. "Quite logical. They *could* have planned it like that. The thing is, though, that they *wouldn't*. Auguste isn't the sort of person to kill anyone. And Ramon bickers a lot with Manfredo, but he wouldn't kill him. Manfredo was killed by someone who *hated* him. I'm positive of that."

"By Sam Borner, then?"

"Not by Sam," said Patrick. He said it in such an odd tone, that his father looked at him again. The boy had gone white.

The idea had not come to him suddenly. It had grown, from little things; things noticed, things heard, half observation, half impression. It was not a logical solution. It was more like a picture. He saw Manfredo, full of wine, muttering and stumbling, climbing through the wire perimeter at the well-known place, steering an unsteady course across the dusty, moonlit compound, towards his caravan and bed. And then – his father had noticed it – something must have diverted him. Patrick did not believe that Manfredo drifted off course. A drunken man has a compass which takes him to his own bed. *Something* had attracted him to the front of the pony-shed and, inside that dark entrance, the murderer was crouched, ready to kill.

It might be proved, too. Only the time was short, and getting shorter.

In three or four days, the main circus would be back, the camp would be full of shouting, working, jostling people; the lights would be on most of the night as they repaired, against time, machinery and equipment for the autumn circuit. The caravans would all be occupied, the clues would be trampled underfoot and the scent would be cold. Also his mother would be back.

She had more belief in the value of an English boarding school than either Patrick or his father. Her first experiment had been unsuccessful. Three years before she had chosen a school on paper and dispatched Patrick to it without further enquiry. A few weeks after his arrival the headmaster's son, a lout of ten, had tried to bully this eight-year-old new boy. He had been half killed for his pains. Patrick had learned about fighting from the small banditti of the slums of Madrid. His methods were unorthodox but drastic. The headmaster had beaten Patrick, but done nothing to his son. That was quite enough, and Patrick had removed himself and made his way home. When his father had heard what he had to say he had supported him and Patrick had resumed the enjoyable freedom of life with his peripatetic family.

Now, he realised, things were different. His mother had departed for England and set about a personal inspection of schools and headmasters coupled with talks to friends who had young sons. This time, no doubt, she would find a decent school for him. And when she got back his liberty would be curtailed.

He spent the next two days on the quayside. Anyone will talk to a polite, good-looking, eleven-year-old boy. Patrick listened. There was a single piece of information that he needed. It was late on the evening of the second day – after nine o'clock – that the son of the proprietor of one of the waterside cafés brought him the news. Patrick went back with him, to confirm it. He wanted no slip-up. The boys stood and peered through the bead-curtained window. Ramon was sitting at a table, staring at the wall. There was a half-empty bottle on the table.

"It's his second," said the boy. "If he makes trouble, my father and his brother will handle him. Shall we stay to watch?"

"No," said Patrick. "I must telephone."

"Why waste money?" said the boy. "Use ours. It is in the passage. I will show you."

Patrick spoke to the housekeeper. His father was out, and would not be back until late.

"When he comes," said Patrick, "tell him – tell him that I am going with some of my friends for a moonlight picnic — "

He cut short her protests by ringing off.

Ten minutes later, he was climbing, alone, into the circus enclosure. When the poodles had inspected him, and the Alsatians had sniffed, and passed him, he walked round the perimeter of the enclosure, keeping as much as possible in the shadows, until he came to the line of caravans. Here he moved very cautiously. He was making for an empty caravan, next to the Borners' at the end of the line. There was a light in the sleeping quarters of the Borners' van. That would be Donna. Even when she got into bed and turned out her light, she would probably not sleep very soundly. She would be worrying about Sam.

Great care was necessary.

Patrick fitted into the lock of the empty caravan the key which Nina had, very unwillingly, lent to him, eased it round gently, and went in. It was not so elaborately equipped as the Borners' caravan, but was constructed on the same lines. There was a cushioned couch under the side window. Patrick climbed onto it, and opened the window.

It was a night of magic. The full face of the moon looked down from a sky of black velvet. It was so bright that it seemed to be generating a light and heat of its own.

And it was very quiet. Patrick could hear the clack of sharp little hoofs on the concrete as Rosalie or Marguerite moved in her stall, and, away on the far side of the compound, a throaty rumble as old Rosso the lion dreamed of the forests of his youth.

From where he knelt, every detail of the living-room of the Borners' caravan was picked out in the cold white moonlight. Opposite to him, on his perch by the open window, sat Nestor, the big green parrot. His eyes were shut. Of Nestor, alone among all the birds and animals of the circus, Patrick was afraid. He had been afraid since he had discovered, in a book of his father's, that Nestor was his real name. *Nestor notabilis,* the sheep-killing parrot of Australia and New Zealand. He had read how they would fly onto a terrified and cornered sheep and peck through its back, into its liver. He had read, too, how the enraged farmers tried to trap them and how the parrots, endowed with almost human cunning and calculation, had avoided all the snares that were set for them, and even set traps themselves in return.

Nestor had opened his eyes. For a moment, Patrick thought he had seen him; that he was going to open his hooked beak, and scream out a warning to the camp. Then he saw that Nestor had his head cocked and was listening.

The next moment, Patrick heard it too. It was the sound of

Ramon returning.

Nestor sidled along his perch towards Leopold and Lorenzo. Patrick could see that they, too, were awake, moving like shadows, noiselessly, from side to side in their cage.

The door of their cage was fastened with a simple bolt, set well out of reach of the lemurs' arms. Nestor reached out with his beak, lifted the arm of the bolt, and struck it. There was a tiny, metallic clang as the door swung open, and the monkeys were gone, out of the cage, and out of the window. Nestor hopped onto the sill, and the next moment, he was gone, too. Only the door of the cage, swinging open, showed Patrick that he had not imagined the whole thing.

As he climbed down the steps of the caravan he could see Ramon clearly. The man had come out from behind the shed, and was tacking, unsteadily, across the open, moonlit square.

Then the voice of Auguste spoke from the shadows by the stable. It called out, "Ramon." The imitation was so perfect that even Patrick, who knew it was Nestor, was deceived for a moment.

Ramon swung to his left. The voice added three unforgivable words in gutter Spanish. Ramon broke into a shambling run. Patrick was close enough to see the moonlight glinting from the knife which he carried, blade upwards, Spanish-fashion, in his left hand. Patrick padded after him, his plimsolls noiseless in the dust. As he rounded the corner, the voice of Auguste spoke for the third time. It came from inside the stable now, rather high up, towards the right.

The moonlight illuminated a small area in the mouth of the shed. In the middle, Ramon stood swaying. On the left – Patrick's heart missed a beat as he saw it – was the pony Rosalie. She had been moved by the lemurs out of her stall, and now stood, fastened only by her head rope, to a ring just inside the door. Leopold sat astride her, jockey-wise. Lorenzo crouched on the edge of the stall by her head.

For a heart-beat, no one moved. Then Lorenzo bent forward and bit Rosalie's ear. At the same moment, Ramon stumbled. The stumble saved his life. Rosalie's steel-tipped hoof, lashing out, missed his head, but hit him, with a splintering crack, in the left shoulder. He went down, rolled like an acrobat, and came up on his feet again. The crack must have been his collar bone going, for his left arm was hanging limp. The shock had knocked all the drink out of him.

Rosalie was whinnying and stamping behind him, but he ignored her. He was staring, his face pale as the moon itself, at the rafter above his head.

Nestor was sitting there. He stared down at him with unblinking yellow eyes. It was a battle of wills, and the stronger will prevailed. Ramon turned on his heel and walked away. As he went the great green parrot gave a scream of derision and triumph.

Ramon broke into a shambling run.

"So," said M. Theron. "The brother, Ramon, has taken himself off. He crossed the frontier, illicitly, in the early hours of the morning. A guardia saw him, but could not stop him."

"Do we want to stop him?" asked Patrick's father. "Going off like that – it amounts to an admission of guilt. You will have to let Mr. Borner go, now."

"Of course. I have done so," said M. Theron. "It is unsatisfactory, all the same. I like a case to be neatly rounded. All the strings tied up. I should like to know why he killed his brother, and what he did it with. And who helped him. For it must have been the work of confederates."

"I don't suppose we shall ever know the real truth," said Patrick's father. And to Patrick, after M. Theron had taken himself off, he said, "You're looking absolutely done. You must have been out very late last night. I didn't hear you come in."

"I was a bit late," said Patrick.

"It was a last fling," said his father. "Your mother's back today. I've had a letter from her. She's chosen the school. She enclosed the prospectus. It's on the South Downs. Association football in the Christmas term and Rugby football in the Easter term. Two headmasters and a qualified matron. It sounds a splendid place, this time. Much better than the last one we tried."

Patrick thought it sounded all right.

27

Detective Constable

Who Has Seen the Wind?

TO Detective Chief Inspector Haxtell education was something you dodged at school and picked up afterwards as you went along.

"All I need in my job," he would say, "I learned in the street." And he would glare down at Detective Petrella, whom he had once found improving his mind with Dr. Bentley's *Dissertation on Fallacies* at a time when he should have been thumbing his way through the current number of *Hue & Cry*.

Petrella was, of course, an unusual detective constable. He spoke four languages. One of them was Arabic, for he had attended the University at Beirut. He knew about subjects like viniculture and the theory of the five-lever lock; and had an endlessly enquiring mind.

The Chief Inspector approved of that.

"Curiosity," he said. "Know your people. If you don't know, ask questions. Find out. It's better than book-learning."

Petrella accepted the rebuke in good part. There was a lot of truth in it. Most police work was knowledge; knowledge of an infinity of small, everyday facts, unimportant by themselves, deadly when taken together.

Nevertheless, and in spite of the Chief Inspector, he retained an obstinate conviction that there were other things as well; deeper things and finer things; colours, shapes and sounds of absolute beauty, unconnected with the world of small people in small houses in grey streets. And whilst in one pocket of his old raincoat he might carry Moriarty's *Police Law,* in the other would lie, dog-eared with use, the *Golden Treasury of Palgrave.*

"She walks in beauty, like the night of cloudless climes and starry skies," said Petrella, and, "That car's been there a long time. If it's still there when I come back it might be worth looking into."

He was on his way to Lavender Street to see a man called Perkoff about a missing bicycle. It was as he was walking down Barnaby Passage that he forgot poetry and remembered that he was a policeman.

For something was missing. Something as closely connected with Barnaby Passage as mild with bitter or bacon with eggs. The noise of the Harrington children at play.

There were six of them, and Barnaby Passage, which ran alongside their back garden, was their stamping ground.

On the last occasion that Petrella had walked through it, a well-aimed potato had carried away his hat and he had turned in time to see the elfin face of Micky Harrington disappear behind a row of dustbins. He had done nothing about it, first because it did not befit the dignity of a plain-clothes detective to chase a small boy, and secondly because he would not have had the smallest chance of catching him.

Even when not making themselves felt, the Harrington family could always be heard. At school? No, too late. In bed? Much too early. Away somewhere? The Harrington family rarely went away. And if by any chance they had moved, that was something he ought to know about too, for they were part of his charge. Six months ago, he had helped to arrest Rick Harrington. It had taken three of them to do it. Rick had fought because he knew what was coming to him. It was third time unlucky and he was due for a full stretch.

Mrs Harrington had shown only token resentment at this sudden removal of her husband for a certain nine and a possible twelve years. He was a man who took a belt to his children and a boot to his women. Not only when he was drunk, which would have been natural, and forgivable, but with cold ferocity when sober.

Petrella paused at the corner, where the blank walls of Barnaby Passage opened out into Barnaby Row. It was at that moment that a line of Rossetti came into his head. "Who has seen the wind?" he murmured to himself. "Neither you nor I."

A casement rattled up and an old woman pushed out her head.

"Lookin' for someone?"

"Er, good evening, Mrs. Minter," said Petrella politely. "I wasn't going to – that's to say, I wondered what had happened to Mrs. Harrington. You can usually hear her family."

"Noisy little bastards," said Mrs. Minter. But she said it

without feeling. Children and flies, hope and despair, dirt and love and death; she had seen them all from her little window.

"I wondered if they'd gone away."

"They're home," said Mrs. Minter. "And Missus Harrington." Her eyes were button bright.

"Well, thank you," said Petrella. His mouth felt dry now that he found his suspicions suddenly come close.

"You're welcome," said Mrs. Minter.

As Petrella turned away he heard the window slamming down and the click of the bolt going home.

He climbed the steps. Signs of calamity were all about him. The brass dolphin knocker unpolished, the steps unwhited. A lace curtain twitched in the front window; and behind the curtain – something stirred.

Petrella knocked.

He had lifted the knocker a second time when it was twitched out of his hand by the sudden opening of the door, and Mrs. Harrington stood there. She was still the ghost of the pretty girl Rick Harrington had married ten years before but life and rough usage had sand-papered her down to something finer and smaller than nature had ever intended. Her fair hair was drawn tightly over her head and all her girl's curves were turning into planes and angles.

Usually she managed a smile for Petrella, but today there was nothing behind her eyes but emptiness.

"Can I come in?" he asked.

"Well – yes, all right."

She made no move. Only when Petrella actually stepped towards her did she half turn to let him past her, up the dark, narrow hall.

"How are the children?" he asked; and saw for himself. The six Harrington children were all in the front room, and all silent. The oldest child, Timmy, and the next oldest, Hazel, were making a pretence of reading books, but the four younger ones were just sitting and staring.

"You're very quiet this morning," he said. "Has the scissor man come along and cut all your tongues out?"

The eldest boy tried out a grin. It wasn't a very convincing grin, but it lasted long enough for Petrella to see some freshly dried blood inside the lip.

I can smell tiger, he thought. The brute's here all right. He

33

must have made his break this morning. If it had been any earlier, the news would have reached the station before I left it.

"I'd like a word with you," he said. "Perhaps you could ask the children to clear out for a moment." He looked at the door which led, as he knew, into the kitchen.

"Not in there," she said quickly. "Out into the hall."

Now that he knew, it was obvious. The smallest boy had his eyes glued to the kitchen door in a sort of dumb horror.

They shuffled out into the hall. Petrella said softly, "I'm not sure you hadn't better go too. There's going to be trouble."

She looked at him with sudden understanding. Then she said, in a loud, rough voice, "I don't know what you're talking about. If you've got anything to say, say it and get out. I got my work to do."

"All right," said Petrella. "If you want to play it that way." He was moving as he spoke. The door to the kitchen was a fragile thing. He ran at it, at the last moment swinging his foot up so that the sole of his heavy shoe landed flat and hard, an inch below the handle.

The door jumped backwards, hit something that was behind it, and checked. Petrella slid through the opening.

Rick Harrington was on his knees, on the floor. The door edge had cut open his head, and he had, on his stupid face, the look of a boxer when the ring gets up and hits him.

Petrella fell on top of him. He was giving away too much in weight and strength and fighting experience for any sort of finesse.

Under his weight Harrington flattened for a moment, then braced himself and bucked.

Petrella had his right arm in a lock round the man's neck, and hung on.

Steel fingers tore at his arm, plucked it away, and the lumpy body jerked again, and straightened. Next moment they were both on their feet, glaring at each other.

In the front room the woman was screaming, steadily, and a growing clamour showed that the street was astir. In the tiny kitchen it was still a private fight.

Then Harrington swung on his heel and made for the window into the garden. For a moment Petrella was tempted. He jumped for the big man's legs, and they were down on the floor again, squirming and fighting and groping.

There was only one end to that. The bigger man carried all the guns. First he got Petrella by the hair and thumped his head on the linoleum. Then he shambled to his feet and, as Petrella turned onto his knees, swung a boot.

If it had landed square that would have been the end of Petrella as a policeman, and maybe as a man, as well; but he saw it coming and rolled to avoid it. And, in the moment that it missed him, plucked at the other foot. Harrington came down and in his fall brought the kitchen table with him. A bowl of dripping rolled on to the floor spilling its brown contents in a slow and loving circle. Petrella, on his knees, watched it, fascinated.

Then he realised that he was alone.

His mind was working well enough to bring him to his feet but his legs seemed to have an existence of their own. They took him out into the front room, which was empty, and then into the hall.

He was dimly aware of the children, all staring at him, all silent. The door was open. In the street footsteps, running.

"You won't catch him now," said Mrs. Harrington.

He turned his head to look at her, and the sudden movement seemed to clear his brain.

"I'm going after him," he said. "Ring the police."

Then he was out in the street, and running. Mrs Minter shouted, "Down there, mister," and pointed. He stumbled, and righted himself. Harrington was already disappearing round the corner. Petrella shambled after him.

When he got to the corner there was one car in the road ahead of him and no one in sight. The car was moving, accelerating; a big, blue, four-door saloon. Too far away to see the number.

"Got away!"

A second car drew up behind him, and a voice said, politely, "Is there anything wrong?"

Petrella became aware that he was standing, swaying, in the middle of the road. Behind him, its bonnet inches from his back, was a neat little sports car in two shades of green, driven by a fat young man with fair hair and a Brigade of Guards moustache.

35

"Police," said Petrella. "Got to get after that car. It's stolen."

The blue saloon was turning into the High Street now. "Move over. I'll drive."

"Hop in," said the young man. "You don't look too fit. I'd better do the driving. It's a tricky little bus this till you get the hang of it."

"All right," muttered Petrella. "But quick."

The young man took him at his word. The little car jumped forward like a horse at the touch of a spur. They cornered into the High Street, under the nose of a bus, and shot down the middle of the crowded road.

The young man hardly seemed to have moved in his seat. He handled his car like a craftsman, insolently exact, both meticulous and careless at the same time.

"Right fork ahead. He's going up to the Heath, I think."

"His neck'll be for sale if he does much more of that," said the young man, calmly. The blue saloon had pulled out, charged past a bus, and only just got back again ahead of the oncoming lorry.

"I say," said Petrella, "you can drive."

"Done a good deal of it," said the man. "Rally stuff mostly, a bit on the track. Name of Blech."

Petrella placed him then.

Time came, and time went, and they were off the Heath and making for the maze of small streets which fills the triangle between Hampstead, Regents Park and Camden Town.

"I'm a bit too light to ram him," said Blech. "No need, really. All we have to do is keep in sight. He'll do himself soon."

It happened, as he was speaking. The road went up in a hump over the canal. The blue saloon hit the rise so fast that it almost took off, came down threshing and screaming, and went into a long, sideways skid, hit the low parapet, and toppled over.

Blech came neatly to a halt, and Petrella was out, and running again.

The blue car was standing on its nose in three feet of water and mud, sinking ponderously. Petrella got the rear door open and pulled. Behind him, Blech pulled. As the car fell away from them, the bulk of Rick Harrington tumbled back on top of them.

Petrella seized him by the hair and hammered his head on the towing-path.

He felt a restraining hand on his arm, and the mists cleared again for a moment.

"I think," said Blech, "that you're being rather too – er – vigorous with him. What he wants is first aid, really."

"Sorry," said Petrella. "Not thinking very straight. Fact is, I think I'm a bit concussed myself."

"That makes two of you. If you helped we might get him into my car." They did this, between them. The street slept in a timeless summer's evening doze. From first to last no other person appeared on the scene.

"Where to now?"

Petrella tried to think. Harrington was out. There was a big purple bruise on one side of his forehead, and an occasional bubble formed in the corner of his open mouth. He was a hospital case. But no hospital would take him in without explanations. Nor would any other police station.

"Home," he said. "The way we came. It'll be quicker in the long run."

They drove home decorously, back up on to the Heath, and west, with the setting sun in their eyes. For a few seconds Petrella dozed. That wouldn't do. No time to sleep. Job not finished. Better talk and keep awake.

"It's very good of you," he said, "to take all this trouble."

"Enjoyed it," said Blech. "What is he?"

"He's an escaped convict," said Petrella. "Called Harrington. Not a pleasant character."

"How did you cotton on to him?"

How had he? It was so many years ago. A great gale was singing through his head. A mighty diapason of sound, that came and went. "It was Rossetti put me on to him," he said, as the gale dropped for a moment.

"Rossetti? The Blessed Damozel — "

"Not Dante Gabriel. Christina. *'Who has seen the wind? Neither you nor I. But when the trees bow down their heads the wind is passing by.'* Fork left here."

"That's nice," said Blech. "Is there any more of it?"

" *'Who has seen the wind? Neither I nor you. But when the leaves hang trembling, the wind is passing through.'* " (That was it!

Hang trembling. It was the children that had made him certain. Sitting there like drugged mice.)

"I must remember that," said Blech. "Here we are. You'd better get some help with your passenger. And then you ought to lie down or something, I think."

Chief Inspector Haxtell reckoned that he was beyond surprise, but the events of that evening tried him hard. First there came two stalwart constables, supporting the drooping figure of a convict of whose escape on transit from one prison to another he had been notified only an hour previously; secondly a diffident figure, whose face he vaguely recognised from the columns of the popular press; and, bringing up the rear, his shirt torn open to the waist, his face rimmed with blood and dried dripping, Detective Petrella.

When he had sorted things out a bit, he sat down to make his report. Plainly it was a case which reflected the greatest credit on all concerned. And a lot of it must, and should, go to Petrella. And, according to Petrella, Blech had behaved very well. A German, but a good chap. So far, so good. But what the Inspector couldn't make out was exactly what credit was to be given to a person called Rossetti. Sounded like some sort of Italian. Further enquiries needed there. His pen scratched busily . . .

The Prophet and the Bird

THE Prophet appeared on an evening of late summer. He drifted along the sun-warmed pavement of the High Street, dressed in the remains of five good suits clobbered together with string. His beard, which veiled the area between his lower lip and his top waistcoat button, was the colour of badly worn snow. Across his shoulder he bore a staff, to the upper end of which was tacked a disc of plywood. On one side, red letters on black said, "Smite and Spare Not." On the obverse was, "Suffer Little Children," in yellow on blue.

The Prophet was suffering little children. A small group was following him, open-mouthed, up the pavement. Every few minutes he would stop to address them, and the children would retreat, their mouths hanging open. They were not out to annoy him. They were just waiting for him to do something.

Detective Constable Patrick Petrella was on his way to keep an appointment when he saw the Prophet. Like all detectives he had his own private, hardly-acquired, scrupulously-guarded, never-to-be-mentioned, list of informers. Useful contacts: some in the underworld, some on the fringes of it; some quite respectable, but with a talent for meddling or a spiteful mind. A few of them sold information coldly, for money. But the payment was so small and the risks were so great that some more complex motive than greed must have been at work in their dark minds.

So that he should never slip into mentioning their real names, Petrella spoke and wrote and thought of them by nicknames. There was the one-legged paper-seller (Peg-leg) and the big, tawny doorman at the local cinema (Leo); and there was the Bird. The Bird was the best of the lot, the only one, so far, who had never let him down.

It was the Bird he was meeting that evening at ten o'clock in a cul-de-sac off the less frequented end of the High Street. If the Bird was willing to sing both loudly and clearly, then it was possible – just possible – that a nasty little collection of thugs, who wore black pantomime masks and carried fish-hooks in their cuffs and called themselves the Cats, might be put where they belonged for a year or two.

The Cats were specialists in shop robbery. They attacked old women in back-street shops, the sort which stayed open until all hours; small dark shops in small dark streets, which often had a surprising amount of money in the till.

He was in plenty of time. The gate in the wall had been left unpadlocked and he eased it open, slipped through, and shut it behind him. It was a small timber yard, on the slope which ran down to the railway, and it was well situated for such meetings. Good contacts could never be hurried. Petrella spread his raincoat and sat down on it. He had spent some hours the previous evening with a nice old lady who had had her face pulled open by the Cats' claws, and for a chance of getting back at them he was prepared to wait a long time.

An occasional electric train curled sparking up out of the mist, oddly silent, teetered on the points and disappeared like a cheerful ghost under the road bridge where the High Street crossed the line. Petrella lit his pipe. An increase of noise on the other side of the fence suggested that the pubs were shutting.

It was at about this time that the landlord of the Feathers looked at his clock and made a sign to his assistant. The assistant read the sign correctly. It meant, "Any trouble, you slip out and fetch a policeman." The assistant edged towards the serving door.

"Now gentlemen," said the landlord. "For the third and last time."

There were five of them at the table in the window. The one they called Len was, perhaps, thirty. He had a hard, white, Londoner's face, sloe-black eyes, and a lack of expression which was more frightening than the animation of the four youngsters with him. They were all drinking whisky. Even Timmy Harrington who hardly looked his sixteen years.

"Don't you hear the gentleman, Len? He says it's time."

"See if you can get another round, Timmy," suggested Len, calmly.

The boy gathered the five thin glasses together in his right hand, a finger in each, and drew them together with a crack. Holding them so, he walked to the counter, stretched out his hand, and opened it. The glasses clattered down on the polished wood. For a moment after he had dropped them, his hand remained, the fingers bent, like a big claw.

"Same again, chum," he said.

"It's ten minutes past time now."

"Len," said the boy over his shoulder. "Gentleman says no."

"Ask him if he wants that luvverly new window of his pushed in," said Len. "Tell him I might lean against it on the way out."

Where the others had drunk themselves gay he had drunk himself quiet and ugly.

The landlord looked quickly over his shoulder and his assistant ducked through the door. But Len saw him go.

He climbed to his feet, walked across to the bar, and said "The boyfriend's gone for help? All right. Don't bother about that drink. We'll put it on the slate this time."

He shook his sleeve, then drew his hand twice, firmly, across the bar counter. The landlord was still staring at the cross, cut a clean half-inch into the polished wood, when the door slammed behind the last of the boys. He wiped his forehead with the beer cloth, and breathed out deeply.

On the pavement the little army gathered itself together.

"Blow me down," said Timmy, "there's that Prophet. We oughter do something about that beard of his. Can't be healthy. What say we trim it for him, Len – ?"

He broke off. Len wasn't looking at the Prophet. His eyes were on a spot, in the shadows, ten yards along the pavement. He moved quickly. The woman looked over her shoulder, seemed half inclined to run for it, then stopped.

Len walked right up to her. She stepped backwards, into the deep doorway of a shop. Len continued to advance until his face was almost touching hers.

"Who've you been drinking with tonight?" he said.

"I never."

"Soon as my back's turned, you're out of the house with some pretty boy."

"I came out to buy some cigarettes."

"Two hours after the shops shut?"

"From the machine."

"Who've you been with?"

"I haven't been with anyone." Her head was twisting from side to side, hopelessly. She was not looking for help. She was nerving herself for what was to come.

A sudden, wicked, stinging slap on the side of the face. Then another. She shook her head. There was a small, dark drop of blood where Len's ring had cut her cheek open.

"Are you going to talk?" said Len. "Or do you want I should use the knuckles on you?"

"Leave that woman alone," said a deep voice.

The Prophet loomed in a doorway.

Len looked up. The madness slowly left him. "You go and chase yourself," he said. "She's my wife. I can talk to her if I want."

41

"I say you shall not strike her," said the Prophet.

"Fix him," said Len shortly.

It was a good fight, while it lasted. One against five is long odds, but the Prophet had a staff and knew how to use it. His first, scything movement cut the nearest boy's legs from under him and his second put Timmy Harrington backwards into a shop window. After that he used the point. When the police arrived, and the boys scattered, he was still on his feet.

Petrella, aroused by the sound of breaking glass, had climbed onto a crate and watched the proceedings over the fence. He saw no reason to interfere. When it was all over he collected his raincoat, came softly out, and went home to bed.

He realised that it was no use waiting any longer for the Bird that night.

The Cats hung out in a loft above a junk store in Parson Street. It was a good place for them, because it had six different ways in and out. And they knew them all. Here Len dispensed justice and wisdom to his followers.

Sober, he was something of a tactician. Under his rule the Cats had learned to steal only money. And to spend it steadily, not in sudden, suspicious bouts of affluence. He had taught them that the clinching argument was a blow. You go in, he said, and you ask for sutthink that costs a few bob and you give 'em a pound note, see? That means they got to open the till. Right? Then you smash 'em, grab what's in the till, and beat it. No clever stuff. Under his guidance they had prospered.

Until recently.

Then came the carefully planned combined operation against a larger shop, with a manager and two girl assistants, which might have been black disaster. At the very last moment, warned by some underground sense, Len had called it off. He had then scouted round by himself, and spotted the police tender parked behind the hoarding across the way.

He had also seen something else. A John the Baptist in beard and rags, motionless at the end of the street.

"Someone put the finger on us," he said. "And I'm wondering just who."

42

"Must have been that flickering prophet," said one of the others.

"Could be," said Len. "Might have been young Timmy."

They looked up to see if he was joking; his face was expressionless as a washed dish.

"Why would it be Timmy?"

"I didn't say it was," said Len. "I said it might be. He's friends with that dick, ent he? I seen 'em talking the other day. He's so young he doesn't think what he's saying, perhaps."

Timmy Harrington came in at this moment. He usually took the route across the roof and through the skylight, because he was still young enough to enjoy climbing for its own sake. This time he was in a hurry, so he came up through the trapdoor.

"I did what you said," he explained. "I watched the back door and slipped by when the old woman — "

"Cut the narrative," said Len. "Tell us what you found."

Timmy, deflated, said, "You know all that old clobber he wears, rags and pieces. Well, he's got a nice suit in his wardrobe. And shirts and shoes and socks. And – and something else."

He held his right hand out and they crowded round him. It was the last, the ultimate argument. A small, old-fashioned, blue-plated pistol.

"And it's loaded," said Timmy.

"I'd better look after that," said Len. No one demurred. He slipped it into his pocket. "What's your idea about this geezer, Timmy?"

"I think he's a copper," said Timmy. "You know – a ghost. Someone they've planted here . . . "

There was an uneasy silence in the loft. It was exactly as if a shadow had stalked across the room.

"What say we lie low for a bit, Len?" said one of the boys.

"Nuts," said Len. The weight in his pocket gave him confidence. "He's no copper. He's a cheap stoolie. When I'm finished with him he'll wish he was back wherever it was he came from. First thing, we want to find out what he's up to. Right? We take it in turns. One of us watch him all the time. Use your loaf. Keep out of sight. We'll soon see what he's at. Then we can fix him."

If the Prophet knew that he was being watched, he gave no

43

sign of it. Most of his day he spent, as before, drifting quietly along the pavements of Pond End and Highside, going no further north than the Main Circular Road, sometimes dropping south as far as the railway terminals and goods depots of Sonning Town.

But most of the time he spent with the children and they, with the instinct of the streets, seemed to realise that he meant them no harm. Hour after hour they would follow him, an early and unusual Father Christmas, carrying no sacks of toys, but big with infinite possibilities of mystery.

"He talks to them," said Petrella.

"As long as he only talks," said big Sergeant Gwilliam.

"The matron of the Highside Children's Home got a bit worried at first. He hangs round there a lot. But from what I can make out he does the children no harm."

"Loitering with intent?"

Petrella considered the matter, but shook his head. Although, as a policeman, he had a well-founded distrust of any unknown character who hung about for long doing nothing, this didn't make sense.

"There's nothing to steal," he said. "The place is just full of kids and beds and bedpans."

"Different thing five years ago when it was a private house. Old Sir Louis Borderer. Then it *would* have been worth a go."

Petrella cast his mind back.

"He was the collector, wasn't he? Died some years ago. A lot of his stuff went to a museum."

"That's right," said Sergeant Gwilliam. "It was before my time. I was in South London then. Why?"

"Was there ever a burglary there? A big one?"

"I expect so," said Gwilliam. "There was plenty worth stealing. Records would be able to tell you. Why?"

"Just an idea," said Petrella.

Sergeant Gwilliam looked at him suspiciously. He distrusted young detective constables who got ideas. Petrella went off to look for the Bird, who had been somewhat elusive lately. He had a feeling that some useful information might by now be forthcoming from that source.

The matron at Highside Children's Home was a single-minded extrovert. A daily life spent in grappling with local authorities, keeping together an underpaid staff, and composing the difficulties of a hundred children left her with little time for reflection.

There came a time in every day, though. The last half hour before she sought her own bed; when her charges were asleep, and the telephone had stopped wrangling. She liked to spend it out in the summer-house. It was a beautiful little baroque temple, lovingly transported, stone by stone, from its native Arezzo by the enthusiastic Sir Louis, as a wedding present for his third wife. In it he had placed, as a sort of table, a pediment of great antiquity, unearthed at Capua. A heavy square of old, hewn stone. On it the matron would place her knitting bag, her spare glasses, and her evening newspaper. Beside it she erected her deck chair.

Her thoughts, as usual, were on the problems of the day. That funny old man. She was inclined to believe the children, when they said he meant no harm.

"Sometimes he talks to us," Lizzie Ferrers had said, "sometimes he asks us questions." What about? "Oh, anything. Getting up time. Meal time. Bedtime. The habits of the staff. The routine of the home." Very odd, thought the matron. Looking up, she saw him.

Clear, in the bright moonlight. Then he was gone. He had dodged in among the trees on the far side of the lawn. Her first thought was to go back and ring for the police. Being a resolute woman she decided to wait for a moment, and watch. The back door of the summer-house led directly to the garden door of the house and there was no chance of being cut off. And there was something else, too. The matron had spent part of her professional life in a home for old people, and as the Prophet came out again into the moonlight at the edge of the trees, she noticed that he was holding himself and moving like a man of half his age.

The next thing she saw was that he was not alone. There were flitting figures behind him, among the trees. Three – no, four – men following him.

She decided that it was time to move. As she turned, the attack developed. Two men flung themselves at the Prophet, who whirled to meet them. A twisting knot of figures went to the ground with a thud which could be heard clear across the intervening distance.

As the matron panted up to the garden door, she received a

further shock. A police car was already coming up the drive. Sergeant Gwilliam jumped from it before it had stopped.

"They're over there." She pointed. "Fighting. Quick, and you'll get them."

"They won't get out without wings," said the Sergeant. "We've had the place surrounded an hour."

He disappeared with his followers at the double. The matron went in and mixed herself a strong drink of brandy from the emergency store.

Chief Inspector Haxtell counted up the score later that evening with Sergeant Gwilliam and Petrella, who had got too close to a flailing Len and had picked up a black eye and a broken nose. They were in matron's sitting-room, which had been turned into a temporary first-aid post.

"First," said the Chief Inspector, "we've got the Prophet, alias Dicky Bird, alias ninety-five other things, who came out of Parkhurst three weeks ago, where he'd been doing a long stretch for burglary. As soon as we get him out of the hospital we'll charge him with – what?"

"Being on enclosed premises," suggested Sergeant Gwilliam.

"I suppose so. I take it that it's some sort of felony to try and re-steal stolen goods."

"Would you very much mind explaining what it's all about," said the matron.

"Certainly, ma'am. This house used to belong to Sir Louis Borderer. Just before his death Bird broke in and cleaned up Sir Louis' collection of Italian Court jewellery – good old-fashioned stuff, gold and diamonds mostly. He was picked up two days later, and charged. Most of the loot was never discovered. The police took all his known hiding-places to pieces, brick by brick. No good. It was even hinted that he might get a remission if he talked. He preferred to take the full rap. He reckoned the stuff was safe enough. It had never left the grounds. He'd lifted that pedestal in the summer-house, and shoved it in the hollow underneath."

"Do you mean to say," said the matron, "that sort of table thing I put my knitting on?"

"That's right, ma'am. Tonight, when he saw the game was up, he told us. I reckon he calculated we couldn't put him away twice for the same job. Which may be right."

"And those others?"

"Ah," said the Chief Inspector. "There we're on much firmer ground. Breaking in with intent to commit violence. And the leader was armed. He'd a loaded gun in his pocket. That ought to take care of *him* for a bit."

"Well," said the matron, "all I can say is that it's very lucky you happened to be there."

"Very lucky indeed," said Haxtell blandly.

Later that evening he talked to Petrella.

"It came out very nicely, didn't it?" said Petrella, happily. "They'd left young Timmy outside, on guard, and he got away. We might pull him in too – but I think it'd be better, don't you, to leave him out of this charge?"

"If you say so," said Haxtell. "Any particular reason?"

"Well, they're bound to work out that *someone* gave them away," said Petrella. "Their first idea was the Prophet. But of course, as it turned out, it couldn't have been him. Then, I think, they suspected Timmy. They knew the boy was friendly with me. If we let him off, they'll be sure they were right."

"Yes," said the Chief Inspector, slowly. "Yes, I suppose that is the best way. May lead to trouble in the future."

It would lead to a lot worse trouble, thought Petrella, if Len ever realised that his wife was the Bird.

Nothing Ever Happens on Highside

To Detective Constable Patrick Petrella the section called Highside was the least interesting part of the manor. It stretched, like the lives of its inhabitants, from the Lying-in Hospital at the foot of the hill to the public cemetery at the top; a honeycomb of tight, respectable streets constructed, as an act of faith, out of yellow brick and second-quality slates by a tight, respectable builder.

The backbone of Highside was Haig Road, and Petrella was walking up it to see a Mr. Gosport who might be able to give him some information about two other men, who might know something about alleged irregularities at the railway depot. A thunderstorm had been hanging over North London all day. The evening was heavy with undischarged artillery; and his feet kept reminding Petrella that he had been on top of them for fifteen hours.

Ahead of him, out of a side road, came Sir Douglas Haig. That was what it seemed like at the time. It was all there, the neat, compact figure, the clipped grey moustache, the kindly, ruthless eye; the eye of Bapaume and Passchendaele, the eye of Ancre and the Somme.

He was walking well, for a man of his age. But that was right, too, thought Petrella. Had not the Field Marshal kept his mind and his figure to the last? Suppose that, as a preliminary penance, great men were condemned to visit every street and square and public house named after them. The Duke of Wellington and Prince Albert would have walked a few miles and drunk a few pints before they won their way to paradise.

When he reached the top of the hill the Field Marshal had disappeared. No, as you were. Petrella, standing on the corner of the pavement, could see his head. He had gone into the cemetery, and was sitting – or was he kneeling? – by one of the new white marble crosses.

Petrella trudged on. Mr. Gosport was not at home. Mrs. Gosport explained that he was on nights now. He might be back in time for breakfast. It all depended on shifts. Or that was what *he* said. She had no way of checking on him. Sometimes he said he'd been working a double shift and came home full of beer. Once she'd found a girl's hair-clip wedged in his top pocket. He hadn't tried *that* lark twice.

Petrella listened with a quarter of his mind and made sympathetic noises at the right places.

When he got out he went back to the cemetery. The grey man was gone. Petrella found a new cross and squatted beside it to read the spidery, gothic lettering.

"Arthur Millichip. The summons came for him in his 84th year. At rest awaiting the last call."

A boy and a girl were walking together on the pavement opposite. Petrella couldn't see them, but he heard the boy say, "Swing in a lovely centre and Sam just nodded it into the net." The girl said, "Go on." She even managed to sound interested.

Courting, thought Petrella. He won't get away with spiels like that once he's married.

He could have gone home himself, to supper and bed. So far as he kept any hours he was long past the end of his duty, and the house where he lodged with Mrs. Catt was only two streets off. Instead, he trudged back to the police station.

As he was climbing the stairs to the CID room he heard Sergeant Gwilliam laughing. It was the sort of laugh which took more than a locked door to contain it. There was sixteen stone of Sergeant Gwilliam, but very little of it was fat, and he had played rugby football for the police in the golden pre-war days when the blue jerseys had carried all before them in London Club football; and twice for Wales.

"What's the joke?" said Petrella.

"Guess who just come in?"

"I'm too tired to guess."

"Ginny Lewis."

"Came in, or was brought in?" asked Petrella. Ginny was a hard character, past his first evil youth; a middle-aged bully grown callous in wrong-doing.

"Walked in on his own feet. The joke is what he came here for."

Petrella could think of nothing save force which would bring Ginny to a police station.

"He came," said Sergeant Gwilliam impressively, "to see could he have police protection."

Petrella laughed too, but absent-mindedly. Something was nibbling at the edges of memory.

When he got home, he was almost too tired to eat, and fell into his bed, and to sleep. It was not the easy sleep of comfortable tiredness and relaxation. He was so near the surface that he saw the lightning, and was wide awake before the thunder rattled the slates of the little house. Then the rain came, in a steady drumming roar, and passed on.

It was in the silence which followed that the still, small voice of conscience said to Petrella, "Of course, you fool, you were looking at the wrong grave."

It took no more than three minutes to throw on some clothes and then he was out in the street, belting his raincoat as he went. The stars were hidden, but the air felt cooler, and there was a tinkle of fresh water running down the gutters. He climbed the cemetery railings without difficulty – they were designed to keep the children out, not the dead in. On the gravel path he paused for a moment. It was not going to be so easy to find the exact spot he wanted.

When he had stood on the pavement earlier in the evening, he had seen the grey man's head. And the man had been sitting, or squatting down. Later, when he himself had knelt beside one of the graves, a young couple had passed, and he had been quite unable to see either of them. *Therefore he had been too far down the slope.* A good deal too far.

The best plan would be to locate Arthur Millichip and move uphill and to the right from there. He used his torch sparingly. There were houses overlooking the cemetery and the last thing he wanted was a prowl car on the scene.

He could almost hear Sergeant Gwilliam laughing.

Away to the south, over the Kent and Surrey hills, the lightning played and the thunder cracked and grumbled. An occasional, single, heavy spot of rain fell onto him out of the black ceiling of the clouds.

He found Arthur Millichip when he had almost given up hope. At rest, awaiting the last call. Up the hill now. When he saw the other cross it was obvious how he had made his mistake. Both were white and both were new. Mass-produced, probably by the monumental mason who had his little shop outside the gates. Petrella hooded his torch, and squatted down beside it.

The moment he read what was there, all his fears became cold certainties.

He stepped back onto the path, trotted to the gate, and hauled himself over. A rapid calculation. Two minutes to the nearest call box. Say ten minutes if he ran, straight down the hill, to the police station. Speed was impossible under the black pall of darkness. He chose the phone box.

Sergeant Gwilliam answered the call himself. It took him a few seconds to understand what Petrella was talking about. Then he said, "I'll get a car to pick you up at Four Ways."

Less than three minutes later – perhaps five, in all, from the moment in which he had read what was engraved on the

50

tombstone, Petrella was in the CID room talking to Sergeant Gwilliam.

"Annie Lewis," he said, "wife of George Lewis, née Cole. And it was Cole I saw this afternoon. I'm sure of that, although I've only seen photographs. He was sent up before I came here."

"Slowly, lad, slowly," said Sergeant Gwilliam. "Let's look at the fences before we jump them. I know Harry Cole well enough. It was me pulled him in. And his daughter, Annie, married Ginny Lewis sure enough. And Lewis and Cole worked as a pair. Housebreaking, screwing, a little smash and grab. But mostly plain, quiet screwing."

"When you sent Cole up for his long stretch," said Petrella, "why didn't Lewis go with him?"

"It was five years ago," growled the Sergeant. "I believe there was some trouble between them."

"Did Lewis buy himself out by turning Cole in?"

"Not exactly. But there was something . . ." The Sergeant put his hand through his hair and stared at the discoloured spot above the door, which looked like old dried blood, but was really a leaking water pipe.

"I'd say that Cole stood the rap for both of them," he said at last. "Lewis was a younger man. And married to Cole's daughter, you see."

"Yes," said Petrella. He knew enough about professional criminals to know that this could be true. "But if Cole thought Lewis hadn't kept *his* part of the bargain . . ."

"If he thought that," said Sergeant Gwilliam, simply, "there'd be trouble."

The telephone sounded.

Sergeant Gwilliam listened like a man who had been expecting nothing but bad news, and at the end of it said "Thank you very much," and replaced the receiver reverently on its cradle.

"That was Control," he said. "I put an enquiry through to them. You are quite right. Cole was released from Chelmsford after breakfast yesterday morning."

Petrella caught a glimpse of himself in the glass as they went out of the door. His pyjama collar had somehow escaped from the neck of the sweater he had pulled hastily over it and was sticking up through the collar of his raincoat. He jabbed it back with nervous fingers.

The car was still waiting.

"Cadsand Cottages," said Gwilliam to the driver. "Stop when you get to the end of the road, and turn your lights out."

And to Petrella, as they ran along the empty High Street, "No wonder Ginny asked for protection."

Petrella agreed. He had seen Harry Cole's face only twice; once in a photograph, once that evening. It was a face with the composed remoteness of a thinker or a killer.

"Stop here," Gwilliam told the driver. "You can put the car across the end of the road, with the lights out. If anyone comes running, grab them."

The driver, a long, gloomy man, called Happy, said, "If you say so, Sergeant," and Gwilliam and Petrella got quietly out. They took care not to bang the car doors. It was very dark but the rain had stopped.

"Ginny lives in the end cottage," said Gwilliam. "He's alone now. Since Annie died."

That was the last thing said. After that, they felt their way. Down the stone-paved lane, across the litter that was part garden, part builders' yard; round the side of the ramshackle brick building.

The Sergeant gave a grunt of displeasure. The back door was ajar. Then they were standing in a small room, a kitchen by the stale smell of it. And a tap was dripping somewhere.

Gwilliam's big torch opened up like a searchlight. It was aimed at the ceiling. In the middle of the grey plaster was a darker mark, the size of a plate. In the middle of the plate something gathered; and another drop fell down to the stone floor with a soft splash.

Upstairs, on the floor of his over-furnished bedroom, lay the empty carcass of Ginny Lewis. He had been neatly butchered and left to lie. There was no one else in the house.

After that there was a lot to be done. For Petrella, pressed down by the double weight of the night and of a mortal weariness, things seemed to pass in slow motion. First the cars arrived, then the doctor, then the men with flashlights and cameras, and policemen, and more policemen, and a real, white-haired Superintendent who, although it was only five o'clock in the morning, had somehow found time to shave his pink chin before coming to Cadsand Cottages.

Petrella, forgotten, propped up the jamb of the kitchen

door. The bulk of Sergeant Gwilliam loomed down upon him. "Go to bed," he said. "There's nothing you can do here."

"Any sign of Cole?"

"Not a sausage. But we've put the net out. Incidentally, it looks as if Ginny was carrying a gun. Only he didn't reach it quick enough."

"Then Cole's probably got the gun in his pocket now."

"Probably," said Sergeant Gwilliam. "It won't make any difference. We'll pick him up as soon as it's light."

Remembering that calm and masterful eye Petrella did not feel so sure. He cadged a lift in a returning car to the foot of Highside and walked off up the hill.

The storm, which had been grumbling about in the background like a much-enduring woman, put out a last long venomous tongue of lightning, and showed Petrella Harry Cole.

He was sitting on a flat gravestone in the cemetery, his head on his hands.

Petrella's first thought was, if they hadn't all been half asleep, that was just exactly where the search should have started.

Then he had jumped the railing, and was walking steadily along the grass verge.

Cole was sitting up now. He had Ginny's gun all right. It was in his hand, and his hand was resting on his knee, steady as the stone he was sitting on. There was enough light in the sky now to see by. Morning was not far away.

"Sit down," said Cole. "Don't come any nearer."

Petrella hesitated for a moment, then his tired legs folded under him and he sat. They both sat, he on one forgotten moss-covered slab, Harry Cole on another, with the new white headstone shining between them.

"She was my daughter," said Cole at last. "You knew that?"

"I found that out tonight," said Petrella.

"A cheap piece of stone. If you killed your wife, you'd give her something better than that, wouldn't you?"

"I'm not married," said Petrella.

"He didn't even pay for it himself. First he let her die, then he let her rot, under a cheap white stone he never even paid for himself."

"I don't — "

"The doctor called it malnutrition. You're educated. You know what that means, I suppose?"

"I don't — "

"It means the bastard starved her to death. I know. I was in Parkhurst. They've got a good news service there. It isn't printed. It comes to you along the hot water pipes, in the evening."

Petrella said, "Look here — " but he might as well have tried to stop a gramophone by talking against it. The light was coming up fast, and the little, cold morning wind blew into his face.

His fingers touched something small and hard. It was the extension switch of his torch. The torch itself was somewhere behind his back slung to the belt of his raincoat. He started to joggle the switch. Three short. Three long. Three short. Someone must be looking from their window by now.

Time went by.

"You're young," said Cole suddenly. "Too young to understand what it is to hate. A man can live on hate. Did you know that?"

"It's a poor food," said Petrella. His fingers kept working.

"It can be meat and strong drink, and a fire to warm you through the long winter nights, when the heating isn't working in the cell, and you've nothing but one blanket over you. It was easy. He knew I was coming. He lived with fear. I lived with hate. It's a good bargain, boy."

"It's a foul bargain," said Petrella. He was suddenly quite cool, for he had heard the sounds he was waiting for. A car, coming fast, up the hill. Its lights went out and it stopped at the corner.

"There's one thing you didn't know," he said. "The grapevine must have missed out on it. Ginny Lewis never killed your daughter. Neither killed her nor let her die."

"Why do you trouble to tell such lies, boy?"

"I'm not lying, and you know it."

Look at him. Talk at him. Keep his attention. Big Gwilliam was over the wall behind Cole, and coming with the fast, controlled rush which had once sent him across the line at Twickenham with half the English pack on his back.

The gun in Cole's hand shifted slightly. It gave a small, sad crack, and he folded onto the ground under an avalanche of bodies. But he was dead before they touched him.

That took a little time to sort out too. And it was the uncomfortable hour of six when Petrella and Sergeant Gwilliam turned their back on Highside Cemetery, and the body that still lay there.

"Funny," said Gwilliam, "that he should have gone without knowing that Ginny Lewis, whatever his sins, had no part in Annie's death. The prison grapevine told him that Annie had died, and been buried by public funds. It forgot to tell him that Lewis was inside as well. On a two-year stretch for receiving."

They both looked at the dead man, flat on the grass, like a doll with the stuffing out.

Petrella thought of Ginny Lewis. Two men, both empty. One empty with fear, the other empty with hate. He looked at his watch. It was too late to think of going to bed. If he hurried, he would just be in time to catch Mr. Gosport.

Cash in Hand

YOU do not mention the Nipper in Highside police circles except with a smile. For in his brief and exciting career he managed to cause quite an extraordinary amount of unpleasantness and ill-feeling.

It started with Chief Inspector Haxtell being summoned to an interview with his Divisional superior, Superintendent Barstow. ("There's a little matter I'd like to discuss with you, Haxtell.") Barstow was big, red and almost permanently angry. In this case, no doubt, there were excuses. He himself had received a rocket from the District Chief Superintendent, and his interpretation of discipline was that if you got a rocket, you passed it on, without delay and at compound interest, to your own immediate subordinates.

Haxtell came back to Highside Police Station, kicked the waste-paper basket, and sent for Detective Sergeant Gwilliam.

"They're getting worried higher up," he said, "about the Nipper."

"Yes," said the Sergeant, cautiously. He was an expert weather-prophet.

"Apparently the local Chamber of Commerce has taken the matter up. I'm afraid the Superintendent and the Mayor haven't been seeing eye to eye since that row they had over the last civic function. Most unfortunate. Now the Mayor sees an opportunity of taking it out on Barstow, so he's jumped in with both feet."

"And the Super jumped on you?" suggested Gwilliam, who had known his Chief Inspector for a very long time.

"Between these four walls, yes," said Haxtell. "Though the interview wasn't remarkable for any really constructive suggestions."

"It's a devil of a problem," said Gwilliam. "Look at it how you will. I suppose it's no good telling these shopkeepers and people that it's largely their fault for keeping so much cash around the place."

"No good at all," said Haxtell. "You know what they'd say: 'What are the police for? What do we pay all these rates for?'"

"Another thing," said Gwilliam. "It can't be a fluke that the Nipper always gets into the office or shop or whatever it is, when it's empty. No doubt he cases each job carefully, but if people would only be a little more discreet . . . "

"A lot of it's their fault," agreed Haxtell. "But we shan't make ourselves any more popular by saying so. Our job's to catch him. You can take one man – Petrella, I suggest – off all outside duty and tell him to concentrate on it. He knows a bit about locks. It's just up his street."

So it caused trouble for Detective Constable Petrella, too. Following a sharp attack of flu, the result of an all-night watch in damp clothes, he had been on the point of asking for a holiday, his first in almost two years. He was going to visit his father, in Barcelona. After that, his plans were vague.

He listened sadly to what Gwilliam had to say, cancelled some tentative reservations, and sat down to serious study of the Nipper.

It was "Square" Peggs, the proprietor of the All-Night

Café in Exeter Street who had first christened him "Nipper."
"He nips in, nips what he wants, and nips out again."

In the last six months, since his work had become
identifiable, the Nipper had visited Solly Moss, the turf-
accountant; Mungo Farnes, the pawnbroker; Mr. Turner,
who kept the big greengrocer's shop on the corner of the
High Street; and Mr. Lowson's garage and repair shop.

He had taken nothing but money. How much he had taken
from each was part of the mystery; but the police, scaling
down the estimate of the outraged proprietors in the light of
experience, came to the conclusion that it was not less than
fifteen thousand pounds in all.

"If he keeps it up for a year," said Peggs, "he'll make
himself twenty thousand nicker. Then maybe he'll retire."

Petrella was fond of Peggs. He liked him for his cynicism,
his philosophy and his lack of conventional morality. Also,
he had found out a long time ago that nothing much
happened in Highside without Peggs knowing about it.

"He'll be after your stocking next," he suggested.

"If he knew where I kept it," agreed Peggs.

"Which is an admission," said Petrella, "that you do keep
your spare cash somewhere round the place. Why the devil
don't you bank it?"

"Might just as well give it away – to the tax collector," said
Peggs. It was, as Petrella knew, a widely held idea.

"What you want to do," said Peggs, "is catch him, and put
him away for a long stretch."

"Tell me who he is, and we'll tab him fast enough."

"If I knew," said Peggs, frankly, "I'd tell you. No honour
among thieves here. He's a perishing little menace."

So Petrella took a bulky folder home with him, that night
and many nights. And studied, in every possible light and
from every possible angle, the depredations of the Nipper.

His methods, in outline, had the simplicity of genius. He
had visited Solly Moss's office at half past one, when Solly
and his two clerks were out at lunch. He had picked, with
speed and efficiency, the mortice lock on the office door,
looked into all the desk drawers until he found the safe key,
opened the safe, removed the cash, closed the safe, replaced
the key, relocked the outer door and departed. Estimated
time, ten minutes. The loss was not discovered until Solly
visited his safe that evening to bank the results of a highly

successful afternoon at Hurst Park. Mungo Farnes, the pawnbroker, and Mr. Turner were both evening jobs. They were bachelors and both lived over their premises, but took an occasional evening out. In each case the Nipper had selected the correct evening, picked the lock of the outer door and, in the case of Farnes, who was a careful man, of the inner door also; gone straight to the place where the money was kept (in one case a desk, in the other a wall cupboard); picked the lock of this, and departed with the contents. At Lowson's garage it had been easier still, since Mr. Lowson did not sleep on the premises, but entrusted his cash to a large, old-fashioned safe, the key of which he concealed, with great originality, by hanging it on a nail behind the door.

"Any leads?" asked Sergeant Gwilliam. Two years had taught him a reluctant respect for Petrella's flair.

"Nothing definite," said Petrella, and stopped himself yawning. He was desperately tired and had been needing that holiday more than he knew. "Just two thoughts. The first is that he hasn't done anything very complicated yet in the way of lock-picking. He hasn't tackled a safe – he either opens them with a key or leaves 'em alone. He hasn't even tried his hand on a Yale lock. It's just been simple three or four-lever locks which he's opened with a couple of picks."

"Why do a thing the hard way if you can do it soft?"

"Surely," agreed Petrella. "All I meant was this. If he could open a really difficult lock, that would make him one sort of person. A professional. And we could get at him through Criminal Records. What I'm afraid of is that he's an amateur. Suppose he's a man who's worked in some place they cut keys – or some little workshop where they make and repair ordinary locks. He'd know just enough about locks to open the simple sort with a bit of practice."

"He's been getting plenty of practice lately," agreed Gwilliam, sourly. "What's your other bright idea?"

"I just thought that if I'm right, the only way of catching him is to find the common denominator of Solly Moss, Mungo Farnes, Mr. Turner and Mr. Lowson."

"They're all in a good way of business. And they're all so damned silly they keep their cash on the premises."

"I didn't quite mean that. I meant that if the Nipper is an amateur, he must have had some easy way of finding out all about these four people – and their money – and what they did with it, and what their habits were, and so on. A professional could buy information like that. An amateur would have to get it for himself."

"It's a thought," said Sergeant Gwilliam, doubtfully, "but it doesn't seem to get us much closer to pulling him in, does it?"

Petrella went out to have another word with Peggs.

"Can you," he said, "think of any sort of link between these four people? They're all men, and they all run businesses. But I mean something more than that. Suppose they all belonged to the same club – or supported the same football team – or had their hair cut by the same barber — "

"Solly hasn't got any hair."

"Just an example."

"Yes. I take your point." Peggs reached down a small bottle, popped two white tablets out of it into a glass of water and swallowed them absent-mindedly. "Blown up like a balloon. It's all that greasy stuff I serve. Supposing they all had the same postman?"

"Would you talk to a postman about your private affairs? What about an insurance agent?"

"Except that none of 'em was insured. That's what they were beefing about." Peggs swilled down the last white drop and said, "What about a Lodge?"

"I don't know much about Lodges," admitted Petrella.

"I don't go for them myself," said Peggs. "Lot of grown-up kids. But I know Solly, Mungo and old Turner belong to one – Sons of Enterprise. Highside Lodge – and come to think of it, I believe Alf Lowson joined 'em lately."

"What do they do?"

"They have outings. Hire a coach and drink their way to Southend and back. And a party at Christmas. Men only."

Petrella extracted the address of the Lodge secretary and went thoughtfully back to Crown Road Police Station. He was aware that he was treading on very dangerous ground. When a lot of grown men got together and called each other brother and elected officers and wore strange emblems, they were apt to be touchy about their privacy.

As it turned out, this was one possible piece of trouble which did not eventuate. At the station he found a message waiting for him. The Nipper had moved in again. Mrs. Porter, owner of a large confectioners in Milton Road, had locked her shop up on the previous evening and gone to visit her sister in hospital. On her return she had noticed nothing amiss. It was not until after lunch next day that she had occasion to go to the cash box in the bedroom cupboard.

"*Mrs.* Porter," said Petrella. "Has she got a husband?"

"A widow," said Sergeant Gwilliam. "Runs the shop herself. It's her life savings, so far as I could make out."

Petrella acquitted the all-male Sons of Enterprise of his unworthy suspicions and began his thinking again. He was aware that time was running against him. By the first post that morning Chief Inspector Haxtell had received a letter which had caused him to go red in the face and beat the desk with his fist.

It was from Councillor Hayes, a notorious local busybody, and it suggested (Councillor Hayes rarely stated anything, but he was a master of suggestion) that the police were applying the rule of "one law for the rich, another for the poor." "I and my fellow councillors notice with regret," it concluded, "that whilst the police are only too active in arresting and persecuting" (this word had been thinly crossed out and "prosecuting" written over the top) "members of the working class who are guilty of the smallest infringement, they do not show the same activity in arresting a man who constitutes a serious threat to the livelihood and savings of the small shopkeeper."

"I wouldn't call Solly a small shopkeeper," said Sergeant Gwilliam, when the letter was read to him. "Anyway, that's only old Hayes blowing his top. He's been wanting to get back at us because we never caught the man who did *his* house. Between you and me I always wondered if he didn't do it himself for the insurance."

Haxtell ignored this slanderous statement.

"How's Petrella getting on?"

Sergeant Gwilliam had to admit that he didn't know. For all his placidity, he too was worried. He knew the power of local politics.

In fact Petrella was back where he had started. He was talking to Peggs.

"Poor old Ma Porter," said Peggs. "How many times I told her it was asking for trouble keeping all her money in the bottom of the wardrobe. Silly old cow."

"She a friend of yours?"

"We use the same pub – when I get a night off. Which isn't often. I knew her old man. He was the only man I ever saw drink a quart of stout without stopping. Stout, not beer. Solly gave him ten to one in dollars he couldn't do it. It's the only time I ever seen Solly pay up cheerful."

Petrella agreed that it was a considerable feat, at any odds, and took his departure. He must have been tired at the time, because he was halfway home before he realised the significance of what Peggs had told him.

It seemed so important, that he didn't waste time going back, but dived into the nearest telephone box and rang back.

"You know what you were saying about Mr. Porter — "

"The one who drunk — ?"

"Yes. What pub were you talking about?"

"The Bull, of course. Everyone goes to the Bull."

"That's what I thought," said Petrella. "Did you ever see Farnes there?"

"Old Mungo? Yes. Once or twice."

"And Lowson? And Turner?"

"Lowson's a regular. I dunno about Turner. I expect so. They all use it. What's the idea? You thinking of organising a stag party?"

"That's just exactly what I am going to do," said Petrella. "All the losers shall drown their losses in quarts of porter," and he rang off.

"Barmy," said Peggs. None the less there was a glint in his small black eyes. He had just begun to realise what Petrella was talking about.

That was Thursday. Two nights later, at about half past nine, the Saloon Bar of the Bull was full, as it usually was on Saturday night, of bright folk, bright lights, smoke and the steady pulling of beer engines and clanking of glasses.

Holding the middle of the floor, gorgeous in a black suit which had first seen the light of day at his wife's funeral, was Mr. Peggs. Facing him, and talking almost as loud, was Mungo Farnes. Behind his left elbow appeared the red face and porcelain smile of Solly Moss.

"What I say is," repeated Peggs, "if you keep your lolly in a safe, you're asking for trouble. What is a safe?"

He paused for breath, and let in Mungo, who told him what a safe was, in language which caused even the barmaid to open her doll-like eyes.

"I'll tell you what a safe is," said Peggs. "It's an advertisement. It says, in letters a yard high, 'Come on, here's where the money is.' Right?"

The company agreed that he was right.

"It's all right criticising," said Solly. "Where d'you keep your stocking, Peggs, my boy?"

"Ah," said Peggs. "One or two people might like to know that. I'll tell you one thing. I don't keep it in the safe. And I don't keep it in the shop. And I don't keep it under my bed."

Petrella, from his post of vantage in the passageway behind the bar, thought that Peggs was doing it very nicely. Not too obvious. Just indiscreet enough to sound natural.

He cast an eye round the bar. Many of them were regulars, and he acquitted them at a glance. Nor did he think the Nipper was a woman. In theory there was nothing to prevent a woman taking to burglary, but as yet it didn't seem to be one of the fields in which they had started seeking equality with men.

There was a youth with red hair and large hands, vaguely attached to a girl, whom he might have brought with him or might have picked up. There was an old man with a white beard, nursing a single half pint of mild in the corner. (Was he as old as he looked? The hand which raised the glass was very steady.) And a clerkly person, sipping a lager, whose eyes flashed round keenly behind a pair of rimless glasses. Nothing to choose between them really.

"Did I do all right?" asked Peggs an hour later. He was mixing himself a powerful sedative.

"Bang on," said Petrella. "If the Nipper was there he'll be after *your* life's savings next."

"You think he'll work it out?"

"Bound to. Not in the shop, not in a safe, not in your bedroom. Really speaking that only leaves the living-room." He cast his eye round the homely apartment. "And it won't be too difficult for him to get in. There's a side door in Exeter Street. Easy lock. Then straight up the stairs. Then he's got a choice. Could be this room, or the room opposite."

"That's the bathroom. Wouldn't keep money in the bathroom."

"Agreed. Now, whereabouts in this room? I'd say the sideboard was the obvious place. Strong doors. And a nice lock. That's the place all right."

"All right," said Peggs. "So that's where I keep my money. Now what? I'm willing to help, but I'm not going to spend three weeks hiding behind a curtain waiting for a little perisher to come and help himself to it."

"Nor you shall," said Petrella. "In fact, it's quite obvious that he won't come near the place until he's seen you safely out of it."

"Are *you* going to hide here, then?"

"No one's going to hide," said Petrella. "It's a little irregular, but this is how I thought we'd do it."

"When you say it's irregular," observed Chief Inspector Haxtell next morning, "what exactly do you mean?"

"I thought, perhaps," said Petrella, "that it might be better if you *didn't* know about it."

"Why?"

"In case it goes wrong."

"And what happens if it goes wrong?"

"It's just possible," said Petrella, cautiously, "that the Nipper might nip no more."

"You mean it might kill him?"

"It's possible, sir."

"I think I'd better know about it," said Haxtell.

"Well – you know how you pick a lock."

"Roughly. But you can tell me again."

"It's more or less the same process, whatever sort of lock it is. You use two picks, one in each hand. The first one's the 'lifter', the other's the 'shifter'. You feel for the retaining spring – that's the spring that puts the weight into the lock. Once you can raise that, the job's more than half done."

Unconsciously, Petrella was demonstrating as he spoke, and Haxtell watched him, half interested, half amused.

"You ought to have been a burglar yourself," he said. "All right. I've got the idea. What next?"

Petrella explained.

"It'll be a lot cheaper than keeping someone on watch," he said. "After all, he mayn't try it for months . . . "

Actually it was three weeks later that Councillor Hayes was walking home down Exeter Street. He was returning from a most interesting council meeting at which he had delivered an address on the subject of inefficiency and dishonesty in the police force. He was reflecting on the pleasures of democracy and free speech when he heard, quite close to him, a piercing shriek.

He looked up. It seemed to come from a darkened first-floor window. Murder? Assault? Bodily harm? Where, oh where, were the police? There was a thudding of feet on the stairs, a door swung back and a figure burst forth. It came straight at him.

Councillor Hayes threw up his arms in a token gesture of self-defence. The next moment they were entangled together in a milling heap on the pavement.

It was at this moment that the bright light of a torch illuminated the scene and a voice said, "Now then. What's all this?"

The police had arrived.

At Crown Road Police Station some sorting out took place. Councillor Hayes was recognised and apologised to. His opponent, who turned out to be a young man with red hair and large feet, was asked for explanations, which he found it embarrassing to give. His case was prejudiced from the start by the fact that during the struggle, an undoubted set of pick-locks had fallen from his coat pocket. The fact that he was wearing cotton gloves and rubber-soled shoes might, of course, have had some innocent explanation; but, having extracted his name and address, Haxtell thought it worth detaining him whilst he sent a man round to his lodgings, where a number of very curious objects came to light including a complete set of key blanks, a high-class set of metal saws and more used one-pound notes than any young man starting out in life ought to possess. Faced with this fresh evidence, the young man decided, at a latish hour that night, to come clean. The Nipper was caught.

The publicity and prestige which Councillor Hayes derived from the matter was so considerable that there seems no doubt that he will be Mayor next year. There was even talk of a public subscription. Had he not, single-handed, succeeded where the whole police organisation had failed?

Haxtell decided, on reflection, to say nothing at all. He was thus spared from having to explain that Petrella had carefully wired the lock mechanism in Pegg's sideboard to the main electricity supply of the house, ensuring an extremely severe shock to anyone who tried to pick it.

Anyway, it would have meant bringing Petrella back from Barcelona where he was enjoying a well-earned holiday.

Source Seven

HOW curious, and how different, are the threads which form the pattern. A titled woman who died in the gutter of Soho; a drunken crane-driver at Tilbury Docks; a pink-cheeked young man fishing off the south bank of the Gironde; a middle-aged gourmet with a house of rose-coloured brick in the hills above Maidenhead . . .

On a fine morning in September, Superintendent Costorphine was studying the entries in his ledger, under the crossreference of Diacetylmorphine, better known as heroin. The book lay open at a page headed with the numeral "7."

Scotland Yard has no separate Narcotics Bureau. Nevertheless, there are men in the Central Office – and Costorphine was one of them – who have come, by accident or design, to specialise in the ramifications of the drug traffic. They are co-ordinators. They work hand in glove with departments whose special interests are Undesirable Aliens, Unlawful Night Clubs, Prostitution, Procuration and Assault with Violence; occasional flowerings of the same shoot.

Superintendent Costorphine was tall, thin, white and untidy – "like a wax candle in a draught," said Superintendent Hazlerigg, who admired, but could not love him. He had the mind of a chess master and the patience of Job. Which was well, because he was fighting a battle in which victory was impossible and the most that could be looked for was a measure of success.

He was speaking to Hazlerigg of this.

"The real trouble," he said, "is that the stuff is no longer manufactured in England. It was tried, in the twenties. Morphia, heroin and cocaine. When we put Eddie Manning, the Negro, inside, they packed it up. It's all made in the Middle East now."

"Why do you class that as a trouble?" asked Hazlerigg. "I should have thought it was a good thing."

"No," said Costorphine. "If you can hit the producer you can stop the line once and for all. Now we can't touch the producer so we have to spread our efforts and go for the carriers. A lot of them are little men – stewards and deckhands and lascars. They're a plague, but they never carry more than tiny quantities. It's the big, regular sources that matter."

He looked down at the ledger open in front of him. It was called "Costorphine's Source Book" – or, by the young and irreverent members of the department, "Mother Costorphine's Cookery Book." In it, numbered serially, could be found set out all the known details of ways and means in which supplies of unlawful narcotics were entering – or were thought to be entering – the country. About some of these sources everything was known, and in these cases a neat red line drawn at the foot of the page indicated one more chapter closed and one more hole stopped.

About other sources, information varied from the moderately complete to the extremely sketchy.

Page seven was practically blank.

"By the way," said Hazlerigg, his mind reverting to the reason that had brought him in to Costorphine's room. "We've found a lot of that jewellery."

They had been discussing a titled woman, in whom they shared an interest. She had disappeared from her family home three months before, with some of her own and some of her family's jewellery, and had just been picked out of the gutter in Dean Street.

"She's been selling it and pawning it," he went on. "She didn't get much for it but the transactions were honest as far as they went. I expect the family will buy it back. She'd no money on her at all. I don't think there's much doubt how she spent it, poor girl."

"No," said Costorphine. He himself never said things like

66

"poor girl" or "poor man" about the victims of drugs; any more than he said "poor fellow" when he captured an unwary chess opponent's queen. "What was the cause of death?"

"Exposure and weakness."

Costorphine pinched his long upper lip. "I've an idea," he said, "that the heroin in her handbag came through Source Seven."

"It's a marvel to me how you keep 'em apart," said Hazlerigg.

"Changes in manufacturing methods, chiefly. This stuff was made almost exactly two and a half years ago. It started to appear on the English market last month. That's always been the peculiarity of Source Seven. A time lag of twenty-seven to thirty months between manufacture and disposal. It's very odd, that. Usually, they're only too keen to get it on the market, you know, and pick up their profit."

"Is Seven a big source?"

"Big enough to be worth stopping," said Costorphine. He was not given to over-statement. "By the way," he added, "did you hear that we had found Thomas?"

"Thomas who?"

"Tiny Thomas."

"Oh him," said Hazlerigg. "When you say 'found' I suppose you mean — "

"Yes. Quite dead. He'd been strangled."

That is where the drunken crane-driver came in. His name was Ricketts and he had been celebrating the return home of his eldest son from Korea; celebrating with such serious concentration that when he came on duty next morning he was not only still drunk, but too drunk to realise it. With the result that he had succeeded in dropping a steel girder weighing five tons from a height of sixty feet. Fortunately no one was underneath it at the time, but the loading jetty had disintegrated as if a bomb had hit it.

Two days later a diver had gone down to assess the damage. While he was down there, he had observed what looked like a roll of cable wire. The scour was carrying it slowly along the river bed towards him. Fearing that it might run foul of him, he had stopped to push it to one side and had noticed two feet projecting from one end.

But for this chance, the little fish and the crabs would have had time to finish what they had begun, and in the end there would have been nothing left but a cocoon of rusty wire, rolling backwards and forwards as the tide ebbed and ran.

As it was, the police were able, with some difficulty, to reconstruct and identify the remains of Tiny Thomas, who was a vendor of newspapers and, in addition, a most useful and successful police informer.

There the matter might have rested, but for the fact that when the experts examined Thomas's coat they took particular care to look out for a secret pocket which they knew it contained. In it they found a sodden piece of cardboard which, under the influence of oblique photography, yielded the single word POYAK.

Since Thomas was known to have been working for some time on Source Seven – to which he said he had some sort of lead – the matter was referred to Superintendent Costorphine.

"What does it mean?" asked Hazlerigg, when all this had been explained to him. "It sounds like a racehorse."

"No one knows what it means," said Costorphine. "It's evidently a name that Thomas heard – or most likely misheard – and since he thought it important he wrote it down and cached it in his inner pocket."

"Po-yak," said Hazlerigg. And then, "Poy-ak." It sounded equally silly either way.

"My first idea was that it might be the name of a boat, or a bungalow on the sea or river. Any of those would have made sense against a smuggling background."

"Have you got anyone particular on it?"

"I haven't been able to spare anyone at the moment," said Costorphine. "Why?"

"I thought it might be something for Petrella to get his teeth into."

"Hmph," said Costorphine. "Well, it would do no harm, I suppose." He didn't sound very grateful.

"Give the boy a run," said Hazlerigg. "It'll be better than leaving him to get stale. I won't let him do anything drastic without asking you or me first."

Detective Constable Patrick Petrella was something of a joke at Headquarters. Hazlerigg had arranged a three-months' attachment for him to Scotland Yard – a welcome respite from his work in North London – when he discovered that he spoke Arabic. He had used him as interpreter in a piece of business he was engaged on in the docks and had discovered that his youthful-looking assistant had other accomplishments. Son of a Spanish policeman and an English school mistress he had started life with the advantage of being bilingual. At the University of Beirut he had learned to speak and read Arabic. After that, at a College of rather peculiar Further Education in Cairo, where most of the teaching was done in French, he had learned, among other things, how to judge wines and pick locks. At Scotland Yard he had come under a certain amount of fire from the old hands. He had accepted the leg-pulling with the same equanimity that he accepted everything else.

"Do some *thinking* first," said Hazlerigg to this young man. "If you strike a line, hunt it yourself, and report results. There's a Thames Conservancy list of motor boats and motor cruisers which you might start on. If you get hold of anything, tell Superintendent Costorphine or myself before you do anything silly."

Petrella saluted gravely and withdrew.

He was back the next morning. "Could you find out, sir," he said, "whether Source Seven could have anything to do with France?"

Hazlerigg telephoned Costorphine. When he had done, he said, "Yes. The stuff starts in the Levant, but there *are* indications that there is an intermediate stage in France. Why?"

"Po-yak," said Petrella. "It's what an Englishman might make of Pauillac, if he overheard it."

"Yes," said Hazlerigg. "So he might. Is it on the coast?"

"In a way, sir. It's on the south bank of the Gironde – that is, the mouth of the Garonne. Quite large boats go past it, I believe, on their way up to Bordeaux. I don't think they stop there. It's not a large place. Perhaps if I could go and have a look round . . . "

The thought of sending a very junior detective constable direct to Bordeaux had not even entered Hazlerigg's head. He opened his mouth to say, Certainly not, and then closed it again.

"I'll speak to Superintendent Costorphine," he said at last. "Meanwhile, get checking those motor boats."

Surprisingly, Costorphine supported the idea.

"Normally," he agreed, "we should ask the French police

to co-operate. But what exactly are we going to ask them to do? Go to Pauillac and look for – what? If there's anything actually sticking out they'd have noticed it before. Unless we can give them rather more to go on, I'm afraid it'll be a routine enquiry and a nil return."

"All right," said Hazlerigg. "Let him go."

And to Petrella, he said, "Look here, son. You're going as a tourist. You've got a fortnight to produce some return for the public money that's being spent on you. I'll give you an introduction to the Commissaire at Bordeaux, but don't use it unless you have to. Behave like a tourist – have you got any hobbies?"

"I used to fish quite a bit."

"Excellent. Take a fishing-rod. It'll be a boring existence but I expect you'll survive. And just what are you looking so pleased about?"

"The finest claret in the world, sir, comes from Pauillac."

"Well, you won't be able to buy much of that on your allowance," said Hazlerigg. "Keep your eye on the fishes."

Which brings us to a young man fishing on the Garonne.

Patrick Petrella never before remembered such a feeling of entire and absolute contentment. He was seated in a clump of reeds. It was not a very good place for fishing, but it was an excellent place for observation. Already he was in love with the misty greys and greens of the Medoc and the broad silver-grey river which ran past his feet. Away, across the river, on the extreme right of his view, were the church and citadel of La Blaye. In front of him spread the willow-covered flats of the Ile St. Louis, with its cheerful-looking lighthouse, like a single-funnelled liner. On his left lay Pauillac jetty, with the mast and bridge of the steamer sticking out of the water exactly as the Germans had left it when they had sunk it as a final act of spite in 1944.

The warm sun was tempered by a breeze which rippled the water. The tide was on the ebb, and a single, battered, tramp steamer was coming up against it.

Petrella settled himself more comfortably and fell into a trance which was part happiness, part the feel of the sun on his back and part genuine tiredness.

It was during the evenings that he did his work, and he had not seen his bed until the very small hours of that morning.

"Garçon très sympathique," declared Madame Jolliot of

70

the Pension Maritime. "One can observe from his accent that he is not a Frenchman. A Belgian, perhaps."

"His passport is British," said Monsieur Jolliot.

"There are all sorts of foreigners in Britain," said Madame. "It proves nothing. To my way of thinking, he is not British. A Pole, perhaps. He is not reserved."

He was certainly not reserved. He took his evening drink at one or more of the four main riverside cafés. He joined in all public arguments. If there was a party, he could usually be relied on to make one of it. He was young and free with his money, and as soon as the ice had broken there had been no lack of parties. It was a fortunate moment, being the last few days before the vintage. Soon everyone would be too tired at the end of the day to do more than eat and tumble into bed. At the moment there was an interval of leisure. The last row had been weeded, the gear overhauled, the casks scrubbed. So there was time for parties.

It was a social routine which left Petrella a little fatigued, but all was compensated for by the long, dreamlike mornings beside the river.

The tramp steamer was abreast of him now. It was alone on the wide reach. Boats usually came in with the flood, instead of battling up against the ebb. She must, he reflected, be running to a schedule which brooked no delay.

A man appeared on the lower well deck. Petrella saw a dark face above white overalls. The man was some sort of galley hand. He was humping a scuttle of rubbish, which he emptied over the side of the boat down wind. Refuse, boxes, paper, tins, flew out. A bag burst as it hit the water and Petrella saw potato peelings. He grinned. You couldn't litter up the sea the same way as you could the land. There were too many scavengers about. Seagulls were already wheeling over the trove.

Soon only one large cardboard carton was visible. It floated high in the water, with a sort of lopsided dignity, and the wind was driving it across the current. Petrella wondered if it would sink before it hit the reeds. At that moment, he became aware that there were other parties interested. Out of a creek, a hundred yards downstream, came a dinghy. There were two boys in it. They handled the boat skilfully, pulling into the current and judging their distance. Another type of scavenger, thought Petrella. Seagulls and boys. He didn't think they would get much for their pains. The way the box floated, he imagined it was empty.

The boat was alongside now. The two boys shipped oars and leaned over. The boat dipped as the box came over the side.

Petrella started to wind in his line. His mind was no longer on fishes. He was trying to work out how a light-looking cardboard carton, which floated high out of the water, could need two strong boys to handle it; and how it could cause a boat to dip when taken aboard; unless it was much heavier than it looked, in which case why had it not sunk? Unless, of course, it had been scientifically buoyed, say with cork or kapok or compressed air.

He packed up his fishing-gear, folded his mackintosh over his arm, and walked back down the river path. When he came to the head of the creek, he saw that the dinghy was already back at its moorings, and empty. The boys were lashing a tarpaulin over a small handcart. He could see that there were nets on the cart. Since there was no sign of the carton, he felt safe in assuming that it was under the nets.

Petrella passed on. He had no intention of following them. Such a course would have been worse than stupid. It was, moreover, quite unnecessary.

After luncheon he fell into conversation with M. Jolliot. Every inhabitant of the commune knows to whom every inch of land belongs. The fields and vineyards, with their infinite divisions and sub-divisions, are spread out for all to see, like a living family tree – a record of marriage, birth, patrimony and descent.

The creek and the landing stage belonged to the owner of Château Maurice-Epinard. The château itself stood some three kilometres away. No, said M. Jolliot, it had not a classified *cru*, but produced a very good patrician wine, of the second class. Two boys? Undoubtedly they would be the sons of Clairambaud, the *facteur*, who acted also as *maître de chai*, or cellar master. In a big château, like Latour or Mouton Rothschild, the offices would be separate, but not in a small one. Both boys were well known.

"Full of *espièglerie*," said Madame Jolliot.

"Full of impertinence," amended M. Jolliet. "Out at all seasons in their little boat. Some day they will come to no good."

Petrella agreed with him and retired to his room for an afternoon nap. What he had to do next needed careful thought.

He got up at half past four, had a cup of chocolate, and then strolled out towards the château. After a short walk, he left the main road and followed a broad track, between rows of vines.

When he reached his destination, he saw that "château" was only a courtesy title. It was a large, flat house, over-shadowed by trees, with a stuccoed front and sham turrets. The long windows were shuttered, and there was no smoke coming from the chimneys. The cellarage buildings, almost as large as the château, formed a separate block, with their own entrance and forecourt. There was some life here. Two men were lounging in the front of the court, and a woman, standing in a kitchen doorway, was talking to a third man, a bulky red-faced person, with the look more of a Gascon than a Bordelaise.

Petrella guessed that he would be the *maître de chai*, and went up to him. He knew that it was not uncommon for visitors to come to a château at vintage time.

"Monsieur Clairambaud?"

"The same," said the red-faced man.

"I wondered if— "

"You wish to see our cellars. Certainly. This way, if you please."

They passed up the courtyard. "You have walked out from Pauillac? You are staying there, perhaps?"

"Yes."

"From England?"

Petrella agreed he was from England. They had reached the door leading down into the cellar. Clairambaud held it open. As Petrella turned to go in, he noticed, pressed to a nearby window, the face of a boy. The expression was an unpleasant mixture of malice and anticipation. The woman had gone inside and the other two men had closed up silently behind him.

He realised that he had not been quite as careful as he imagined.

"Go ahead," said Clairambaud. His face was still smiling, but Petrella saw, for the first time, his great red butcher's hands. He walked down the steps. "Straight ahead." It was an order. The three men followed him closely. They were walking down an aisle, dimly lit, between rows of barrels. At the far end there was a grating. Clairambaud pushed past him, took out a key, and opened the door.

"Our inner cellar," he said, "where we keep some of our most precious vintages. It is useful also for a multitude of other purposes. Please go in."

"I suppose you know what you are doing," said Petrella.

"Of a certainty," said the man calmly.

"My friends at the hotel will be enquiring after me when I do not return. I informed them, of course, where I was going."

"I think that is a lie," said Clairambaud. "My son tells me that you spoke to no one before leaving. In any event, when you do not return, they will think, no doubt, that you are at some party – busy asking questions. That seems to have been your occupation on all other evenings. To ask questions."

Petrella had nothing to say to that.

"By tomorrow morning, no doubt, some enquiry will start. Believe me, my little detective, they will have to search long and closely if they wish to find you then."

The two men standing behind M. Clairambaud laughed.

"One other thing. If you shout and scream it may be necessary to tie you up with cords. That will be very uncomfortable for you. And you will, in any event, have wasted your time. At this point you are three metres below the ground and the walls are of great thickness."

"I shall not shout," said Petrella.

"I was sure of it," said Clairambaud. He walked out, snapped shut the lock of the grille with his big key, and turned out the light. Then he turned it on again for a moment to say: "Look out for the spiders. They grow, in this darkness, to the size of a man's hand." Then he turned it out again. The three men tramped away. When they reached the steps, the cellar light went out as well, and Petrella heard the heavy outer door being shut and bolted.

He sat still for some minutes. It was not that he was afraid of the spiders, whose existence he doubted, but he decided to wait until his flickerings of panic had died down. Then he could start to work things out.

Slowly, the darkness cleared to a dim, shadowy dusk. There was no direct source of light in his cage, but it was not quite black. There must be ventilators, up near the roof, to let in the necessary air, and they let in some light as well. He could see the bars of his door black against the lesser darkness beyond. The atmosphere was quite fresh.

What a fool he had been. And he had imagined he was being clever. He had only succeeded in being obvious. They had suspected him all along. They had not minded – that was the galling part. They had not even minded his seeing how the goods came ashore from the steamer. They had known, only too well, that he would come to the château. Everything was arranged. He had no doubt at all that a long, limp bundle would go back on the handcart that night, and that in the early hours of the morning a heavily loaded dinghy would pull out from the jetty into midstream.

That, or something like it, was their intention. One thing mattered: would they visit him again before night? Even if they intended to kill him that night they would hardly dare to move him before midnight. More probably it would be later than that. Would they visit him first? In the circumstances they would be unlikely to waste food and drink on him.

All the same, he thought they would look in once – just to make sure that all was well. Perhaps at about nine or ten o'clock. That gave him three hours to make his preparations.

He was confident that he could open the door. It would take time, but it could be done. The lack of light did not bother him, because you always have to open a lock by touch, and not by sight. He would need two strong, thinnish pieces of iron, bent to the correct angle.

In a clumsy great lock like this one the retaining spring would be very powerful. It would be the sort of spring that needed a thick key with a long shaft and a wide handle to lift it at all. Little pieces of bent wire were going to be no use. In his hip pocket he had a relic of his Egyptian experiences, a pair of pliers with a fine saw edge in one handle and a triangular file in the other.

There was plenty of metal in the wire racks around him. He selected a cross-strut of half-inch angle iron, out of sight of the door, and started to work on it.

It took him two hours to make the necessary tools. When he had perfected them, and knew that he could open the door quickly, he hid them in the dust at the foot of the cellar wall. Then he waited. The waiting was the hard part.

He might be making a stupid mistake by waiting at all. Equally, he could spoil everything by starting too early. He decided to compromise. He would give them until eleven o'clock.

It was ten minutes to eleven when they came again – the same three men. This time they searched him. They found the pliers, but made no comment on them. Petrella got the idea that they were emptying his pockets less to deprive him of chances to escape than as a first step in stripping all marks of identity from him. His tailors' tabs would go next. Then, perhaps, his fingers and his face. One man had brought a can of coffee.

"You had better drink it," said Clairambaud.

"Later," said Petrella.

"As you wish."

When they had gone, he sniffed at the contents of the can and decided that there was more in it than coffee. He emptied it out into the corner.

At eleven fifteen he opened the grating, and stepped out into the cellar. The door at the head of the steps offered him nothing. It was massive and was bolted on the outside.

There was an inner door, at the top of a ramp, in the left-hand wall, and this was unlocked. It led into the *chambre-des-cuviers*, where the fermenting-vats stood, stretching from floor to ceiling. They were empty now, scrubbed and ready for the coming vintage, but the room stank of bygone grape harvests. Unfortunately, its outer door was bolted, too.

He made another circuit of the two cellars and confirmed that there were only two ways out. Then he sat down again to think.

He might hide in the cellar. But for how long? Or he might conceal himself behind the door and try to slip out, or fight his way out, when the men came for him. It seemed a slender chance. And, at the back of his mind, maddening him . . . he knew that there was a way out.

It was a chance thought about scrubbing the vats that brought it back to him.

In olden days they had, literally, to be scrubbed: by men with brushes, who were lowered from the opening at the top. In modern vats there was often a device in the back at ground level enabling a man to get through. He would drag a pressure-hose with him, and so the work would be done in a tenth of the time.

Petrella prayed that the march of science had reached the Château Maurice-Epinard. It had, and a minute later he was inside the vat itself. He had armed himself with a pole from the cellar, and with it he pushed at the big trapdoor in the ceiling of the vat. It swung up under his pressure. So far, so good. The chance existed, but at the moment it was three clear feet out of reach of his fingertips. He needed something to stand on.

The empty barrels in the main cellar would be tall enough to set on end, but they were too wide to get into the vat. He stumbled around in the dark for ten minutes and discovered two brooms and a rake, but nothing more.

Twelve o'clock.

Sweating now, he went back into his prison and took all the bottles from one of the racks. Then he set to work at loosening a section. It was a very bad time indeed before it came away from the wall. But it was thin enough to be squeezed through the opening in the vat, and just strong enough to take his weight.

The last piece was a nightmare. He dared place very little weight on the rack, and he had to stand on it and lift a heavy trapdoor, using a thin wooden pole. That done, he had to pull himself up through the opening. His arms were trembling with fatigue, and twice he thought he would drop. It was only the realisation that if he failed he would never be able to try again that got him through onto the floor of the loft.

And that was almost the end of his difficulties. The loft door was bolted, but on the inside. Five minutes later, he was in the open, creeping between the vines, heading for the main road.

It was seven o'clock in the morning, in London. Superintendent Costorphine had been dragged from his bed at six, but he seemed neither surprised nor excited. He listened silently to the outline of Detective Petrella's adventures.

"How did you get back, then?" he said.

"I got a lift in a lorry to Bordeaux," said the battered young man. "I got in touch with Commissaire Michel and he took me to the airport. We were lucky. The plane from Marrakesh had to touch down and he got me a seat in her. Did you get my telephone message?"

"I got nothing."

"There's a forest fire south of Paris. A lot of the lines are down."

"I expect that's it," said the Superintendent.

He pondered for a moment. "Let me have your ideas about it," he said. "What do you think these people do with the stuff – after they've picked it up out of the water?"

"I found out," said Petrella, "that a lot of the vineyards – particularly the smaller ones which don't go in for château-bottled wines – will sell you a barrel or more at a time. They arrange the shipping and the customs clearance. You just pay the money and in due course the barrel or barrels are delivered. It's new wine, of course – not very drinkable."

"I see," said the Superintendent. "Your idea is that they hide the stuff in the wine and export a barrel or two to a contact on this side?"

"Yes, sir. If they used a Perspex container – or something of the sort – they could regulate the weight so that it wouldn't either float or sink. It would be suspended, so to speak. It would be almost impossible to detect without actually draining the cask."

"You would appear to have a natural talent for smuggling. Perhaps you can tell me why the man who received it leaves it alone for two years. Just plain caution, would you think?"

Petrella said earnestly: "Oh, no, sir. Once a claret is in cask you must *never* touch it for two years. You'd do endless harm to the fermentation. After two years you draw it off and bottle it. That would be the time to get the stuff out, without hurting either it or the claret. In 1952 you get a 1950 heroin . . . "

"Hmph," said the Superintendent. "We're in the realms of guesswork there. The first thing to do will be to ask the customs people to give us a list of private buyers from this château. It can't be a very long list. You'd better go to bed."

"You wouldn't like me to — "

"No, no," said the Superintendent testily. "I can handle it now."

Which brings us to a lovely house of rose-coloured brick in the hills above Maidenhead, and a portly man with a white

78

face and red lips, who started by protesting, then screamed with rage, and ended by whimpering.

And promotion recommended for Detective Constable Petrella.

And one more neat red line in Superintendent Costor-phine's drug book.

The Night the Cat Stayed Out

MATRIX Street is an outpost. On both flanks rise the advancing tide of bedsitting rooms and shops; behind it, in the open space caused by a landmine in 1940, office blocks have risen. In Matrix Street the little houses, with their three white steps leading to their gay front doors, still belong to people. People live in them.

They are not the sort of people who trouble the police except when their chimneys catch fire or they lose their dogs. Detective Constable Patrick Petrella was on his way to see a retired Colonel, who had been using a real Smith and Wesson .445 revolver to shoot imaginary rats in his back garden, and he was using Matrix Street as a short cut. Outside No. 15 he noticed Miss Flint's large tortoiseshell cat, Tinker, sitting on the low wall beside Miss Flint's porch. As he went past Tinker looked at him and lifted the side of his velvet mouth in the lightest of protests. Petrella said, "Good morning, Tinker," but his mind was on the Colonel.

Nearly an hour later he was on his way back. The Colonel had proved amenable to reason, and the right-hand pocket of Petrella's raincoat was weighed down by a Smith and Wesson .445 revolver. Tinker was still sitting on the wall. As Petrella approached he jumped down, ran to the front door, and scratched it delicately.

Petrella stopped.

Now that he had time to consider the matter it occurred to

79

him that No. 15 still wore an overnight appearance. The downstairs curtains were drawn. The end of a folded newspaper protruded from the letter-box. Petrella looked at his watch. It was eleven o'clock.

It was, of course, possible that Miss Flint was away. But before going away she would surely have made proper arrangements for Tinker. In some households cats were left to fend for themselves when the family went on holiday. Not in Matrix Street. Petrella climbed the three white steps and pressed the bell. He heard it buzzing in the bowels of the house; and then, so faintly that it might have been the echo of an echo, he thought he heard a cry.

He stood for a moment, and heard nothing but his own heart; then went down the steps, through the little green side door, which stood on the latch, and down the narrow side passage. Outside the back door was an untouched bottle of milk. He felt a pressure on his ankle. Tinker had followed him.

The window which looked most hopeful was the smallest of the lot. Petrella, by a torpedo–like manoeuvre, and at the expense of a coat button, injected his thin body through the opening, and found himself in a larder. The door was held by a thumb–catch on the outside but yielded to treatment.

In the tiny front hallway he stopped again and called out. This time, he heard the answer. It was a feeble hail, and it came from upstairs.

He tried the two bedrooms, without success, noticing that neither had been slept in. Then the voice spoke again.

"Stop pottering about, whoever you are," it said. "I'm in the bathroom. The door isn't locked."

Petrella opened the door and looked inside with caution. It was a long, narrow, coffin-shaped bath with high sides and Miss Flint was sitting in it. She had a towel wrapped round her shoulders.

"This is no time for modesty, young man," she said. "I've been here all night."

Petrella found another towel, wrapped this also round the old lady, picked her up bodily and carried her into the bedroom. She was surprisingly light. Here he tucked her up as best he could.

"Shout and shout. People must be very deaf in this street. I thought no one would ever come."

"It was Tinker brought me in," said Petrella.

"Darling Tinker," said Miss Flint. "As soon as I'm up and about he shall have a whole haddock for himself. If it hadn't been for him, I might still be in that horrid bath – how I hate it – bawling my head off."

"How did it happen?"

"I got in," said Miss Flint. "I couldn't get out. That's all. Something's wrong with my legs. I managed to pull the plug out, and all the water went away. And I got hold of a towel *and* the bath mat. Lucky it was a warm night."

"Yes," said Petrella. A sudden thought of what it meant to old people to live quite alone came into his head. "You lie quiet. I'll send the ambulance round."

"Ambulance?"

"Certainly," said Petrella. "Just lie still."

"But what about Tinker?"

"I'll look after Tinker. My landlady's very fond of cats."

"It's very good of you," said the old lady, doubtfully. "I don't even know your name. Who are you?"

"As a matter of fact," said Petrella, "I'm a policeman."

Two days later he called in at the hospital to tell Miss Flint that Tinker was settling down nicely in his new home. He had a word with the doctor before he went in.

"She's a marvellous old lady," he said. "It would have killed some people a lot younger than her."

"Will she be all right?"

"Certainly she'll be all right. The delayed shock was the worst part of it. That and the very slight stroke which affected her legs. She'll be up in another week. They don't make 'em like that nowadays. You go and have a gossip with her. She thinks very highly of you."

Petrella found Miss Flint in a reminiscent mood. She talked of her father, who had been a Colonel, and of her great-uncle, who had been a Canon Residentiary of Salisbury; and quite suddenly she stopped, and said, "You don't think I'm mad, do you?"

"I've rarely met anyone saner in my life," said Petrella, sincerely.

"Then let me tell you something. I was helped."

"Helped?"

"During that dreadful night. Quite late. I'd heard the church clock strike midnight and I knew I was there until

81

morning. Perhaps for ever. For the first time, I really thought about that. Suppose no one came. Not for days, or even weeks. And I started to scratch at the side of the bath – what good I thought it could do – and I think I opened my mouth to scream, and I knew, for my father often talked to me about panic, that if I started to scream I should be finished, and at that moment I saw it."

"Yes," said Petrella, in what he hoped was a soothing voice; but it is doubtful if Miss Flint heard him. She was back, in the night, fighting the Terror with only the shades of a long line of hard-living, hard-headed ancestors to help her.

"It was the most beautiful thing. A face, bearded and strong, and lit up from behind by a glow of goodness and kindness. Every time I weakened, I saw it. I don't know how many times. And in the end I went to sleep. Now do you think I'm mad?"

"I'm not sure," said Petrella, truthfully. "How good is your eyesight?"

"As good as yours," said Miss Flint, tartly. "I still use my own eyes and my own teeth."

"How far away did this – er – face seem to be? I mean – was it just outside the window – or further away?"

"If it wasn't inside my own head?"

"If it wasn't inside your own head," agreed Petrella.

Miss Flint considered, and then said, "You're so rational. About a hundred yards. Do you believe me?"

"I believe you saw it," said Petrella. "The interesting question, to my mind, is whether anyone else, similarly placed, would do the same."

Miss Flint fumbled in the old black bag on her bed table.

"Here's the key," she said. "Why don't you go and have a look for yourself."

It was mad, of course.

Petrella told himself so, quite firmly, more than once during the course of the afternoon and as the afternoon faded into the smoky grey of evening. A dream, a vision, a hallucination, born of strain and nurtured by shock.

He told no one.

At eleven o'clock, feeling curiously guilty, he let himself into No. 15 Matrix Street, climbed the stairs to the first floor and stopped to listen. The clock in the hall ticked loudly back at him.

Using his torch discreetly, he moved an old wheelback chair from Miss Flint's bedroom across to the bathroom, and padded it with two cushions. He had a long wait in front of him.

He positioned the chair in front of the bathroom window and settled himself into it. After which he took from his pocket a small but powerful pair of night glasses, and placed them ready.

The gardens of Matrix Street run sharply down to the railway, a branch line, little used at night. Beyond the railway, the ground rises again, to the backs of the big new shop and office blocks which have risen there since the war. These, in their turn, front on the High Street.

Petrella dozed. Behind him, Matrix Street slept the deep sleep of clear consciences and small incomes. An occasional car passed the end of the street, dipped down – what was it called? – a funny little street of cellars and warehouses – which ran through the arch under the railway embankment, then rose again to join the High Street at the war memorial. He could trace the progress of each car quite clearly, the run down, in top gear, the slight booming noise as it passed under the arch, the gear change for the steep rise beyond, then a glimpse of the lights as the car slowed at the corner.

What *was* the name of the street? Petrella was irritated. He prided himself that he knew his . manor forwards and backwards.

Piggott Street? Parrot Street? Perrin Street?

Not street, hill.

Pearson Hill – Pearlyman Hill – Purton Hill. That was it!

At this point Petrella, who had had a long day, most of it on his feet in the open air, fell fast asleep.

When he woke he found himself looking at a face. Bearded and strong and lit from behind by a glow of light. Even as he fumbled for his glasses, it faded.

Petrella shook himself.

"Now did I dream that?" he said. Outside the window everything was dark and quiet. There was a faint flicker of lights from the High Street as a car ran past the corner. He looked at his watch. A quarter to one. And getting cold. He moved across to the bedroom, pulled the patchwork quilt off the bed, and swathed it round him. There was no question now of going to sleep. He had rarely felt more wakeful.

Ten minutes. A quarter of an hour.

Another car – it sounded like a homing taxi – came slowly past the end of Matrix Street, hesitated, then dipped down Purton Hill.

Suddenly the face was there again.

Petrella snatched up his glasses, focused them, steadied them, saw nothing but blackness.

When he lowered them the face was gone.

Speed was going to be essential. If I knew when it was going to happen, he thought, I could be ready with the glasses actually up. Otherwise I don't know how I'm going to catch it. On – off, on – off, like a blessed magic lantern.

At three o'clock he suspended his vigil. The face had appeared no more. He got stiffly to his feet and went home to snatch a few hours' sleep.

The following day, after turning matters over in his mind, he telephoned Nicholas Freeman. It took him four shots to mark him to earth for Nicky was a bird of passage, a young man of a type now almost extinct, who did nothing and did it beautifully.

"Will I do *what?*" said Nicky.

"I don't think I can explain over the telephone," said Petrella. "Meet me at the Crown and Anchor, on Highside, in half an hour."

"Highside?"

"It'll broaden your mind," said Petrella. "Jump to it."

Half an hour later they were sampling the excellent mild beer of the Crown and Anchor and Petrella was drawing a little sketch for Nicky.

"You'd better have a girl with you. Can you manage that?"

"Leave it to me," said Nicky, stroking his small moustache.

"Then you drive twice down this street. Once, at a normal pace. Don't stop. The next time, go slowly, as if you were looking for somewhere to park. Stop at the bottom of the slope – spend about five minutes."

"You can leave that bit to me," said Nicky. "What happens next? Is it Jack the Ripper? Does some character jump out of the shadows and cosh us?"

"If I knew exactly what was going to happen," said

Petrella, "I wouldn't be bothering you. Now be a good chap, and don't ask questions."

At eleven o'clock that night he again let himself into Miss Flint's house. The eight-day clock had run down, otherwise everything seemed much the same.

At one minute to midnight he heard the unmistakable exhaust of Nicky's car and gave that gilded young man full marks for punctuality. It turned the corner, passed the end of Matrix Street and headed for Purton Hill. Petrella had his glasses up to his eyes and practice enabled him to focus them on roughly the right spot.

There was no doubt about it.

A window, a pane of glass; a somewhat dusty pane of glass which reflected back the light of a torch and showed up the face of the man holding it. On, for a count of just three seconds. Then off.

Petrella lowered the glasses and looked again at his watch. He had some time to wait for the more serious part of the performance.

Punctually at half past twelve he heard the car once more. It was idling this time. Very slowly it approached the top of Purton Hill. Then it changed gear, rolled down, and stopped.

"That's shaken him," said Petrella with satisfaction. This time the torch in the window was performing a fandango of dots and dashes. "They don't like that. I only hope they don't assault Nicky."

All was now dark and quiet. Four minutes later Petrella breathed a sigh of relief as he heard the car start, and glimpsed its lights as it swept away. He put back his glasses, and went downstairs, and home to bed.

"It was a swindle," said Nicky, indignantly, the next morning. "Nothing happened. Except to the girl."

"On the contrary," said Petrella. "It went excellently. You were an important part of an experiment. A most successful experiment."

"What d'you mean? Nothing happened at all. And I'd promised the girl there'd be some excitement."

"What sort of excitement?"

"Don't be coarse," said Nicky. "I thought someone was supposed to jump out and cosh us. I had a loaded revolver

85

ready under the dashboard, but I never had a chance of using it."

"Thank goodness for small mercies," said Petrella.

Later that morning he paid an unostentatious visit to the office block in whose window he had seen the torch. It fronted the High Street, and was an ambitious building, with a reception hall, a glass-fronted board of tenants' names, and, more unusual in that part of London, a commissionaire.

He knew Petrella, and invited him into his sanctum.

"No trouble, I hope."

"Not for you," said Petrella. "Just some information. Which offices would it be that possess a window on the third floor, six from the left-hand corner as you look at it from the back?"

The commissionaire consulted the letting plan and did some calculations on his fingers. "That's Solly Moss, the turf accountant. No. As you were. Six from the *left*. That's a new crowd. Novelty Projects."

"What do they do?"

The commissionaire scratched his head. "I don't rightly know," he admitted. "They took two rooms – let me see – three weeks ago. But they haven't started up yet."

"But they've got the keys."

Yes. They had the keys. And a key of the front door. That was the right of all tenants, since the commissionaire went off duty at six. The last man out locked up. They'd never had any trouble yet. Had someone been complaining?

"No one's complained yet," said Petrella. He discovered that the commissionaire had never actually seen any of the members of Novelty Projects and jotted down the name and address of the letting agents.

Midday found him strolling down Purton Hill. It was a curious little street. First came the blind side of the corner house of Matrix Street, then a high blank wall, which no doubt marked the garden of this property. Thereafter the road curved slightly, before running down to the railway arch, and at this point there was a building, fronting on the road and backing on the railway. It had the look of a disused warehouse. A stubby crane projected at first-floor level, and three low, arched openings, heavily barred, at pavement level suggested the presence of a considerable cellar.

Instinct told Petrella that he had found what he was

looking for, and it also warned him not to stop. He walked past without a further glance. It could have been an indiscretion to walk down Purton Hill at all. He only hoped it had not been a fatal one.

His next call was on Messrs. Ryan & Gosport who managed most of the worthwhile property in Highside. Old Mr. Ryan greeted him with an enthusiasm which suggested a guilty conscience, but which was actually nothing but good nature.

"The warehouse in Purton Hill," he said. "Now that is odd. It really is odd. Fancy you mentioning that. A month ago you could have had it for the asking. A white elephant. No market for it. Now I've let it."

"Not by any chance," said Petrella, "to a firm called Novelty Projects?"

"That's them. Nothing wrong with them I hope?"

"Nothing that I can prove," said Petrella, cautiously. "Who actually did the negotiations?"

"A most respectable-looking man. With a beard. I've got his name somewhere here. Henniker."

Petrella made a note of the name and the address, but without much hope. It had the look of an accommodation address. As he turned to go he said, "What was so special about these premises? Why were they so difficult to get rid of?"

"They were put up fifty years ago," said Mr. Ryan, sadly, "by a wine firm. Lovely cellars. Just the thing for storing wine. Then the railway came. Too much vibration. Spoilt the wine. No one else wanted them."

"And those are the cellars you look into, at pavement level? I see. Yes. Thank you very much."

He spent a busy afternoon in the Criminal Records Office, and then sought out his ally, Sergeant Gwilliam, who had a shrewd Welsh head on top of his vast bulk.

He told him all he knew, from beginning to end, including the rescue of Miss Flint, at which the Sergeant laughed immoderately, but when Petrella had finished he scratched his head and said, "It certainly sounds like something, but *what?*"

Petrella said, "The CRO are inclined to think that my friend with the beard, Mr. Henniker, may be none other than 'Artful' Andrews. He's out of nick just now. And he works with a little mob."

"Andrews," said Gwilliam, thoughtfully. "Shop robbery?"

"Specialising in small jewellers' shops and pawnbrokers."

"Yes," said the Sergeant. "You might have something there. I think we'll bring the Inspector in on this."

So Petrella told his story all over again.

"And your idea is — ?" said Chief Inspector Haxtell.

"I couldn't see at first how it worked, sir. But when you walk down Purton Hill it's obvious. There aren't any street lamps until you get under the railway arch, and it's a nasty little slope with a half turn at the bottom. Any car which comes into it would be almost bound to flick on its headlights. And they would shine straight into one or other of the arched openings. They're at pavement level where the road curves. And I should imagine, though I didn't stop to look, that they give directly onto the old cellar."

"I see," said Haxtell. "So if you happened to be doing a little quiet work in the cellar – after midnight, say – something you couldn't very well hide, like swinging a pick-axe – you'd be likely to be spotted."

"That's just what I thought," said Petrella. "They could have blocked up the arches – but that would have been even more suspicious. I haven't quite worked out all the angles, but I should imagine they'd need two guards – one near at hand to warn them about patrolling policemen and pedestrians and so on. And a second one in the office, with a torch, to give them plenty of warning when a car was coming."

Haxtell had been studying a large-scale street plan and directory.

"I see," he said, "that Samuelson's shop is in Comber Street – that backs on to Purton Hill. If it's a tunnel they'd need to go about forty yards. I wonder how far they've got."

A few days later when, at the consummation of two weeks of hard work, the Andrews mob stepped through a carefully cut hole into the cellar of Mr. Samuelson, the well-known pawnbroker and jeweller, they found an interested reception committee awaiting them. 'Artful' Andrews was a professional, and he acknowledged a fair cop.

"I suppose I been shopped," he said, glaring round at his

associates. "Which of you's the rat?" Petrella, who was present, felt tempted to point out that it was not a rat, but a large tortoiseshell cat, which had been responsible for his downfall. But he refrained. Junior Detectives were not expected to make jokes, even if recommended for promotion.

Detective Sergeant

Breach of the Peace

"READING aloud," said Sergeant Gwilliam. "Writing, including handwriting, spelling and punctuation, and the first four rules in arithmetic, including imperial weights and measures and simple fractions."

"Simple fractions."

"Right. Vulgar fractions are for inspectors. Also decimals." The Sergeant contemplated the tattered copy of *Police Regulations* sourly. "You may have wondered why I'm still a sergeant . . . "

"As a matter of fact," said Petrella, "I had."

"Vulgar fractions," said Gwilliam. "Next comes geography. Especially the geography of the British Isles. Most important that. Suppose you're sent off to arrest someone in Edinburgh. No good saying 'Where the hell's that?' is it?"

The vexed subject of promotion was once again under discussion. Normally, as *Police Regulations* points out, a constable must have completed five years' service ("the last two being free from punishment other than reprimand or caution") before he can be considered for the lofty rank of sergeant; and four years before he can even take the exam. But there is a wise proviso. If he manages to "satisfy the Chief Officer of Police" that he is a special case he may be allowed to jump the queue. And in the three months that Petrella had spent at Scotland Yard and the two years he had been at Highside, quite a few Special Reports had found their way on to his superior's desk.

Chief Inspector Haxtell had even gone so far as to suggest that he might be able to skip the exam. "You're educated," he said. "Got School Certificate, or O-levels or whatever they call it nowadays, I expect."

But Petrella was doubtful. He had been comprehensively educated, but on somewhat unorthodox lines.

"I've got a Spanish Certificate of Instruction," he said, "and a pass degree at Beirut University. Also a Certificate of the Elementary Degree of Competence in Viniculture — "

"I think you'd better take the exam," said Haxtell.

So Petrella borrowed the necessary text-books and renewed

his acquaintance with imperial weights and measures and the geography of the British Isles. He was memorising the rivers of the east coast, when the riot call came through.

"Church Hall," said the telephone. "And make it snappy."

Petrella grabbed his hat, and was out of Mrs. Catt's lodging house and running down the street. He considered, but abandoned, the idea of fetching his bicycle. He would be quicker on his feet. A police tender overtook him, and he jumped onto the running board.

"What's up?" he asked.

Sergeant Gwilliam, who was sitting beside the driver, said, "A lot of little bastards started roughing up the Church Hall, but they got a bit more'n they bargained for." Then to the driver, "Stop at the top of the street. We'll form up and go in together. Use your weight."

There were five of them including Petrella. Five men who keep together and know how to behave are a formidable force.

At one moment Petrella saw a milling crowd of youth, flailing arms and dark bodies, the next, they had broken through and were on the steps of the Church Hall. There had been no need to do anything. The sight of police reinforcements had had its usual effect and the crowd was shredding away.

The Reverend Philip Freebone, a stalwart young man, had been holding the doorway with a hockey stick. He had the beginnings of a black eye, his hair was on end, and there was a purely secular light in his eye.

"Glad you've got here," he panted.

"Who started it?" said Gwilliam.

"Young Corky – him and his friends."

Gwilliam said to Petrella, "Grab Corky."

Petrella knew Corky Williams of old. He looked for a mop of blond, almost white, hair; and saw it, in the dusk, under a lamp post.

Petrella ran. The remains of the crowd was melting fast, but he had to jump one prostrate body and push past two boys who were quietly finishing off a private argument. For a moment he lost sight of Corky. Then he saw him, and put on speed. Corky ran. Petrella ran. The chase lasted the length of two streets, and then Corky, seeing he was going to lose the race, slowed down and Petrella grabbed his arm.

"Come back and do some explaining."

"Sure, I'll come with you, Mr. Petrella," said Corky. He had the appearance of a lost waif and a voice that had melted harder hearts than Petrella's. "What do you want me for? It's nothing to do with me. I was just passing."

"Save it," said Petrella. "We'll hear what the parson has to say."

"You needn't hold my arm," said Corky. "I won't run away."

"I'm glad to hear it," said Petrella, and held his arm twice as tight.

Back at the Church Hall volunteers were clearing up the mess. Four boys were being guarded by a policeman in the changing-room, and Sergeant Gwilliam was being talked to by the Reverend Freebone.

"What that Corky wants," he said, "is the repeated application of a hard-heeled shoe to his bottom. He looks like a cherub, his mother spoils him, and if someone doesn't do something drastic, he's going to grow up to be a gangster."

"I know his mother," said Sergeant Gwilliam, shortly. "What happened tonight?"

"A week ago I threw young Corky out of the club. For what seemed to me good reasons. I found he'd been using the recreation circle as cover for a pontoon school. And not even" – the reverend gentleman choked slightly – "an honest pontoon school. The cards were marked. And if a boy complained about his losses, he was intimidated by some of the older boys – you've got three or four of the worst of them in there. But they weren't the organisers. They did what they were told – by Corky."

"I see," said Gwilliam, "and tonight — ?"

"Tonight he turned up, with his supporters, and started shouting at the boys who were coming into club night. They didn't like it – but it wasn't until they threw a stone through the window that the trouble really started — "

"I can take it from there," said Gwilliam. "Who threw the stone? Was that Corky?"

"I don't think so. He kept very much in the background. But he was there all right. That head of hair's unmistakable."

"I'd better have a word with him," said Gwilliam.

A quarter of an hour later, he returned. He looked frustrated.

"Either he's the most accomplished liar I've ever listened to –

95

or we're all dreaming," he said. "You're sure he was here, when the trouble started, I mean?"

"Absolutely sure. Does he deny it?"

"He says that his mother sent him out on an errand – he's got all the times and details pat – that he came past the end of the road, heard a lot of noise and shouting, and stopped to see what it was all about."

"Let's see the other boys," suggested Petrella.

The four youths in the changing room all said the same thing in suspicious unison. They'd been walking past the end of the road. (They hadn't taken the same trouble as Corky to construct an elaborate alibi, Petrella noticed.) They had heard a row. They had stopped to watch. It was nothing to do with them.

"Someone must have started it," suggested Gwilliam. "Did you happen to see anyone – throwing a stone, for instance?"

They had seen no one.

"You didn't happen to notice young Williams?"

They had none of them noticed Corky.

The police retired, baffled.

"Ask Corky," said Petrella, "why he ran away from me."

Corky was brought in. His blue eyes grew large as he understood the purport of the question. "*Me*, run away," he said. "Why, it just isn't true. I was walking away – I didn't want any part of it. I was two streets away when this other man came running after me. And grabbed me by the arm. He grabbed so hard it hurt."

Petrella could almost see the blue eyes filling with tears.

He looked at Sergeant Gwilliam, and shook his head.

The Sergeant drew a visible breath. "I'm charging you all," he said. "Breach of the Peace."

Petrella had early discovered that it was useless trying to set aside periods for study in his spare time. He had no spare time. Three times in his nominal rest hours he had retired to his lodgings with his text-books and three times he had been snatched from them by the calls of duty. Now he kept the books in the CID room – a small room, up a flight of stairs at the back of the Crown Road Police Station, which he shared with Sergeant Gwilliam – and studied when he could.

He was committing to memory that difficult table which

starts, "Twenty-four grains, one pennyweight, twenty penny-weight, one ounce," when Chief Inspector Haxtell looked in.

"This Williams case," he said. "It looks as if it's blowing up into something. They've asked for a remand so that they can brief counsel. And the high-ups are getting worried and talking about bringing in a big gun themselves."

"It's that woman," said Gwilliam. There was no need to ask. They both knew who he meant.

"They're building up a lovely case of persecution," said Haxtell. "Here's how it goes. Six months ago we charged Mrs. Williams with receiving property – one portable wireless set – knowing the same to have been stolen. So she did, and so it had been. Only we weren't able to prove it. We knew it had been looted from the Sonning Town Goods Depot. Knowing isn't proving. She produced a receipt, from a wireless shop, now defunct. And a neighbour, who swore blind she'd had that set for two years. And the court gave her the benefit of the doubt."

"I see now, sir," said Petrella, "where Corky gets his eye for detail."

"They're both very high-class liars. Now, the story goes on, having failed to convict Mrs. Williams, we try and get at her by trumping up a story about her son. Sounds quite convincing, too. I'd believe it myself if I didn't know it was all lies."

It was the lunch hour, on the following day, that Mrs. Williams called to see Petrella. There was, in theory, nothing to prevent people visiting the CID room, but in fact this was the first occasion he could remember of an outsider penetrating it. An apologetic constable put his head round the door, and said, "She had something very important to say – I thought I'd better bring her up."

"That's all right," said Petrella, pushing a work on Elementary Punctuation back into the drawer. "Show her in."

A sight of Mrs. Williams at close quarters showed where Corky had got his good looks from. She must have been nearer forty than thirty but she possessed those firm, regular, very slightly exaggerated lines of beauty which are so popular in saloon bars and on the music-hall stage. The suggestion of a flower garden in the month of August advanced with her into the room.

As Petrella studied her she repaid him the compliment. She seemed surprised that he was so young.

"Please sit down," he said. "What can I do for you?"

97

Her surprise seemed to increase when he spoke.

"You're educated, aren't you?" she said. "What are you doing in this crowd?"

"Earning my living."

"Must be better ways than this." Her glance comprehended the bare and dusty room, the worn linoleum, the shiny patches on Petrella's hard-worked elbows.

"I'm endeavouring to better myself," said Petrella seriously.

"So I heard. You're going for sergeant, aren't you?"

If Petrella was surprised he managed to conceal it.

"That's one of the reasons I came to see you. You heard of Micky Malone?"

Petrella said nothing. Everyone had heard of Micky Malone, housebreaker extraordinary. And every policeman in North London would have given his belt and buttons for the chance of presenting a real, watertight, lawyer-proof case against him.

"If you pulled him in – with the stuff on him – that'd do you some good, wouldn't it?"

Petrella sat very still. He had been a policeman long enough to know that just so had all great criminals been caught. By some woman, like Mrs. Williams, coming quietly to a CID room and speaking a few simple words. What sordid story of intrigue and violence, of passion and treachery lay behind those words was often not known.

"If you know anything about Malone," he said, "I'd be glad to listen to it."

"So you shall," said Mrs. Williams, crossing one shapely leg over the other, "when the charge against my son is dismissed."

"I'm not the magistrate," said Petrella.

"Now don't you come that sort of stuff with me. I've talked to the boy, and I know just where he stands. There's only one thing against him. That he ran away when he saw you coming. All you've got to do is take it back. Say you made a mistake. It was some other boy. He was walking away quietly, like he said."

"How can I say it when it isn't true?"

"That's up to you," said Mrs. Williams. "It won't be the first lie the police have told. What about it? Do we deal?"

If Petrella hesitated, it was nothing to do with his decision. He had come to that minutes earlier. It was just that there were certain angles which still puzzled him. At last he said, almost absent-mindedly, "No, of course I can't make any bargain with you. Now if that's all . . . "

Mrs. Williams was on her feet and she suddenly looked ten years older and a great deal uglier.

"I'm warning you," she said. "You're young. You don't understand how things go. I've got friends."

"Mind the step," said Petrella.

"Certainly she's got friends," said Gwilliam, when Petrella told him about it. "And that perishing little jack-in-office, Councillor Hayes, is one of them. He's had it in for the police ever since we didn't find out who did *his* house nine months ago. If he didn't do it himself."

"I don't think Hayes is a crook," said Petrella. "Just a busybody. He's certainly got a bee in his bonnet about the police."

"As long as he keeps it in his bonnet, and doesn't let it get out and sting us."

"I've just been reading a book on civics," said Petrella. "It points out that whilst, outside London, the police forces are under the control of the Borough Council or the County Council as the case may be, in London they are answerable only to the Home Secretary."

"And who's *he* answerable to?" said Gwilliam. "Parliament. And who are they answerable to? I'll tell you. Any nosey little busybody who chooses to make a fuss and get the press moving."

Superintendent Barstow at Division was saying the same thing, but in different words, to Chief Inspector Haxtell.

"This is one case we want to *win*," he said. "I hear the defence have got Marsham-Tallboys – you remember him? He's the man who gave the Chief Superintendent such a bad time in the warehouse case. We've briefed Collins."

"What's all the fuss about?" said Haxtell, uneasily.

"It's just one of those things," said Barstow. "If the boy gets off, people will believe we have been persecuting the Williams family. Councillor Hayes is bound to raise it for them. He's not a crook, but he's a susceptible old fool. And Mrs. Williams has got him round her little finger. The press have been a bit restive lately, and this'll be a Roman holiday for them."

Haxtell didn't enquire who would play the role of early Christian martyr. He knew.

"There's more to it than that," said Barstow. "I'm told there's a sort of pressure group trying to put the Home

Secretary down. And criticism of the police is the best ammunition they can have."

"Do you think we ought to drop the case, sir?"

Superintendent Barstow slowly turned a dusky red. "By God, I don't," he said. "What you've got to do is win it."

Unconscious of the clouds of political magnitude which were banking in the west, Petrella made his way quietly home that evening to his lodgings. His path took him through Barnaby Passage, and in the darkest part of the passage two figures came out to meet him. His heart gave a jump, then steadied again. They were only boys; as he now saw, two of the Harrington children, Ron, the ten-year-old, and a smaller one whose name he had forgotten. Ron seemed to have something he wanted to say, but as he spoke in a disjointed and breathless whisper it took quite a long time for him to get it across.

When at last he had made his meaning clear, Petrella was filled with a deep and unholy joy.

"Are you absolutely sure?" he said.

"Course I'm sure," said Ron. "Hazel's got a friend whose sister chars for Missus Williams. She saw it. She didn't like to say anything, see. But it's there all right. On a little plate. It's inside the back of the clock. That's why Missus Williams never seen it."

"Ron," said Petrella, "next time I'm here I'm going to bring you the biggest and most unsuitable box of sweets that money can buy."

"S'all right," said Ron. "Corky, he won my money, by cheating, see. That's why we thought we'd tell you. We don't want no sweets."

"You shall have 'em all the same," said Petrella.

The Case of the Police against Williams (and others) was one of the most remarkable ever heard in Helenwood Magistrates Court. And its crises were none the less real for not all being apparent on the surface.

The presiding magistrate, Mr. Benkall, was not what is popularly called a "policeman's magistrate." He decided cases on the evidence produced and in the light of his own rugged common sense. But even he could not be unaware of the implications of the case he was hearing; of the crowds round the door, of the packed public benches, of eminent counsel in their places, and of a press box, usually occupied by one elderly reporter from the *Highside Mercury*, but now bulging with representatives of the national press.

It took an hour to clear the routine matters and the case was called just before midday.

By four o'clock in the afternoon it was apparent that the police were winning. The insidious Mr. Marsham-Tallboys had done his best with Mrs. Williams and his worst with the police, but on the whole it seemed probable that the evidence of one clergyman, six boys, one detective sergeant and one detective constable was going to be preferred to that of a mother, however sympathetically represented.

It was time for the defence to call up its reserves. At four o'clock Mr. Councillor Hayes entered the box. He appeared as witness to character and told the magistrate that he had always found Williams a cheerful, honest and truthful boy, of very good family. He knew his mother well. A widow and a very worthy citizen. The family was a credit to Highside. He could not for a moment believe that a boy from such an excellent family would do the things imputed to him.

When Mr. Collins rose to cross-examine, he seemed, for a moment, to have forgotten what he wanted to ask. He was an amiable teddy bear of a man, with the untidiest wig at the Old Bailey, and his kindliness and apparent vagueness had been deceiving criminals to their undoing for the past twenty-five years. He said at last, apologetically, "I'm afraid I missed your names – Mr. Hayes. Your Christian names, I mean. Could you repeat them?"

Mr. Hayes, surprised, said, "Cedric Winstanley," in the strangled tones of a man unexpectedly asked to repeat his Christian names in public.

Mr. Collins repeated, "Cedric Winstanley Hayes," in a dreamy voice and made a careful note on the margin of his brief. "You have, I believe, always been interested in local government topics?"

"That is so."

"Am I right in saying that you gave a series of lectures on them, some years ago, to the London Institute of Civic Studies?"

"That is correct."

"In fact, I believe, so appreciative were your students that they presented you, at the end of the course, with a handsome walnut clock with a small plate inside the back as a token of their appreciation."

"I – yes – That is so."

"And this was one of the articles stolen from your house, some nine months ago, and never recovered."

"The police," said Mr. Hayes with heavy sarcasm, and a glance at the press, "have not succeeded in restoring it to me – yes."

"Really, Mr. Collins," said the magistrate. "Wide though the latitude is that is permitted to counsel in this court, I fail to see — "

He was interrupted. Mrs. Williams was observed to be on her feet and fighting her way through the crowd, towards the exit. The face that she turned over her shoulder as she reached the door was as white as paper.

"I was only going to ask the witness," said Mr. Collins gently, "whether he was aware that the clock was at this very moment to be found on Mrs. Williams' drawing-room mantelpiece. It can easily be identified from a plate in the back . . . "

"How *very* satisfactory," said Superintendent Barstow. "How really very satisfactory." He ticked the points of satisfaction off on his fingers. "First, of course, that we won the case. I notice that has killed the news story dead. Secondly, that old Hayes should have made a perfect fool of himself in public – giving evidence about that woman's respectability when all the time she'd got a clock *stolen from him* on her drawing room mantelpiece. Thirdly, that clock's going to be a very useful bit of evidence when we go against Mrs. Williams for receiving goods stolen within the last twelve months: Section 43 of the Larceny Act, I needn't tell you – and if she doesn't go down this time, what with all the rest of the stuff we found in her cellar, I'm a Dutchman. And fourthly — " his finger waggled for a moment. There was, he knew, a fourth cause for satisfaction.

"Oh, yes. Petrella's promotion has come through. He's a sergeant now. Probationary, of course."

Voyage into Illusion

THE steward was young, and the band of freckles across the top of his nose made him look even younger. He was carrying, not very expertly, a tray with glasses on it.

A tall glass of iced lager went to the savage-looking woman who wore her bangles with the air of an experienced gladiator coming out for another dusty battle in the arena of life. A brandy-and-soda for the savage lady's red-faced, white-moustached husband. Major and Mrs. Corret, said the steward to himself. A large part of his job was getting the right names attached to the right faces.

A medium-sized gin with French vermouth for the girl in the cut-away linen dress with the gold hair and the biscuit-coloured suntan. French. Marianne something-or-other. You could always get by with a French girl by calling her M'selle.

A large gin to Mr. Clinton, the owner of the yacht *Medea*. Mr. Clinton was his employer and had a smooth, round face, a smooth, round smile, and a sharp pair of eyes. A very large gin for Captain Harbert, the certificated skipper of the yacht. The second part of the steward's trade was observation, and he saw that the Captain was already a little drunk. The large gin with a splash of water would take him a long step further.

As he turned to go, the girl said lazily, "Oh, steward."

"M'selle?"

"I take it you mixed this martini yourself?"

"Yes, M'selle."

"By the light of your own unaided intelligence?"

"Certainly, M'selle."

"Next time I suggest you use the book. It requires half as much gin, twice as much vermouth, and a dash of bitters."

The steward flushed, bowed slightly, and withdrew. As he closed the door he heard Clinton say reproachfully, "Stewards aren't all that easy to get, Marianne."

The steward, moving away down the passage, shook his head like a diver surfacing after a deep dive. But there was no time for resentment. There was too much to do.

The *Medea*, though all of two hundred tons' capacity, could

103

hardly be expected to carry such a luxury as a second steward. Until the four passengers were all safely tucked up in their own, or each other's, bunks he was going to be on the run. If the weather had been bad, his job might have been easier, but the Solent had never looked calmer. The afterglow of a long summer's day lay on the smooth sea like a mantle. How lovely it would be, he thought, to strip off the tight white uniform and dive into the water and swim to some beach where the sand was still warm from the sun.

Major Corret's cabin. There were two suitcases thrown on the bunk, one opened, the other one closed but unlocked. And a battered leather holdall containing brushes and a razor. A seasoned traveller, the Major. The steward's fingers moved deftly, removing clothes and packing them neatly away in the built-in cupboard under the bunk. He seemed, somehow, to be cleverer at this part of his trade than he was at handing round drinks. One of the ties that he unpacked bore the broad stripes of the Brigade of Guards. Lower down in the case he found a Rifle Brigade blazer and a Royal Artillery silk square. An all-round man, the Major.

His next call was the galley. The Breton cook, twenty stone of well-laid yellow fat, was in a temper. He had been in a difficult mood ever since the company had come on board at tea-time, and had been made no pleasanter by a criticism of his gateaux uttered by Mrs. Corret and incautiously passed on to him by the steward.

He was chopping carrots with a very heavy, very sharp knife, and looking as if he wished it was Mrs. Corret's fingers that he was shortening. "Any further grunts from the sty?" he enquired gracefully.

"They're drinking now."

"And soon they will stop drinking and start — " The cook employed a farmyard metaphor which lost nothing from being in earthy Breton.

The bell in the little pantry sounded. With a sigh the steward picked up the tray. It occurred to him to wonder if the job was going to be as amusing as it had seemed when he was offered it.

At ten that evening, on the top of the tide, the mooring-cable was slipped and the *Medea* headed down the Solent. At eleven o'clock Major and Mrs. Corret retired to their cabins. At half past eleven Marianne followed. The steward, who happened to be in the companion-way outside the saloon, held open her cabin door for her and was rewarded, this time, with a smile. A minute later he heard the bolt click in the lock. At a quarter to twelve he fetched a drink for Mr. Clinton. At twelve o'clock, a further drink. At half past twelve he found the saloon empty, cleared up the glasses, and washed them in the sink in the pantry.

The bell sounded, this time from the bridge. The steward frowned slightly, and made his way forward.

At the wheel in the small, enclosed bridge-house he found the mate, Cairns, a monkey-like man who rarely spoke and never drank. The skipper was sitting against the side of the bridge-house, his head on his chest.

"The skipper," said Cairns, "would like some coffee. Black coffee."

"At once, sir."

"And I could do with some, too."

The coffee took time to brew. When the steward came back with it, the skipper was stretched flat, his head pillowed on a life-jacket.

"The skipper no longer requires any coffee," said Cairns. "You may have the other cup yourself."

The *Medea* was dipping softly now as it cleared the southern tip of the island and met the up-channel swell. The twin diesel engines purred like cats with a full night's work in prospect. A big liner, remote but ablaze with light, snailed across ahead of them.

"You'd better get your head down," said Cairns. "You'll have a lot to do tomorrow."

By eleven o'clock next morning the steward felt that he had already finished a heavy day's work. The Correts had breakfasted and were reading in the saloon. Neither Clinton nor Marianne had appeared. The steward snatched a moment's respite to creep on deck and see just where the enchantress *Medea* might have set them down.

They lay in the land-locked estuary of the River Odet, half a mile above the fishing village of Benodet. The steward had never been to southern Brittany before, but he was aware of a feeling of familiarity. Indeed, it was more Cornish than Cornwall itself. The steep, high, enclosing river banks, close-carpeted with blue-black woods; the river, dark in colour, but clear; the glimpse of a grey stone roof among the treetops.

Came a pattering of steps on the deck beside him, and a body went through the air in a kingfisher flash of blue and gold, and smashed the looking-glass of the river. He held his breath until she came up, twenty yards nearer the shore. Then he moved.

Down in his cabin, a tiny cupboard off the pantry, he kept a pair of binoculars. His porthole commanded the eastern river bank, and presently he picked out the white bathing-cap. The girl was making for a wooden hulk, beached on the mud. She went on until she could hold the wooden stern post, and there she rested for a moment. Then she turned and started back, swimming lazily but happily, as if water was her element.

A fat laugh blew off in his ear, nearly making him drop the glasses. The cook, silent in rubber soles, had padded in behind him.

"Ravishing," he agreed. "But not on the menu for you, *mon gars*. Now, suppose we get on with laying the lunch?"

Clinton appeared in time for a pre-lunch gin. The steward was an adaptable young man. It had not taken him long to realise that if a servant behaved discreetly people would talk in front of him as though he did not exist. Perhaps he did not exist. Perhaps nothing was real in this floating world of silver and polished wood and old-young people . . . perhaps it was all an illusion.

"I've never been treated so before in my life," said Mrs. Corret. Her ugly little mouth was well shaped for sentences like that. "What do they suppose we are? A boatload of weekend trippers?"

"Hardly, my dear. Hardly," said her husband.

"Then why should they come to my cabin this morning, when I was barely out of it, and search my luggage? They were there for an hour."

"You were lucky," said Clinton. "*I* was still in bed."

"Bit unusual, isn't it?" said the Major.

"The routine varies," said Clinton. "They're well within their rights, of course. Benodet's a customs station. But it's the first time I've known them search the baggage."

"And what's this about not going ashore?"

"I think there's been some confusion over that," said Clinton. "A message from Paris that's been misunderstood. It will all be cleared up by tonight, I'm sure."

"Meanwhile," said the girl, "I am the only one of you whose

106

feet have touched the soil of France. And very muddy soil it was." She wriggled her bare toes in her sandals.

"They're not being unreasonable," said Clinton. "I told them the cook would have to go ashore for stores this afternoon. They raised no objection."

"Decent of them," drawled the Major.

The steward made a mental note. He would have to see whether he could go with the cook. Actually it was quite easy. The cook raised no objection. He appeared to have taken a liking to the steward.

They put two large store baskets into the dinghy and rowed the half mile downstream to the ferry and the landing stage. The cook, for all his bulk, handled the oars daintily; every time he leaned forward at the top of his stroke his singlet gapped away from his chest and showed the words TOTO CHÉRIE in startling purple relief.

They tied up below the Bac and went ashore. It took an hour to find all the fruit and vegetables and fish they wanted. At the end of it the cook headed for a fisherman's bistro near the port.

"But I ought to be serving tea," said the steward.

"Let the pigs forage for themselves," said the cook. "I require a drink."

It was a small, dark place, which looked like a general store, but had a bar tucked away at one end. The cook ordered pineapple squash and rum, which he mixed together and drank with slow enjoyment. The steward had a cup of gritty chocolate. As they were finishing, the man behind the bar said something in the harsh local dialect and the cook hauled himself up and rolled across. For a minute the conversation continued.

The bulk of the cook obscured the space in front of him, but it seemed to the steward that something was being pushed across the zinc counter. He got to his feet and moved over. The cook's big hand closed on something. It looked like a flat packet of cigarettes. The next moment it was gone.

"Really," said the steward, "it is past five."

"Let us go then," agreed the cook.

Nothing was said as they walked back to the dinghy. Nothing as the cook bent again to the oars. As they neared the yacht, however, he paused for a moment in his labours and said, "Nothing, I suggest, need be mentioned of a visit to the bistro."

"I agree, of course," said the steward solemnly. Neverthe-less, he seemed to be deeply preoccupied.

So much so that he made several mistakes in serving drinks that evening and was pulled up sharply by Clinton. There was a feeling of tension in the saloon, which was not improved by the fact that general permission to land, though expected, had not yet been received. When, at last, the steward got to bed, he did something he had not done before. He slipped home the bolt on the door of the little steel cupboard where he slept.

Next morning the atmosphere was lightened. A customs officer arrived, full of smiles and apologies. A grave mistake had been made. Of course the passengers might land.

It was too late to organise a lunch ashore, but a picnic tea was packed by the steward into a hamper and lowered into the dinghy. He had half expected that he would be detailed to accompany the party, but in the end it was one of the deck-hands who rowed them to the jetty at the foot of the wooded slope and shouldered the basket as the party set out on the winding path, the girl running ahead, and disappeared into the bluey-green of the woods.

The steward had out his useful glasses and watched them as they went. His attitude seemed to suggest that he felt some crisis in his affairs to be approaching.

But for the next hour frustration awaited him at every turn. Three times he found himself outside Marianne's cabin, and three times he was interrupted. First it was the Captain, who wanted his shoes cleaned. Then the engineer appeared from the depths and demanded hot water.

Then the cook wanted to borrow a cup and saucer from the saloon crockery, which was the steward's department. He indicated the empty shelf where the white kitchen crockery, fat cups and thick, plain plates and saucers, had been stored. "The pigs," he said, "have taken it for their picnic. Am I therefore to be without a cup of coffee?" The steward unlocked the saloon china cupboard and got out two cups. He felt in need of some coffee himself.

The fourth time he was lucky. All seemed quiet. He turned the handle and went in. The little room was full of the faint but lovely scent she used. It was as if, her physical self being absent, she had left behind a sweet-smelling ghost to watch over her belongings. The steward wasted no time.

He pulled on a pair of cotton gloves and opened the drawers

of the built-in cupboard. Then he turned his attention to the
suitcases crowded together at the foot of the bunk. The first
two were unlocked and empty. The third – and smallest – was
locked. The steward pulled out a bunch of tiny keys, selected
one carefully by size and shape, tried it, and rejected it. He was
neat, precise, and infinitely patient. The tenth key worked.

It was a dressing-case. At first sight he thought that this, too,
was empty. Then he saw that there was a wallet flap inside the
lid. By its bulk, it contained papers. The steward pulled out the
contents and stared at them for a moment, the oddest
expression on his face. Curiosity. Then incredulity. Finally,
something which looked oddly like relief.

"So that's it," he said to himself. Carefully but quickly he
fastened the lock. Carefully replaced the cases where he had
found them. Quietly left the cabin.

He did not notice that the galley door was fractionally open.
Nor was he aware that from the darkness behind it the cook
was watching him.

The guests were back on board by six o'clock clamouring for
attention. They were soaked with sun and surfeited with the
unusual exercise of walking up and down a steep hill. "Worth
it, though," said the Major. "Reminded me of the view from
the top of Jakko."

Clinton, too, seemed in high good humour. He had ordered
claret, and as he passed round the third bottle the steward was
glad to see that even the Major's wife was drinking level. He
reckoned that the red wine and the sun would work together to
his advantage; and it fell out as he had calculated.

By eleven o'clock the Correts had rolled to their cabins, and
ten minutes later the girl followed. Clinton lit his second cigar,
called for a brandy, and settled down at the table with a
portfolio of papers. When the steward arrived with his drink he
said, without looking up, "I shan't be needing you any more.
You've had a long day."

If the steward felt surprised he managed to conceal it. In three
days he had learnt a good deal about concealing his feelings. He
went quietly out.

In the passage he paused. From the nearest cabin came the
sound of a reassuring snore. Under the door of the girl's cabin a
light showed. Again he paused, then drew in his breath as if

plunging into cold and unknown water, and knocked lightly on the panel.

With the slightest pause he heard her voice say, "Who is it? A moment, if you please." Then, "Come in."

He pushed the door open. She was sitting in the low chair beside the bunk, smoking a cigarette. Her feet were bare but she had not undressed. She might almost have been expecting him. He shut the door quietly behind him.

"If you wish us not to be disturbed," she suggested coolly, "you had better slip the bolt. That's right. Mr. Clinton, who does not lack for persistence, usually tries my door when he comes past to his cabin."

The steward said abruptly, "This afternoon, I opened your dressing-case."

"Yes," said the girl. "You replaced the cases carefully. But not quite carefully enough."

"I know, therefore, your real name and your job. You are of the French police."

"And you, I judge, of the English police. What is your real name, if I may be permitted — "

"Petrella," said the young man. "Sergeant Petrella."

"And there is another name?"

"Patrick."

"Tres gentil. Pat-trick." She made two equal syllables of it, as if it rhymed with hat trick. Petrella thought it sounded delightful. "Now, how can I help you? How much do you know?"

"I know," said Petrella, "that the police of both our countries have been watching Clinton for a long time. I know that he is a receiver of stolen goods. That he specialises in precious stones. Some historic pieces have passed through his hands. He breaks them up. Sometimes the stones are re-cut. Then they are shipped abroad, in this yacht, and sold on the continent."

"That is all conjecture."

"It is all conjecture. If it were more than conjecture, he would be in gaol. But it is conjecture based on some remarkable coincidences. Half a dozen times, stones of great value have been stolen. Up to a certain date we know – we positively and actually know – that they are in England. That's the date when Clinton takes his yacht and sails to Benodet in her. Then, a little time later, we hear that the stones are in Europe. It's as simple as that."

"Simple," said the girl, "but not simple. There are a thousand places on a boat like this where a few precious stones might be hidden."

"While they are on the ship, yes. But sooner or later the moment comes when they must go ashore. They cannot walk, or fly. They must be carried. And until your picnic this afternoon only two people have touched the soil of France. The cook and myself."

"You are wrong." She stretched out one bare foot. "I have touched it. And very muddy it was."

"Yes. I watched you through my glasses."

"Then you saw me using the old hulk as a post office?"

"I saw you do something," said Petrella. "But you were too quick, and it was too far off for me to be certain. That is why I searched your things and discovered the truth."

"I took ashore a note," she said, "containing a suggestion. It was not an order – I am not in charge of this operation – but I suggested that the embargo be lifted and Clinton and his guests allowed ashore, and I with them. You may be certain that not one step we took, not one move we made, was unobserved."

"Tell me what happened."

"Nothing happened. We walked up a steep path through the woods. The sailor – the one they call R-r-ron – carried the tea hamper. Do you think, by the way, that he is concerned?"

"No," said Petrella. "We've checked on the crew very thoroughly. I think they just sail Clinton's ship for him. The Captain's an astonishing old soak, but I don't think that any of them, except perhaps the cook, are concerned. Please go on."

"We reached a plateau – an open space of grass, where there is a ruined church; you can see the top through the trees. In the middle of the field there are three stone pillars. They are common in Brittany. They are very old, I think."

"Dolmen stones?"

"Yes. We sat with our backs against them. It was very pleasant. We had our tea."

"Was Clinton ever out of your sight?"

"Not for a minute. He sat next to me. He was very gallant."

"I can believe it."

"So much so that he nearly spoilt my dress. He — " She broke off, and said, "Don't talk."

Footsteps were tip-tapping down the linoleum-covered

111

passageway. They seemed to pause for a moment, then passed on. The door of Clinton's cabin slammed.

"Really!" said the girl. "I hardly call *that* gallant. He might at least have tried the handle." She reached up her hand and clicked off the switch. Only the soft bunk lamp glowed.

"You were telling me about your dress."

"It was nothing, really. We were drinking from our cups at the same time. He leaned across and clinked his against mine – as if they were wine glasses, you understand. Only they were not wine glasses. They were common crockery cups, and they both broke. In a drawing-room there would have been a mess. In a field it did not matter."

A memory stirred. Something he had seen. In the galley, with the cook. "Common, white crockery cups?" he said. "With thick bases?"

"That is so." He saw the sudden gleam of interest in her eye. "Is it important?"

"It might be," said Petrella. "They are cups that the cook used, for himself, in the galley. Why should they be used for the passengers? There are plenty of china cups in the saloon."

She considered it, and shook her head slowly. "There is nothing in that," she said. "They would not take good cups. In case they got broken – as they did."

"What did you do with the pieces?"

"When we had finished, R-r-ron dug a hole, and buried the scraps. And the paper, and the broken cups – good Lord!" He heard her catch her breath.

"So it's occurred to you, too, has it?" said Petrella. "What better hiding-place for the journey out? To bake the stones into the bases of a pair of thick china cups, and hang them in the galley, under the cook's own eye."

"You sound so sure."

"You saw Clinton this evening," said Petrella. "You must have noticed the change from this morning. Relaxed, at ease. The job done. It was clear that the stones had gone ashore somehow. And we know how it was done."

"What are you going to do?"

"I am going to do some digging," said Petrella. "Where were they buried?"

"Under the left-hand stone as you stand with your back to the river. What do you propose?"

112

"It would be better, I think, not to take the boat. It is a warm night."

"Take this, though," she said. It came out from her bunk. An automatic pistol. No lady's toy, with inlaid mother-of-pearl grip; but a man's gun, in shining blue steel.

Petrella put it into his pocket. As he handled it, the metal was still warm from the warmth of her bed. She leaned forward, said, "Good luck, little Sergeant. Be careful when you get among the trees."

Back in his cabin, Petrella stripped naked. Then from his kit-bag he picked out and put on a pair of old khaki shorts and a pair of rope-soled deck shoes. The gun was the real problem. In the end he dropped it in his sponge bag and knotted the cords of the bag to one of the belt-loops in his shorts. It swung awkwardly as he walked, but the arrangement left his hands free.

As he made his way towards the deck he noticed that the cook's cabin door was on the hook. He looked in. The moonlight showed an empty cabin and an unused bunk. Also, as he saw when he reached the deck, the dinghy was gone. He had heard no sound but it would have been easy enough to cast off and float down with the current until out of earshot.

If the cook was already ashore he would need twice as much care; and twice as much luck.

The gangway, which ran past the porthole of Clinton's cabin, represented an unnecessary danger. Petrella climbed through the stern rail, hung by his hands, and let himself drop. The water was warm to the touch. He drifted quietly downstream. The tide was near full ebb, and the current of the Odet was asserting its strength. His feet touched mud a hundred yards below the landing-stage.

The river bank here was built up with concrete blocks against the scour and he pulled himself onto them and sat, for a moment, to disengage the gun and get back his breath and improve his night sight.

Above him the line of trees was unbroken, but they were mostly pine and oak and he guessed that, with a little care, he could walk through them as quickly, and with less noise than on the beaten track.

At first it was scrambling, with hands and feet. Then the slope levelled off. Soon after that he saw dim light ahead of him. He pushed through the last of the bushes and was looking out at the upland plateau which the girl had described.

Under the pale, full moon it was a place of ancient and potent beauty. The grass looked as smooth as a college lawn. In the middle stood the three crooked dolmen stones, throwing long shadows behind them. On the edge of the clearing, the old chapel, silvery-grey in the moonlight.

Under that soft light, time went back. Black shades of priest and congregation were moving in the doorway, and the lights were on in the chancel.

Petrella rubbed his eyes. Surely it was a trick of the moon?

It took an effort of the will to move away from the friendly shelter of the wood. The feel of the heavy gun in his hand helped him.

As he started to move, the voices started. When he stopped, they stopped too. He told himself that it was the noise of his feet, passing through the dry ankle-high grass.

When he reached the dolmen stones, he looked across to the chapel, but it had gone. It was hidden in mist, which crept up, unnoticed, to his knees. If it rose higher and thicker, it might be a nuisance. The left-hand stone, she had said. Petrella knelt beside it. A large piece of turf had been cut. It moved to his fingers. Needing both hands, he laid the gun carefully down beside him. At that moment he looked up and saw the cook, five paces away, staring at him. His hand went to the gun. A foot was on it, a booted foot, which stamped on his fingers.

As he cried out, men came from everywhere: from behind the stones, from the hollow in the field, they rose from the ground. Then the world stopped short on its axis and he himself was diving, upwards and outwards, into space, towards the upside-down river of stars which formed the sky. As he went he heard shouts, and the braying of a siren, but faintly, and more faintly, as he left the busy earth behind him and journeyed outward into space.

There was sunlight in his eyes when he opened them, and a very pretty girl in a nurse's uniform was doing something to the slats of the venetian blind, and saying, "Only five minutes, then. No more."

Petrella turned his head painfully, and saw Superintendent Hazlerigg, with his bowler hat between his hands and a look of sardonic interest on his brick-red face.

"Where am I?" said Petrella.

"At Quimper," said Hazlerigg, "in hospital."

Petrella gathered from his tone of voice that all was well.

"Have you got the stones?" he said. "What were they?"

"The Ladbrook emeralds, none other," said Hazlerigg. "Six lovely stones. But no thanks to you. Or was it? I'm not sure. This has been rather a muddled trip. As I said to the Commissioner, we ought either to have told you a lot more, or a lot less."

"You warned me to expect help from the French police," said Petrella. "When it turned out to be that girl — "

"Marianne," said Hazlerigg thoughtfully. "Yes. She's in gaol with Clinton. You realise she was not being candid with you?"

Petrella said nothing. He lay and stared.

"The papers you were allowed to discover in her suitcase – the ones that seemed to indicate that she was in the French police – they had, of course, been planted there for you to find. Not that we lied to you. There was help on board. I expect you realise that now. The cook. A very experienced hand. The trouble was, *he* hadn't been told about *you*. A bad lack of liaison. But he came to the conclusion that you might be on the side of law and order when he caught you watching the girl through binoculars. That was why he took the shore trip. When you insisted on coming with him, and breathed down the back of his neck in the bistro, he knew exactly where he was."

"If he knew I was on his side," said Petrella faintly, "why didn't he tell me?"

"By then it was too late. Clinton and his friends were wise to you, too. I'm not sure they hadn't suspected you all along."

Petrella grasped at the disappearing skirts of reality. "Do you mean," he said, "that the girl – that she knew? All the time? Then why did she tell me about the broken cups? Why not just send one of her own side to dig them up? Wasn't it incredibly risky?"

"It would have been risky," agreed Hazlerigg, "if the stones had ever been in the cups. But they never were. You were told that story simply to make you go on shore. But the cook heard it. He'd fixed a microphone in her cabin."

"He'd *what*?"

"He'd got them in all the cabins. I tell you, he is a professional, that man. When he heard what was up, he took

115

the boat and went ashore ahead of you and tipped *us* off. It was a close race, but we got there more or less together. Not in time to stop you getting hurt, but in plenty of time to round up *their* party. She'd left a message for them on her early-morning swim, so they knew what the plan was."

Petrella said feebly, "I've no idea what you're talking about. What plan? How did the stones go ashore?"

"That bit was really quite simple," said Hazlerigg kindly. "*You* were carrying them. Six stones wrapped in cotton wool, in the magazines of the gun she gave you."

At this point the nurse reappeared. "Do you wish to kill the boy," she said sternly, "with your chattering? Out with you this moment! No, not another word!"

The Oyster Catcher

THE table was the first thing which caught your eye as you came into the room. Its legs were of green-painted angle-iron, bolted to the floor; its top a block of polished teak.

Overhead shone five white fluorescent lights.

On the wide, shadowless, aseptic surface the raincoat looked out of place, like some jolly, seedy old tramp who has strayed into an operating theatre. A coat is such a personal thing, almost a second skin. As it loses its own shape, and takes on the outlines of its wearer, as its pockets become a repository of tobacco flakes and sand and fragments of leaves, and its exterior becomes spotted with more unexpected things than rain, so does it take on an intimate life all of its own.

There was an element of indecency, Petrella thought, in tearing this life from it. The earnest man in rimless glasses and a white laboratory overall had just finished going over the lining with a pocket-sized vacuum-cleaner with a thimble-shaped container. Now he was at work on the exterior. He cut a broad strip of adhesive tape and laid it on the outside of the coat, pressing it firmly down. Then he marked the area with a special pencil, and pulled the tape off. There was nothing visible to the naked eye on the under-surface of the tape, but he seemed satisfied.

"We'll make a few micro-slides," he said. "They'll tell us anything we want to know. There's no need for you to hang about if you don't want to."

Sergeant Petrella disliked being told, even indirectly, that he was wasting his time. Let the truth be told, he did not care for Scientific Assistant Worsley at all. Worsley had the very slightly patronising manner of one who has himself been admitted to the inner circles of knowledge and is speaking to unfortunates who are still outside the pale. It was a habit, Petrella had noticed, which was very marked at the outset of a scientific career, but which diminished as a man gained more experience and realised how little certainty there was, even under the eye of the microscope.

"All right!" he said. "I'll push off and come back in a couple of hours."

"To do the job completely," said Worsley, "will take about six days." He looked complacently at the neat range of Petri dishes round the table, and the samples he had so far extracted. "Perhaps another three to tabulate the results."

"All the same," said Petrella, "I'll look in this evening and see what you have got for me."

"As long as you appreciate," said Worsley, "that the results I give you will be unchecked."

"I'll take a chance on that."

"That, of course, is for you to decide." His voice contained a reproof. Impetuous people, police officers. Unschooled in the discipline of the laboratory. Jumpers to conclusions. People on whom careful, controlled research was usually wasted. Worsley sighed audibly.

Sergeant Petrella said nothing. He had long ago found out that it was a waste of time antagonising people who were in a position to help you.

He consulted his watch, his note-book, and his stomach. He had a call to make in Wandsworth, another in Acton, and a third in South Harrow. Then he would come back to the Forensic Science Laboratory to see what Worsley had got for them. Then he would go back to Highside and report to Chief Inspector Haxtell. He might have time for lunch between

Acton and South Harrow. If not, the prospect of food was remote, for once he reached Highside there was no saying that Haxtell would not have a lot more visits lined up for him.

All this activity – and, indirectly, the coat lying on Worsley's table – stemmed from a discovery made by a milkman at No. 39 Carhow Mansions. Carhow Mansions is a tall block of flats overlooking the southern edge of Helenwood Common.

Miss Martin, who lived alone at No. 39, was a woman of about thirty. Neither beautiful, nor clever, nor ugly, nor stupid. She was secretary to Dr. Hunter, who had a house and consulting-room in Wimpole Street. She did her work well, and was well paid for it.

The flat, which was tucked away on the top storey and was smaller than the others in the block, was known as a "single" which means that it had about as little accommodation as one person could actually exist in. A living-room which was also a dining-room. An annexe which served as a bedroom. One cupboard, called a kitchen, and another, called a bathroom. Not that Miss Martin had ever been heard to complain. She had no time to waste on housework and ate most of her meals out. Her interests were Shakespeare and tennis.

Which brings us to the milkman, who, finding Friday's milk bottle still unused outside the door of Flat 39 on Saturday, mentioned the matter to the caretaker.

The caretaker was not immediately worried. Tenants often went away without telling him, although Miss Martin was usually punctilious about such matters. Later in the morning his rounds took him up to No. 39 and he looked at the two milk bottles and found the sight faintly disturbing. Fortunately, he had his pass-key with him.

Which brought Chief Inspector Haxtell on to the scene in a fast car. And Superintendent Barstow, from District Head-quarters. And photographic and fingerprint detachments, and a well-known pathologist, and a crowd on the pavement, and a uniformed policeman to control them; and, eventually, since Carhow Mansions was in his manor, Sergeant Petrella.

Junior detective sergeants do not conduct investigations into murders, but they are allowed to help, in much the same way as a junior officer helps to run a war. They are allowed to do the work, whilst their superiors do the thinking. In this case there was a lot of work to do.

"I don't like it," said Barstow in the explosive rumble which was his normal conversational voice. "Here's this girl, as ordinary as apples and custard. No one's got a word to say against her. Life's an open book. Then someone comes in and hits her on the head, not once. Five or six times."

"Any one of the blows might have caused death," agreed the pathologist. "She's been dead more than twenty-four hours. Probably killed on Friday morning. And I think there's no doubt that that was the weapon."

He indicated a heavy, long-handled screwdriver.

"It could have belonged to her," said Haxtell. "Funny thing to find in a flat, though! More like a piece of workshop equipment."

"All right!" said Barstow. "Suppose the murderer brought it with him. Ideal for the job. You could force a front door with a thing like that. Then, if the owner comes out, it's just as handy as a weapon. But it's still" – he boggled over using the word and its implications – "it's still mad."

And the further they looked, and the wider they spread their net, the madder it did seem. Certain facts came to light at once.

Haxtell was talking to Dr. Hunter, of Wimpole Street, within the hour. The doctor explained that Miss Martin had not come to work on Friday because he himself had ordered her to stay in bed. "I think she'd been over-using her eyes," said the doctor. "That gave her a headache, and the headache affected her stomach. It was a form of migraine. What she needed was forty-eight hours on her back, with the blinds down. I told her to take Friday off, and come back on Monday if she felt well enough. She's been with me for nearly ten years now. An excellent secretary, and such a nice girl!"

He spoke with so much warmth that Haxtell, who was a cynic, made a mental note of a possible line of enquiry. Nothing came of it. The doctor, it transpired, was very happily married.

"That part of it fits all right," said Haxtell to Superintendent Barstow. "She was in bed when the intruder arrived. He hit her as she was coming out of her bedroom."

"Then you think he was a housebreaker?"

"I'd imagine so, yes," said Haxtell. "The screwdriver looks like the sort of thing a housebreaker would carry. You could force an ordinary mortice lock right off with it. As a matter of fact he didn't have to use it in this instance, because she'd got a simple catch lock that a child of five could open. I don't doubt he slipped it with a piece of talc."

"Why did he choose her flat?"

"Because it was an isolated one, on the top floor. Or because he knew her habits. Just bad luck that she should have been there at all."

"Bad luck for her," agreed Barstow, sourly. "Well, get the machine working. We may turn something up."

Haxtell was an experienced police officer. He knew that investigating a murder was like dropping a stone into a pool of water. He started two enquiries at once. Everybody within a hundred yards of the flat was asked what they had been doing and whether they had noticed anything. And everyone remotely connected, by ties of blood, friendship or business, with Miss Martin was sought out and questioned.

It is a system which involves an enormous amount of work for a large number of people, and has only got one thing in its favour. It is nearly always successful in the end.

To Sergeant Petrella fell the task of questioning all the other tenants in the block. This involved seven visits. In each case, at least one person, it appeared, had been at home all Friday morning. And no one had heard anything at all, which was disappointing. Had anything unusual happened on Friday morning? The first six people to whom this enquiry was addressed scratched their heads and said that they didn't think anything had. The seventh mentioned the gentleman who had left census papers.

Now Petrella was by then both hot and tired. He was, according to which way you looked at it, either very late for his lunch or rather early for his tea. He was on the point of dismissing the man with the census papers when the instinct which guides all good policemen drove him to persevere with one further enquiry. Had he not done so the Martin case would probably have remained unsolved. As he probed it, a curious little story emerged. The man had not actually left any papers behind him. He had been making preliminary enquiries as to the numbers of people on the premises so that arrangements for the census could be put in hand. The papers would be issued later.

Petrella trudged down three flights of stairs (it is only in grave emergency that a policeman is allowed to use a private telephone) and rang up the Municipal Returning Officer from a call box. After that he revisited the first six flats. The occupants unanimously agreed that a "man from the Council" had called on them that Friday morning. They had not mentioned it because Petrella had asked if anything "unusual" had happened. There was nothing in the least unusual in men from the Council snooping round. Petrella asked for a description and collated, from his six informants, the following items. The man in question was "young," "young-ish," "sort of middle-aged" (this was from the teenaged daughter in No. 37). He was bareheaded and had tousled hair, he was wearing a hat. He had a shifty look (No. 34), a nice smile (teenaged daughter), couldn't say, didn't really look at him (the remainder). He was about six foot, five foot nine, five foot six, didn't notice. He had an ordinary sort of voice. He was wearing an Old Harrovian tie (old gentleman in ground-floor flat No. 34). He seemed to walk with rather a stiff sort of leg, almost a limp (four out of six informants).

Petrella hurried back to Crown Road Police Station, where he found Haxtell and Barstow in conference.

"There doesn't seem to be much doubt," he reported, "that it was a sneak thief. Posing as a Council employee. I've checked with them and they are certain that he couldn't have been genuine. His plan would be to knock once or twice. If he got no answer he'd either slip the lock or force it. He drew blank at the first seven. Someone answered the door in each of them. When he got to No. 39 I expect Miss Martin didn't hear him. The migraine must have made her pretty blind and deaf."

"All right!" said Barstow. "And then she came out and caught him at it, and so he hit her."

"The descriptions aren't a lot of good," said Haxtell, "but we'll get all the pictures from the CRO of people known to go in for this sort of lark. They may sort someone out for us."

"Don't forget the most important item," said Barstow. "The limp."

Petrella said, "It did occur to me to wonder, sir, whether we ought to place much reliance on the limp."

He received a glare which would have daunted a less self-confident man.

"He would have to have somewhere to hide that big screwdriver. It was almost two foot long. The natural place would be a pocket inside his trouser leg. That might account for the appearance of a stiff leg."

Haxtell avoided Barstow's eye.

"It's an idea," he said. "Now just get along and start checking on this list of Miss Martin's known relations."

"There was one other thing — "

"Do you know," observed Superintendent Barstow unkindly, "why God gave young policemen two feet but only one head?"

Petrella accepted the hint and departed.

Nevertheless the idea persisted; and later that day, when he was alone with Haxtell, he voiced it to him.

"Do you remember," he said, "about six months ago, I think it was, we had an outbreak of this sort of thing in the Cholderton Road, Park Branch area? A man cleared out three or four blocks of flats, and we never caught him. He was posing as a Pools salesman then."

"The man who left his coat behind."

"That's right!" said Petrella. "With Colonel Wing."

Colonel Wing was nearly ninety and stone deaf, but still spry. He had fought in one Zulu and countless Afghan wars and the walls of his top-floor living-room in Cholderton Mansions were adorned with a fine selection of assegais, yataghans and knobkerries. Six months before this story opens he had had an experience which might have unnerved a less seasoned warrior. He was not an early riser. Pottering out of his bedroom one fine morning at about eleven o'clock he had observed a man kneeling in front of his sideboard and quietly sorting out the silver. It was difficult to say who had been more taken aback. The man had jumped up, and run from the room. Colonel Wing had regretfully dismissed the idea of trying to spear him with an assegai from the balcony as he left the front door of the flats, and had rung up the police. They had made one curious discovery.

Hanging in the hall was a strange raincoat.

"Never seen it before in my life," said Colonel Wing.

"D'you mean to say the damn' feller had the cheek to hang his coat up before starting work? Wonder he didn't help himself to a whisky and soda while he was about it."

Haxtell said that he had known housebreakers to do just that. He talked to the Colonel at length about the habits of criminals; and removed the coat for examination. Since the crime was only an abortive robbery, it was not thought worth while wasting too much time on it. A superficial examination produced no results in the way of name tabs or tailor's marks; the coat was carefully placed in a cellophane bag and stored.

"I'd better have a word with him," said Petrella.

He found the Colonel engaged in writing a letter to the *United Services Journal* on the comparative fighting qualities of Zulus and Russians. He listened to the composite descriptions of the intruder, and said that, as far as one could tell, they sounded like the same man. His intruder had been young to middle-aged, of medium height, and strongly built.

"There's one thing," said the Colonel. "I saw him in a good light, and I may be deaf, but I've got excellent eyesight. There's a tiny spot in his left eye. A little red spot, like a fire opal. You couldn't mistake it. If you catch him, I'll identify him for you."

"The trouble is," said Petrella, "that it looks as if he's never been through our hands. Almost the only real lead we've got is that coat he left behind him at your place. We're going over it again, much more thoroughly."

Thus had the coat grown in importance. It had improved its status. It was now an exhibit in a murder case.

"Give it everything," said Haxtell to the scientists. And the scientists prepared to oblige.

That evening, after a weary afternoon spent interrogating Miss Martin's father's relatives in Acton and South Harrow, Petrella found himself back on the Embankment. The Forensic Science Laboratory observes civilised hours and Mr. Worsley was on the point of removing his long white overall and replacing it with a rather deplorable green tweed coat with matching leather patches on the elbows.

"I've finished my preliminary work on the right-hand pocket," he said. "We have isolated arrowroot starch, pipe tobacco and a quantity of common silver sand."

"Splendid!" said Petrella. "Splendid! All I have got to do now is to find a housewife who smokes a pipe and has recently been to the seaside and we shall be home and dry."

"What use you make of the data we provide must be entirely a matter for you," said Mr. Worsley coldly. He was already late for a meeting of the South Wimbledon Medico-legal Society, to whom he had promised a paper entitled: "The Part of the Laboratory in Modern Crime Detection."

Petrella went back to Highside.

Here he found a note from Haxtell which ran: "A friend of Miss Martin has suggested that some or other of these were, or

might have been, boyfriends of the deceased. I am seeing ones
marked with a cross. Would you tackle the others?" There
followed a list of names and addresses ranging from Welwyn
Garden City to Morden. He looked at his watch. It was half-
past seven. With any luck he could knock off four of them
before midnight.

In the ensuing days the ripples spread, wider and wider,
diminishing in size and importance as they became more distant
from the centre of the disturbance. Petrella worked his way
from near relatives and close friends, who said: "How terrible!
Whoever would have thought of anything like that happening
to Marjorie," through more distant connections who said:
"Miss Martin? Yes I know her. I haven't seen her for a long
time," right out to the circumference where there were people
who simply looked bewildered and said: "Miss Martin – I'm
sorry, I don't think I remember anyone of that name," and, on
being reminded that they had danced with her at a tennis club
dance two years before, said, "If you say so, I expect it's right,
but I'm dashed if I can even remember what she looked like."

It was in the course of the third day that Petrella called at a
nice little house in Herne Hill. The name was Taylor. Mr.
Taylor was not at home, but the door was opened by his wife,
a cheerful redhead who banished her two children to the
kitchen when she understood what Petrella was after. Her
reactions were the standard ones.

Apprehension, followed, as soon as she understood that
what Petrella wanted was nothing to do with her, by a cheerful
communicativeness. Miss Martin was, she believed, her
husband's cousin. That is to say not his cousin but his second
cousin, or something like that. Her husband's father's married
sister's husband's niece. So far as she knew they had only met
her once, and that was quite by chance, six months before, at
the funeral of Miss Martin's mother, who was, of course, sister
to her husband's uncle by marriage.

Petrella disentangled this complicated relationship without
difficulty. He was already a considerable expert on the Martin
family tree. Unfortunately, Mrs. Taylor could tell him
nothing. Her acquaintance with Miss Martin was confined to
this single occasion and she had not set eyes on her since. Her
husband, who was a commercial traveller for Joblox, the
London paint firm, was unlikely to be back until very late. He
was on a tour in the Midlands, and it depended on the traffic

when he got home. Petrella said he quite understood. The interview remained in his memory chiefly because it was on his way back from it that he picked up his copy of the laboratory report on the coat.

They had done themselves proud. No inch of its surface, interior or exterior, had escaped their microscopic gaze. Petrella cast his eye desperately over the eight closely typed foolscap pages. Stains on the exterior had been isolated and chemically tested and proved beyond reasonable doubt to be in two cases ink, in one case rabbit-blood and in one case varnish. A quantity of sisal-hemp fluff had been recovered from the seam of the left-hand cuff and some marmalade from the right-hand one. A sliver of soft wood, originally identified on the Chatterton Key Card as *Pinus sylvestris,* was now believed to be *Chamaecyparis lawsoniana.* In the right-hand pocket had been discovered a number of fragments of oyster shell and a stain of oil shown by quantitative analysis to be a thick oil of a sort much used in marine engineering.

Petrella read the report in the underground between Charing Cross and Highside. When he reached Crown Road he found Haxtell in the CID room. He had in front of him the reports of all visits so far made. There were two hundred and thirty of them. Petrella added the five he had completed that afternoon, and was about to retire when he remembered the laboratory report, and cautiously added that, too, to the pile. He was conscious of thunder in the air.

"Don't bother," said Haxtell. "I've had a copy." His eyes were red-rimmed from lack of proper sleep. "So has the Superintendent. He's just been here. He wants us to take some action on it."

"Action, sir?"

"He suggests," said Haxtell, in ominously quiet tones, "that we re-examine all persons interviewed so far," his hand flickered for a moment over the pile of paper on the table, "to ascertain whether they have ever been interested in the oyster-fishing industry. He feels that the coincidence of oyster shell and marine oil must have some significance."

"I see, sir," said Petrella. "When do we start?"

Haxtell stopped himself within an ace of saying something which would have been both indiscreet and insubordinate. Then, to his credit, he laughed instead.

"We are both," he said, "going to get one good night's rest first. We'll start tomorrow morning."

"I wonder if I could borrow the reports until then," said Petrella, wondering at himself as he did so.

"Do what you like with them," said Haxtell. "I've got three days' routine work to catch up with."

Petrella took them back with him to Mrs. Catt's, where that worthy widow had prepared a high tea for him, his first leisured meal for three days. Sustained by a mountainous dish of sausages and eggs and refreshed by his third cup of strong tea, he started on the task of proving to himself the idea that had come to him.

Each paper was skimmed, and put on one side. Every now and then he would stop, extract one, and add it to a very much smaller pile beside his plate. At the end of an hour Petrella looked at the results of his work with satisfaction. In the small pile were six papers: six summaries of interviews with friends or relations of the murdered girl. If his idea was right, he had thus, at a stroke, reduced the possibles from two hundred and thirty-five to six. And of those six, only one he knew in his heart of hearts was a probable.

There came back into his mind the visit that he had made that afternoon. There it was, in that place and no other, that the answer lay. There he had glimpsed, without knowing it, the end of the scarlet thread which led to the heart of this untidy, rambling labyrinth. He thought of a nice red-headed girl and two red-headed children, and unexpectedly he found himself shivering.

It was dusk before he got back to Herne Hill. The lights were on in the nice little house, upstairs and downstairs, and a muddy car stood in the gravel run-in in front of the garage. Sounds suggested that the red-headed children were being put to bed by both their parents and were enjoying it.

One hour went by, and then a second. Petrella had found an empty house opposite, and he was squatting in the garden, his back propped up against a tree. The night was warm and he was quite comfortable, and his head was nodding on his chest when the front door of the house opposite opened, and Mr. Taylor appeared.

He stood for a moment, outlined against the light from the hall, saying something to his wife. He was too far off for Petrella to make out the words. Then he came down the path.

He ignored his car, and made for the front gate, for which Petrella was thankful. He had made certain arrangements to cope with the contingency that Mr. Taylor might use his car, but it was much easier if he remained on foot.

A short walk took them both, pursuer and pursued, to the door of the King of France public house. Mr. Taylor went into the saloon. Petrella himself chose the private bar. Like most private bars, it had nothing to recommend it save its privacy, being narrow, bare and quite empty. But it had the advantage of looking straight across the serving counter into the saloon.

Petrella let his man order first. He was evidently a well-known character. He called the landlord "Sam," and the landlord called him "Mr. Taylor."

Petrella drank his own beer slowly. Ten minutes later the moment for which he had been waiting arrived. Mr. Taylor picked up a couple of glasses and strolled across with them to the counter. Petrella also rose casually to his feet. For a moment they faced each other, a bare two paces apart, under the bright bar lights.

Petrella saw in front of him a man of young middle-age, with a nondescript face, and neutral coloured, tousled hair, perhaps five foot nine in height, and wearing some sort of old school tie.

As if aware that he was being looked at, Mr. Taylor raised his head; and Petrella observed, in the left eye, a tiny red spot. It was, as the Colonel had said, the colour of a fire opal.

"We showed his photograph to everyone in the block," said Haxtell with satisfaction, "and they all of them picked it out straight away, out of a set of six. Also the Colonel."

"Good enough!" said Superintendent Barstow. "Any background?"

"We made a very cautious enquiry at Joblox. Taylor certainly works for them. But he's what they call an outside commission man. He sells in his spare time, and gets a percentage on sales. Last year he made just under a hundred pounds."

"Which wouldn't keep him in his present style."

"Definitely not! And, of course, a job like that would be very useful cover for a criminal sideline. He would be out when and where he liked, and no questions asked by his family."

Barstow considered the matter slowly. The decision was his.

"Pull him in," he said. "Charge him with the job at Colonel Wing's. The rest will sort itself out quick enough when we search his house. Take a search warrant with you. By the way, I never asked how you got on to him. Has he some connection with the oyster trade?"

Petrella said, cautiously, "Well, no sir. As a matter of fact, he hadn't. But the report was very useful corroborative evidence."

"Clever chaps, these scientists," said Barstow.

"Come clean!" said Haxtell when the Superintendent had departed. "It was nothing to do with that coat, was it?"

"Nothing at all," said Petrella. "What occurred to me was that it was a very curious murder. Presuming it was the same man both times. Take Colonel Wing – he's full of beans – but when all's said and done, he's a frail old man, over ninety. He saw the intruder in a clear light, and the man simply turned tail and bolted. Then he bumps into Miss Martin, who's a girl, but a muscular young tennis player, but he *kills* her, coldly and deliberately."

"From which you deduced that Miss Martin knew him, and he was prepared to kill to preserve the secret of his identity. Particularly as he had never been in the hands of the police."

"There was a bit more to it than that," said Petrella. "It had to be someone who knew Miss Martin, but so casually that he would have no idea where she lived. Mightn't even remember her name. If he'd had any idea that it was the flat of someone who knew him he wouldn't have touched it with a barge-pole. What I was looking for was someone who was distantly connected with Miss Martin, but happened to have renewed his acquaintance with her recently. He had to be a very distant connection, you see. But they had to know each other by sight. There were half a dozen who would have filled the bill. I had this one in my mind because I'd interviewed Mrs. Taylor only that afternoon. Of course, I'd have tried all the others afterwards. Only it wasn't necessary."

There was neither pleasure nor satisfaction in his voice. He was seeing nothing but a nice red-headed girl and two red-headed children.

It was perhaps six months later that Petrella ran across Colonel Wing again. The Taylor case was now only an unsatisfactory

128

memory, for Mr. Taylor had taken his own life in his cell at Wandsworth, and the red-headed girl was now a widow. Petrella was on his way home, and he might not have noticed him, but the Colonel came right across the road to greet him, narrowly missing death at the hands of a motor-cyclist of whose approach he had been blissfully unaware.

"Good evening, Sergeant!" the old man said. "How are you keeping?"

"Very well, thank you, Colonel," said Petrella. "And how are you?"

"I'm not getting any younger," said the Colonel. Petrella suddenly perceived, to his surprise, that the old man was embarrassed. He waited patiently for him to speak.

"I wonder," said the old man at last, "it's an awkward thing to have to ask, but could you get that coat back – you remember — ?"

"Get it *back*," said Petrella. "I don't know. I suppose so."

"If it was mine, I wouldn't bother. But it isn't. I find it's my cousin Tom's. I'd forgotten all about it, until he reminded me."

Petrella stared at him.

"Do you mean to say — "

"Tom stayed the night with me – he does that sometimes, between trips. Just drops in. Of course, when he reminded me, I remembered — "

"Between trips," said Petrella, weakly. "He isn't by any chance an oyster fisherman?"

It was the Colonel's turn to stare.

"Certainly not," he said. "He's one of the best-known breeders of budgerigars in the country."

"Budgerigars?"

"Very well known for them. I believe I'm right in saying he introduced the foreign system of burnishing their feathers with oil. It's funny you should mention oysters, though. That's the thing he's very keen on. Powdered oyster-shell in the feed. It improves their high notes."

Petrella removed his hat in a figurative but belated salute to the Forensic Science Laboratory.

"Certainly you shall have your coat back," he said. "It'll need a thorough clean and a little stitching, but I am delighted to think that it is going to be of use to someone at last."

Dangerous Structure

HELENWOOD House was built in the early years of the last century by a successful Special Pleader. He built generously (for he had a wife and eleven children to house), in brickwork, cream-painted stucco and imitation Bath stone; and he surrounded his home with a garden and a high iron fence. Those were spacious days, when tea-brokers from Mincing Lane drove out to their mansions on Muswell Hill, and the nightingale sang on Highside.

The years went past, Highside descended in the social scale and Helenwood House descended with it, but more slowly for it was insulated from the march of time by its high fence and by an ever-thickening jungle of shrubs and trees.

Its barrister-owner died, but the complex settlement which he had made lived after him, and the tentacles of the law gripped Helenwood House more tightly even than the ivy which now enshrouded it. Had it been taken in hand in the twenties or thirties it might have been rescued, and opened up and turned into an apartment house (for which there is great demand in Highside), but by this time it was under the control of trustees and was occupied by two elderly ladies, and five cats. *Buprestidan*, the borer, and *Anobium domesticum,* the death-watch beetle, made lodgement in the timbers; and, creeping out from the shrubberies, *Polyporus destructor,* curiously miscalled dry-rot, cast its dripping cloak over the brickwork of the basement and reached up white and yellow fingers to make a meal of the ground-floor woodwork.

The best thing for all concerned would have been a direct hit from Hitler's air force, but where so many more useful buildings suffered Helenwood House remained, decrepit but intact.

In the late forties it was inhabited by one old lady and seventeen cats, and the local authority toyed for a time with the idea of serving a dangerous structure notice on the occupant, and might have done so, had the old lady not quietly died, leaving only the cats to serve the notice on. The property then became the subject of protracted litigation.

Detective Sergeant Petrella knew a certain amount about all this, as he knew a certain amount about most of the houses and people in his manor. To him Helenwood House was a place whose defences had constantly to be watched and strengthened against the incursion of children to whom the ruined house and rampant shrubberies were a fascinating playground; jungle and enchanted palace in one. And against tramps who would force one of the many broken and boarded-up windows and sleep quite happily in the basement, along with *Anobium* and *Buprestidan*.

It was Mrs. Catt, Petrella's amiable landlady, who called his attention to Helenwood House one morning when she brought him his tea.

"Someone's going to do *what*?" said Petrella sleepily. He had spent much of the previous night in unsuccessful watching of a warehouse and brought himself back reluctantly to the problems of a new day.

"Do it up," said Mrs. Catt. "Regardless of expense."

"That old mausoleum," said Petrella. "It'd be cheaper to start over again than mess about with that."

"It's a house of great character," said Mrs. Catt, who had the sort of mind that believed in house agents' advertisements. "Architect designed, on four storeys."

"It's a death trap," said Petrella, and finished his tea at a gulp. He had a lot of work to do that day. Most of it was connected with young Maurice Meister, who was fast qualifying as Highside's leading juvenile delinquent. His current activity was "milking" telephone boxes, and he had a sideline in stealing from parked cars. Crime was the hereditary occupation of the Meisters. Maurice's father was none other than "Bull" Meister, the suspected organiser of the famous mail-van robberies in which fifty thousand pounds' worth of old pound notes, on their way to the pulping mills, had been diverted into the pocket of Bull and his gang. He was at that moment serving a three-year sentence, not for any of his more lucrative crimes but for cutting off the right ear of one of his subordinates with whom he had had a difference of opinion.

"His mother's just as bad," said Petrella to Chief Inspector Haxtell. "I'd say she was running the Meister crowd herself now. Keeping it warm till Bull comes out again. What do you expect a boy like Maurice to do? Sell tracts?"

"I expect him to behave," said Haxtell, sourly. "And if he doesn't, I expect you to tell him where he gets off. So don't let's have you getting soft about juvenile delinquents."

That evening Mrs. Catt re-opened the subject of Helen-wood House.

"What I was telling you," she said without preamble, "it's being converted. Into six self-contained apartments, of convenient size."

"You're not thinking of moving, are you?" said Petrella. The thought was alarming. He knew that he would never find lodgings which suited him so well.

"S'not me," said Mrs. Catt. "S'my married daughter. They've been living with his family. S'not a good arrangement."

Petrella agreed. Highside, being within easy travelling distance of the centre of London, had an even more acute housing problem than most boroughs.

"They've saved money, both of them. Not enough to buy a house, but then they don't want a house. They want a flat."

Almost everyone in Highside wanted a flat.

"How much are they paying?" said Petrella. He was wide awake, this time, and the implications of what he was being told did not escape him.

"Each applicant," quoted Mrs. Catt, "is asked to put down the sum of five hundred pounds. Three hundred of which will be used towards conversion of the premises, two hundred being considered as rent for the first year."

"How many apartments?"

"Six."

"There's a catch somewhere," said Petrella. "Work it out for yourself. I don't say the house would cost much to buy. The owners would be glad to get rid of it. But there'd be legal fees and so forth. Say you did all that for a thousand pounds. Right? Well, six times three is eighteen. That leaves you eight hundred pounds to develop the property with. Why, that wouldn't deal with the dry-rot alone."

The gloom on Mrs. Catt's face deepened.

"It did sound almost too good to be true," she said.

"Who's the operator?"

Mrs. Catt produced a piece of paper from her pocket, and the fact that she had it ready confirmed Petrella's suspicion

132

that his landlady had not introduced the subject of Helenwood House entirely by chance. He read: "Utopia Building and Development Projects Limited."

"It's a good-sounding name," said Mrs. Catt.

"It sounds all right," said Petrella, pocketing the paper. "But the only word I should believe in myself is the last one."

Scotland Yard possesses a small Company Fraud Department, and Petrella knew Sergeant Brennan who was in charge of it. Brennan had spent his early years on a beat round the Old Kent Road. He had been promoted to his present job when his superiors discovered that he possessed the sort of mind that delighted in solving difficult crossword puzzles or in playing several games of chess simultaneously.

"These sort of people make me sick," he said to Petrella. "Give me a drunken Irishman with a bottle. You do know where you are with him. It'll take a few days to ferret out, because all the shares, you can bet, will be in the names of nominees. We can usually dig out the real holders, but it takes time."

Petrella thanked Sergeant Brennan, and made his way back to Highside. He found Mrs. Catt looking even more worried.

"I bin asking round," she said. "From what I hear this company's been showing these flats to dozens of people. There ought to be a law against it."

"I thought it must be something like that," said Petrella. Having no further duty that evening he strolled out on a course which would bring him past the top end of Helenwood House. Sure enough there was a triumphant red SOLD notice nestling amongst a clump of giant elders. Petrella noted the name of the agents, Messrs. Prentice and Partners, and was on the point of moving on when something caught his eye.

Bending forward, he gripped the rusty, spiked, iron upright which formed part of the formidable boundary defences at this point. He twisted it, and it lifted, coming up through the rail. A foot from the top the metal was worn bright with friction in the socket. What he had found was a well-used back door. The gap was wide enough to admit a large boy, or a slim policeman. Petrella squatted down and eased his way through, replacing the bar behind him. For the next few yards he had to crawl, then he got to his feet.

He was standing in a hollowed-out space in the heart of the shrubbery. And somewhere ahead of him – his nose told him – a wood-fire was burning. He tiptoed forward. Then stopped. He knew that he was being watched. He heard a rustle, swung round, and something hit him on the cheek. It was an iron-hard pellet of folded paper, and it had been shot with such force that it stung like an adder. Then the silence was broken by laughter, and the crackling of running steps. Petrella did not give chase. He followed his nose through the labyrinth, until he found the fire. It was smouldering damply among the moss and leaves, and he stamped it out. Then he returned the way he had come. As he stooped to lift the railing he looked back. A face was watching him from the nearest thicket; a face which split into a grin when it saw it was observed.

"You get out of there," said Petrella. "And your pals. Before you get into any more trouble."

Young Maurice continued to grin but said nothing.

Petrella saw Mr. Prentice next morning and warned him to strengthen the defences of Helenwood House. But he knew it was a waste of time. There were a dozen places in the boundary where a determined boy would break through.

"If we blocked one, they'd open another," said Mr. Prentice. "And that'd mean more damage. Thank goodness it'll soon be off our hands."

"How's the sale going?" asked Petrella.

"A deposit's been paid," said Mr. Prentice, cautiously. "And a contract signed. Otherwise we wouldn't have handed over the keys." He added that it was not his firm that had the job of showing prospective tenants round. That was done personally by the managing director of the new company.

Petrella was on the point of asking for the name of the managing director, but realised, just in time, that Mr. Prentice would refuse to give it to him. In fact, he need have answered none of his questions. No offence had been committed. A swindle was in the course of being perpetrated in front of his eyes. A swindle in which a number of people, of slender means, were to robbed of their life's savings; but if it happened to be legal robbery there was nothing to be done about it.

What Sergeant Brennan told him two days later confirmed his first instinctive feeling.

"This company of yours," said Brennan. "It's run by a chap called Clark. Neighbour of yours, actually. He's got an office in Crown Road. Clark's his present name. He changes it about once a year. All by due process of law. And he must have operated at least a hundred companies. Some have done quite well. Others have gone bust. I guess the Utopia Whatsit & Whatsit is one which is going to fold up."

"Can't it be stopped?"

"It's difficult," said Brennan. "Here's this company. The company mind you, not Clark. It says to you, we're buying certain properties and converting them into flats. As a gesture of good faith it pays a fifty-quid deposit on some old shambles of a property, and gets hold of the keys. Then it starts showing people over it. And collects five hundred pounds from all of them. Ten, twenty, thirty people – or however many it can get interested."

"It's clearly a fraud," said Petrella. "You couldn't make twenty flats out of Helenwood House."

"Of course you couldn't," said Brennan wearily. "But what's to prevent the company buying more houses? It might too, if things go well. But sooner or later, and in this case probably sooner, it'll go bust."

"This Clark character. He's got money of his own?"

"You bet he's got money."

"Then if I was one of his customers, I'd sue him for my five hundred pounds."

"You're not dealing with him. You could sue the company, of course. Only by that time it's got no money left. What there was has been spent. On management expenses."

"That means by Mr. Clark on Mr. Clark."

"Right."

"God, what a set-up," said Petrella. He thought of Mrs. Catt, and her daughter and her daughter's husband, and the money which they had saved.

"What can anyone do?"

"There's just one chance," said Brennan. "If you strike the right moment, near the beginning of the ramp, when there *is* a little money in the kitty and all the mugs aren't in, and slap in a writ, you might get your stake back just to keep you quiet."

"I'd judge it's already too late for that," said Petrella. "This particular racket's been running for weeks. Would it be any good if I called on him and tried to scare him?"

"Certainly. If you want him to get straight through on the blower to your boss enquiring what authority you'd got for threatening him."

"I see," said Petrella.

Nevertheless he made a point of being at the end of Crown Road when Mr. Clark emerged from his office that evening. He saw a small, stout person with a figure like a ripe pear and a face like a frog; if you can imagine a frog wearing rimless glasses. Behind the glasses a pair of liquid brown eyes looked out on the world. Nor did the eyes miss much. Mr. Clark came straight across the road to where Petrella was standing, said "Good evening, Sergeant," and passed on. Petrella was on the point of departing himself when the door of the office block opened for a second time, and a girl came out. A girl, moreover, whom he recognised.

Later that evening he visited the All Night Café in Exeter Street and had a word with its proprietor, Mr. Peggs.

"I never knew your daughter worked locally," he said. "I thought you told me she'd got a job with some solicitor in Lincoln's Inn."

"So she had," said Mr. Peggs, who was a large man and served large meals to his customers, but himself lived almost entirely off bismuth tablets. "And a good job, too. But I had to fix it so's she could be home lunchtimes. Her mother's been bad lately."

"So she works for Mr. Clark?"

"That's right," said Peggs. "He's in house property. Nothing wrong with him, I suppose?"

Petrella took a deep breath. He liked Mr. Peggs, and had always found him trustworthy.

"If your daughter can turn up anything," he said quietly, "I'd just like to hear about it."

"Like that is it?" said Mr. Peggs thoughtfully. "Well, she might be able to help. Between you and me, I don't think she's got a lot of use for him. Personally speaking. He keeps her late – after hours – you know."

"You mean he makes passes at her?"

Mr. Peggs loosed a sudden bellow of laughter which rattled the coffee urn.

"You want to brush up your psychology, boy," he said.

136

"He keeps her late and *don't* make passes at her. That's what makes a girl mad."

After which a week went by. A week in which Petrella got on with a lot of other jobs and tried to forget about Helenwood House. And was reminded of it every time he saw Mrs. Catt.

He gathered that the conversion had not started yet. "He's going to have a narkiteck round soon. Measuring up," said Mrs. Catt, but she didn't say it very hopefully.

Then, at ten o'clock one night, just as Petrella was leaving the CID room, the telephone rang. It was Mr. Peggs, and even allowing for the distortion of a bad line, Petrella could tell that he was excited.

"Drop in for a cuppa on your way home," he said. "I heard something that's going to make you laugh."

Five minutes later Petrella was listening to Peggs with growing incredulity.

"Are you sure?" he said.

"Certain," said Mr. Peggs. "She's a good girl. Wooden make a mistake about a thing like that. The switchboard's in her room. She's only got to plug in. Listen to everything."

"And he turned it down?"

"Turned it down flat. You asked for something funny, and if that isn't funny, what is? He gives five hundred pounds for a rotten old house – and when I say gives it, he hasn't even done that yet. Just paid fifty for a deposit. And now this woman comes along and offers him three thousand for it. And he turns it down. Flat."

"Perhaps he really does intend to develop the property."

"Develop my second-best trousers," said Mr. Peggs. "From what my girl tells me, it's a stone-cold ramp."

"Then why did he turn down a nice quick profit of two thousand five hundred?"

"You haven't heard half of it. Hour later she rings again. Now she's offering three thousand five hundred. That's her last word, she says. Only the way she says it makes it sound as if she might raise a bit more steam if you pushed her."

"And Clark turned that down too?"

"He's wavering," said Mr. Peggs.

"Look here," said Petrella. "This sounds like a miracle. I want to know the minute Clark says yes. And I want an introduction to the solicitor your daughter used to work for.

137

If what I've got in mind comes off, I know someone who'll buy your daughter a new evening-dress. And I'll take her dancing myself the first time she wears it."

"Do what we can," said Mr. Peggs.

The following afternoon the call came through.

"Old Clark's done it," said Mr. Peggs. "After lunch. Four thousand smackers."

"Is it just talk? Or is it settled?"

"Signed, sealed and delivered. Very business-like lady. Brought round a contract with her, signed it on the spot."

"Excellent," said Petrella. "Excellent. The first thing Clark'll find on his desk tomorrow will be a writ for five hundred pounds. Let's see him wriggle out of this one."

"Another funny thing," said Mr. Peggs. "Guess who the lady was."

"Whoever she was, she was an angel in disguise."

"Heavily disguised," said Mr. Peggs with a throaty chuckle. "It was Bull Meister's old lady, Annie."

"Mrs. Meister!"

"S'right."

Petrella said "Good God" softly and put down the telephone. Up to that point he had been obsessed with the personal aspect of his battle of wits with Mr. Clark. Now, quite suddenly, he forgot about Mr. Clark and Mrs. Catt and Mrs. Catt's married daughter and Utopia Developments, and started thinking like a policeman again.

And as he did so, a pattern came to light. A pattern of startling simplicity.

The redoubtable Bull Meister, perpetrator of the mail-van robbery, earns himself a three-year sentence, which still has a month or two to run. Bull's own share of the robbery, between twenty and thirty thousand old, but still quite serviceable, pound notes, is never recovered. And now Mrs. Meister is prepared to lay out four thousand hard-earned pounds, and for what? For an ancient and decaying building like Helenwood House. A building in whose grounds, moreover, he had himself caught young Maurice Meister, only a day or two before.

"It's a snip," he said enthusiastically to Chief Inspector Haxtell. "And what brought Mrs. Meister finally out into the open?"

"You tell me," said Haxtell.

"Why, the fact that Clark announced that he was going to put an architect in to measure up for conversion. He probably

138

didn't mean it. It was done to keep his subscribers quiet. But it produced Mrs. Meister, in a sweat, with four thousand pounds in her pocket."

"Yes," said Haxtell. "It looks as if you could be right. What do you suggest?"

"I'd suggest," said Petrella, "that we borrow a couple of professional searchers from Central and go right in tonight. Unofficially. If anyone makes a fuss we can always say we were looking for tramps."

Haxtell considered the matter carefully, from all possible angles, and then said, "Do you know, I think I'll come with you myself. It's a long time since I've been on a treasure hunt."

They found Bull Meister's hoard, packed in biscuit tins, sealed with adhesive tape, and stacked in an old recess beside the chimney front in the best bedroom. It was a neat job. The recesses on both sides had been masked with plywood and covered with distemper. The cache came to light only when the professional searchers, one of whom was a qualified architect, had made certain measurements and deductions. On Haxtell's suggestion they replaced the plywood as carefully as they had removed it. So far as they were aware no one observed them either coming or going.

"There's no problem about the notes," said Haxtell. "We'll tell the bank they've been recovered and they can continue quietly on their journey to the pulping mill. The real question is, what else do we do?"

"I don't really see, sir," said Petrella slowly, "that we need actually do anything at all. My landlady's married daughter got a cheque for five hundred pounds this morning. And the rest of the business looks like sorting itself out very satisfactorily. Really, very satisfactorily indeed."

"What's in your mind?"

"Well," said Petrella, and there was an almost ecstatic note in his voice, "don't you see? Bull's due out very shortly, and he's bound to think that Clark found the notes and removed them. And not only removed them, but sold the house to Bull's wife for four thousand pounds. I should think he'd cut off *both* his ears, wouldn't you?"

Death Watch

DURING his tour of duty at Highside, Detective Sergeant Petrella encountered quite a number of memorable people, but he never remembered anyone quite like Judge Vereker.

James Vereker was an official of the Colonial Service and had held judicial office in Palestine, in Kenya and, more recently, in Cyprus. He was a small, cheerful, birdlike person who dragged a club-foot behind him, and possessed the whole of a right hand and part of a left hand – the missing fingers had been blown off by an ingenious greetings telegram sent him on his fiftieth birthday, by Irgun Zvai Leumi. Vereker was a bachelor, which may have been as well in all the circumstances. When Petrella encountered him, he was under sentence of death.

The Judge told him so himself, perched on the fender seat in his cosy, second-storey flat in the new block on Heath Hill, while Petrella sat, ill at ease, in the single armchair.

"They're an offshoot – a sort of foreign working party – of Anorthotikou Komonia Ergezonienou Laou. That's really another name for the local communist party."

"Just why should they want to kill you, sir?"

"Expediency," said the Judge. "Of course, that's not what they say. The ostensible reason is revenge. I sentenced one of their members, George Antinas, to death for terrorism. They made a terrific fight to save him. It was last year. You may have read about it."

Petrella nodded. Like everyone else in England, he had read about it. Half the Press had made out that George, who had spent most of his life in England, was a young William Tell; the other half had presented him as a vicious paid-assassin. Overpaid, apparently, for he had badly bungled his last job, which was the blowing-up of a police station, and had fallen alive into the hands of the men he had set out to destroy.

"My own theory," said Judge Vereker, "is that the whole thing had precious little to do with politics. George's employers had got tired of him. Both he and his brother,

Antar, were wild young men, and not always discreet. So they sent George on this job – but tipped off the police in advance. Thus they had the best of both worlds. George was removed; and they got themselves a useful martyr."

"I should have thought they had enough martyrs already," said Petrella.

"Timing," said the Judge. "They want an up-to-date martyr. One they can use right now. As I said, it's purely a question of expediency. If they succeed in murdering me, in some spectacular way, in the next few weeks, it will strengthen the hands of the extremists on both sides. By November I should guess the best time for them will be over."

He stroked his tortoiseshell cat with his sound hand. He might, Petrella thought, have been talking about oysters coming in and going out of season.

"Who are they?" said Petrella.

"The leader is, I think, an Egyptian. His animosity against this country has nothing to do with recent events. I doubt if he harbours animosity. He is a professional terrorist, and his present name is David. Incidentally he is one of the finest amateur conjurers in the world."

David, noted Petrella, *conjurer.*

"If he is working with his usual number two, that will be Stefanos, a Greek engineer, who specialises in electrical devices."

"Stefanos," said Petrella. "Electrician. And the third?"

"Oh, the third, I should think, would be George's brother, Antar. There would be a touch of poetic justice in that, don't you think? Also, Antar, like George, was brought up in England and looks and speaks like an Englishman. That could be useful to them in their operations."

As Petrella sat, some days later, in the porter's cubicle, watching the clock with one eye and the main door with the other, he was thinking of David and Stefanos and Antar, implacable figures of Grand Guignol. David with his long, strong, conjurer's fingers. Stefanos with his engineer's skill; and Antar – Antar, who might appear in any form at any moment, beneath some commonplace mask, a brother's blood crying out for vengeance.

141

They were known to be in England. The Special Branch had confirmed it. And they were thought to be operating from the area of the docks where they had friends. But, apart from that, there was nothing but speculation.

A quarter to midnight. The last pubs had shut some time before and thrown their noisy contingents into the streets. In eight and a quarter hours' time, Petrella's relief would arrive, and he could go home and sleep. Ten hours was a long spell, when you couldn't relax for a minute of it.

Heath Hill Mansions was not a difficult fortress to defend. It was a great deal easier than a private house. The Judge had a flat on the second storey of the annexe. Underneath him, on the ground floor, lived a South African dentist. Above the dentist, a woman journalist, above the journalist the Judge, and above the Judge a practising faith healer. All the tenants had been there considerably longer than the Judge; and all had been carefully and unostentatiously checked, with the result that the faith healer was now strongly suspected of being a receiver of stolen goods. Such were the unexpected by-products of criminal investigation.

A single main staircase led to the flats, and ended in a front hall conveniently commanded by the porter's cubby-hole, in which Petrella sat watching the clock. This part of the block was L-shaped; and in the angle of the L at the back was a small-walled courtyard, the gate to which was locked at night. In ordinary times an iron fire-escape staircase led up from this courtyard to the back doors of the flats; but, by arrangement, the bottom section of it was removed at night. After all, as Chief Inspector Haxtell pointed out, there was very little chance of a fire starting undetected if they had a policeman actually on the premises.

What else, thought Petrella. There was a goods hoist beside the back staircase, which was locked during the hours of darkness, and was in any event far too small for the smallest terrorist to use. And to baulk assault from the roof with packets of explosive swung from cords – a method developed in Palestine – a fine wire mesh had been fixed across all the windows of the Judge's flat.

A car – no, not a car, a heavy lorry – rumbled past the end of the road, slowed for a moment, then changed its mind, and went on, picking up speed.

Could any precautions be effective against determined,

accomplished killers? Were there not a dozen ways into the fortress, even without physical access? The vegetables, the groceries, the milk. All carefully examined, it was true. Likewise the letters and parcels, the books from the library, the shirts from the laundry.

But the men they were up against were ingenious and ruthless. They had learnt the art of secreting a damaging charge of explosive in a minimum of space. Petrella thought of the story the Judge had told him of the Inspector of Constabulary, who had lived in a similar state of siege for three months in Haifa. And how, in the end, Irgun had bribed or terrorised the local cobbler to repair his shoes with hollow heels full of explosive, which had blown both legs off the first time the Inspector wore them. Or the case of the Governor's bodyguard, whose ammunition pouches had been filled with explosive timed to go off at the moment when the Governor was inspecting them; a plan which had failed because the Governor, on this occasion and most unusually, was two minutes late.

"I can tell you an even sadder story," Judge Vereker had said, swinging his legs and looking like a mischievous boy. "About my predecessor in Cyprus. It was not a story which received any publicity. AKEL had sworn to kill him. He was closely guarded, more closely than I am here. Perhaps too closely. You must always preserve a sense of proportion in these matters. It lasted for three months. By the end of that time, AKEL had made no move. But they had succeeded."

Judge Vereker paused, and added, "Poor fellow. He went mad. I saw him the other day. He's a little better now, but he'll never be much use. The slightest unexpected sound or movement makes him scream." That, thought Petrella grimly, was a type of assault that was very unlikely to succeed in this case.

He guessed that at that moment Judge Vereker was sleeping soundly. A lot more soundly than the anxious policemen who were trying to guard him, or, for that matter, than the men who were working to destroy him.

Funny – what was that?

A faint, scintillating light had appeared, over the trees and bushes in the strip of park that ran along the closed end of the road. If it had been the fifth of November he would have written it down as a cheap firework. It rose, dipped, and went out. Nothing else happened.

One o'clock. A dog barked. Then another. He heard footsteps coming along the next street. Two pairs of feet. They stopped at the corner, and then the voices started. Too low to determine sex. Much too low to hear what was being said. One was insisting, Petrella thought, the other protesting.

The voices stopped abruptly, and the footsteps came on. Peering through the open front door, Petrella saw them. A man and a girl by their silhouettes. They reached the porch two doors away, and the footsteps stopped and the voices started again, louder this time.

They were just outside the range of his comprehension, but the cadences were clear enough. The man insisting, repeating. The girl saying no. No. No.

Suddenly they broke off. There was a muffled scuffling noise. A cry. Then the man slipped out of the porch, turned his head for a quick look up and down the road, and took to his heels.

Behind him, from the porch, came a little sobbing moan, and the girl staggered after him. Took two paces, stumbled and went down on her knees in the middle of the road. Clutched her stomach, and pitched forward and sideways onto her face.

He's done her, thought Petrella. His hands were on the door. He jerked it open, and his foot was actually lifted to go through, when reason took charge of his instinct.

Anyone watching Petrella at that moment would have seen something as shocking as a car that is rolling forward being thrown suddenly into reverse. For a count of seconds, he stood quite still. The girl lay motionless in the road, the lamp casting a pool of light round her. Then Petrella moved, like one released from a spell.

Very slowly his hand unfolded, and he let the door swing shut. Very slowly and very softly he walked back into the porter's cubicle, picked up the telephone, and dialled a number.

"Police," he said. "It's Detective Sergeant Petrella. On duty at Heath Hill Mansions. There's been some trouble. Out in the street. A girl's been hurt."

The other end of the telephone said something.

"Yes," said Petrella. "I thought so, too. Perhaps if you

closed both ends of the street. Just in case." He replaced the receiver and, almost on tiptoe, walked back to the street door.

As he stood there, for the second time that night, a faint glimmering light arose, over the line of bushes at the end of the road, hung for a moment, and disappeared.

In the succeeding blackness and stillness he heard a sound, small but distinct.

It came from behind him. From the courtyard at the back.

He ran across the hallway and jerked at the back door. It refused to budge. He put his shoulder to it, but realised that he was wasting his time. The door was built to open inwards.

Quickly. Think quickly. He pressed the doorbell of the ground-floor flat. Almost at once the door was opened. The South African dentist was wearing a dressing-gown. He seemed surprisingly wide awake.

"Trouble?" he said.

"I don't know," said Petrella. "Would you stand here a minute? Shout if anything happens. There'll be a squad car along any moment."

"Sure," said the dentist. "Sure."

Petrella ran past him, into the kitchen, and snapped on the light. The back door of this flat also opened on the court. It was bolted, but when he had slipped the bolt it swung open.

The light from the kitchen window lit up the little enclosed space. It was quite empty. Petrella had had visions of a ladder spanning the missing section of the fire-escape, but there was nothing at all. And all the upper windows were dark.

He went out cautiously. A wire, he discovered, had been passed through the handle of the door that led into the hall, and secured to a window bar opposite. And the back gate into the street behind swung open to his touch.

Petrella walked thoughtfully back into the kitchen, bolting the door carefully behind him. He found the stout dentist on guard.

"Here come your chaps," he said.

It was Haxtell, who must have been sleeping in his clothes. "Where's the girlfriend?"

145

Petrella peered out into the street, lit now by the powerful spotlight of the police car. It was empty.

"We had both ends of the street blocked within three minutes of your phone call," said Haxtell. "She moved pretty quick for a dead girl."

"It was a put-up job, all right," said Petrella.

He told him what had happened, and they went back into the courtyard.

"We'd better move the wire," said Haxtell. "We'll leave the rest as it is. The boys may get something out of it in the morning."

They thanked the dentist, who observed that it had been quite an evening.

"What do you think it was all about?" said Haxtell as they stood together in the hall.

"Plainly," said Petrella, "they expected me to run out and help the girl. I don't know what was next on the bill. Possibly they planned to cosh me as I was bending over her. They had the back door ready wired, so something quite elaborate was planned to happen in the yard. Maybe a ladder up to the start of the fire-escape. And they'd have had a shot at breaking in through the Judge's kitchen. It wouldn't be easy. The back door's locked and bolted and the windows are barred and wired."

"Maybe," said Haxtell. "What about the fireworks?"

"Some sort of signal?"

"Signal of what?"

Petrella considered the matter. "Suppose," he said, "that they had the telephone from the flat tapped. Somewhere down the road. The first signal would be to start operations. The second would mean, 'Break it off. He hasn't fallen for it and he's telephoned for reinforcements. Get out quick.'"

"Could be," said Haxtell. He was still worried. What he really wanted to do was to go up and see if the Judge was all right. But he realised that it might be difficult to wake up a sleeping man simply to explain that something was going on which he couldn't understand himself.

In the end he said, "All right. Keep your eyes open," and drove away.

Petrella was troubled, too, but about something else. He was trying to place the noise that he had heard, in the darkness, after the second light signal. At first he thought that it was the back gate of the courtyard. He even went out and tried opening and shutting it, but he couldn't induce it to make the right sort of noise – a rackety click.

He was still worrying about it as the sky paled and the light came back and a new day hauled itself sluggishly over the horizon.

At seven o'clock the milkman arrived. He had, besides the milk, a box of fresh eggs, butter, and two loaves of bread for the Judge. Petrella knew him well by now. Nevertheless he went through the careful routine of search, even unwrapping and piercing each loaf with a steel needle.

"Wooden' like to search the eggs as well?" suggested the milkman, who was a cheerful young cockney.

"That's enough of that," said Petrella. "You can send 'em up."

The Judge, who was an early riser, used to take the stuff in himself and cook his own breakfast. His daily woman wasn't due till nine. Petrella was just reflecting, with pleasure, that by nine o'clock he would be safely in bed himself, when he heard the noise again.

Unmistakably, the same rackety click.

He jumped to the back door and jerked it open. Outside, the courtyard was empty. The milkman had gone. Nothing moved. It came again, above his head this time. Then he saw the wheel rotating and the wire running. It was the goods lift going slowly upwards.

Time stood still.

Then Petrella was in the passenger lift, the sweat pouring off him in a steady stream. First floor, second floor. And he was pelting down the passage. He placed a finger on the bell and kept it there.

After an eternity the door opened and Judge Vereker looked out.

"Why, Sergeant – "

"Have you lifted them out?" croaked Petrella.

"Lifted what?"

"I'm sorry." Petrella recovered his breath and his heart stopped pounding. "The stuff that was coming up in your service lift?"

"As a matter of fact, I'd just opened it when you rang."

"But you hadn't touched anything?"

"No. It looked all right to me, though."

"The stuff's all right," said Petrella. "I examined it myself. It's the lift. They tampered with it last night."

As he spoke they were walking into the tiny, spotless kitchen. The doors of the service lift stood open, and the cardboard box of groceries lay where the milkman had placed it.

Petrella said, "Have you got a torch?"

The Judge hobbled off to his bedroom. When he came back with the torch Petrella said, "It's right, isn't it, that no one else can use this lift while your doors are open?"

"Quite right," said the Judge. "That tiresome woman in the flat underneath once went away for the weekend and left hers open. What's the catch?"

Petrella was on one knee, shining the torch through the tiny gap between the bottom of the lift box and the top of the boarding.

"There's something there," he said. "I'm going to get help on this. If we leave the doors open and the lift where it is, it can't hurt us."

He went into the Judge's sitting-room, and dialled a number which is not in the telephone book. A bored voice said, "Heath Hill Mansions. No. 27. All right. We'll send a car round straight away."

Five minutes later a man in a raincoat, carrying a heavy bag of tools, and looking like a superior plumber, had arrived and introduced himself as Sergeant Oliphant.

"Is it safe to watch?" said the Judge. "Or do you want us to clear out?"

"Safe enough now you've spotted it," said Oliphant. "Neat, though. Very neat." He got a long steel rod with a tiny light bulb at the end of it out of his bag, and inserted it under the lift.

"Care to look?" he said.

Petrella saw that three solid-looking blocks of some dark toffee-like substance had been clamped to the underside of the box. Oliphant took a thin pair of pliers, slid them in, and snipped twice.

"Clever, really," he said.

He lifted off the box of groceries, and as he did so the

whole floor of the lift rose for a fraction of an inch then checked.

"They've slipped in a double floor. See? The sort of thing you get in a passenger lift. Spring-loaded. The weight of those groceries would be quite enough to keep it down. That makes an electrical contact. When you lifted the box off, you'd touch off the stuff underneath. About six pounds of gelignite, I should say. Do you no good at all. By the way, how did they know your man'd be the first to use it?"

"He had a special early delivery," said Petrella. "Every morning."

"Great mistake," said Oliphant, "if you don't mind me saying so. Never do things the same every day. Not with these types. It's playing into their hands. I'll get up the steamer from the car and disinfect this lot."

Petrella stood for a moment, listening to Oliphant's footsteps disappearing down the passage. He felt both breathless and deflated. Then he was aware that the Judge was speaking. "I notice," he said, "that our friend has left his tool bag behind. I think we'd better get moving."

Petrella stared.

The Judge gripped his arm. "There's really no time to waste," he said urgently. "Come on!" The next minute they, too, were out in the passage, and running.

"Down the stairs," said the Judge. "This'll do. You won't catch him now."

Together they flopped down on the stairs. Two floors below them a door slammed and they heard a car start. Then all sounds were blotted out in the solid roar from the flat they had just left.

Petrella raised his nose from the stair carpet. His ears were singing. Fragments of plaster were still dropping from the ceiling and the air was full of dancing dust.

"How did you know that that man was a fake?" said Petrella.

"It was Antar," said the Judge. "I recognised him as soon as he came in. He's very like his brother."

"Why didn't you tell me?"

"He had a gun. Neither of us had. It seemed safer to let him think he'd got away with it."

"The tool bag was full of explosive."

"With a very short time fuse, yes."

"How did he know — " Petrella started. And then stopped. He was asking himself questions to which he knew the answer: "Of course. They had the telephone line tapped. It was a double precaution, in case we spotted the lift."

"They're very persistent people," said the Judge. "I expect they'll get me in the end. You'd better go and comfort our lady journalist. By the sound of it, she's having hysterics."

Lost Leader

THE late afternoon sun, shining through the barred skylight, striped the bodies of the four boys sprawled on the floor. Nearby, the Sunday traffic went panting down the Wandsworth High Street, but in this quiet, upper back room the loudest noise was the buzzing of a bluebottle. The warm, imprisoned air smelt of copperas and leather and gun oil.

The oldest and tallest of the boys was sitting up, with his back propped against the wall. In one hand he held a piece of cloth, something that might once have been a handkerchief, and he was using it to polish and re-polish a powerful-looking air-pistol.

"They're beauties, ent they, Rob?" said the fat boy. He and the red-haired boy both had guns like their leader's. The smallest boy had nothing. He couldn't take his eyes off the shining beauties.

"Made in Belgium," said Rob. "See that gadget?" He put the tip of his finger on the telltale at the end of the compression chamber. "You don't just open it and shut it, like a cheap air-gun. You pump this one up slowly. That gadget shows you when the pressure's right. It's accurate up to fifty yards."

"*It* may be accurate," said the fat boy. "What about us? I've never had a gun before."

"We'll have to practise. Practise till we can hit a penny across the room."

"Why don't we start right now, Rob?" said the red-haired boy. "These things don't make any noise. Not to notice. We could chalk up a target on the wall — "

"Yes?" said Rob. "And when the geezer who owns this shop comes up here tomorrow morning, or next week, or whenever he does happen to come up here, and he finds his wall full of air-gun pellets, he's going to start thinking, isn't he? He's going to check over his spare stock, and find three guns missing. Right?"

"That's right," said the fat boy. "Rob's got it figured out. We put everything else back like we found it, it may be months before he knows what's been took. He mayn't even know anyone's broke in."

The leader turned to the smallest of his followers. "That's why you can't have one, Winkle," he said. "There's plenty of guns in the front of the shop, but we touch one of them, he'll miss it."

"That's all right, Rob," said Winkle. But he couldn't keep the longing out of his voice. To own a big, bright gun! A gun that went phtt softly, like an angry snake, and your enemy fifty yards away crumpled to the ground, not knowing what had hit him!

"What about Les?" said the red-haired boy.

"What about him?"

"He'll want a gun when he sees ours."

"He'll have to go on wanting. If he's not keen enough to come with us on a job like this."

" 'Tisn't that he's not keen," said the fat boy. "It's his old man. He's pretty strict. He locks his bedroom door now. Where are we going to practise, Rob?"

"I've got an idea about that," said the tall boy. "You know the old sports pavilion? The Home Guard used it in the war, but it's been shut up since."

The boys nodded.

"I found a way in at the back, from the railway. I'll show you. There's a sort of cellar with lockers in it. That'll do us fine. We'll have our first meeting there tomorrow. Right?"

151

"Right," they all said. The red-haired boy added, "How did you know about this place, Rob?"

"My family used to live round here," said the tall boy. "Before my Ma died, when we moved up to Highside. As a matter of fact, I was at school about a quarter of a mile from here."

The fat boy said, "I bet I get a strapping from my old man when I get home. He don't like me being away all day."

"You're all right," said Winkle. "You're fat. It don't hurt so much when you're fat." He looked down with disgust at his own slender limbs.

It was nine o'clock at night nearly a month after that talk and in quite another part of London, that Fishy Codlin was closing what he called his Antique shop. This was a dark and rambling suite of rooms, full of dirt, woodworm, and the household junk of a quarter of a century. Codlin was in the front room, locking away the day's take, when the two boys came in.

"You're too late," he growled. "I'm shut."

He noticed that the smaller of the boys stayed by the door, while the older came towards him with a curiously purposeful tread. He had a prevision of trouble, and his hand reached out for the light switch.

"Leave it alone," said the boy. He was a half-seen figure in the dusk. All the light seemed to concentrate on the bright steel weapon in his hand. "Slip the bolt, Will," he added, but without taking his eyes off Codlin. "Now you stand away from the counter."

Codlin stood away. He thought for a moment of refusing, for there was nearly twenty-five pounds in the box, the fruits of a full week's trading. But he was a coward as well as a bully and the gun looked real. He watched the notes disappearing in the boy's pocket. There was no hurry. When one of the notes slipped to the floor the boy bent down and picked it up, but without ever removing his steady gaze from the old man.

When he had finished, he backed away to the door. "Stay put," he said. "And keep quiet for five minutes, or you'll get hurt."

Then he was gone. Codlin breathed out an obscenity and jumped for the telephone. As he picked it up, "I warned you," said a gentle voice from the door. There was a noise

152

like a small tyre bursting and the telephone twisted round and clattered to the floor.

Codlin stood, staring stupidly at his hand. Splinters of vulcanite had grooved it, and the blood was beginning to drip. He cursed, foully and automatically. Footsteps were pattering away along the road outside. He let them get to the corner before he moved. He was taking no further chances. Then he lumbered across to the door, threw it open and started bellowing.

Three streets away Detective Sergeant Petrella, homeward bound, heard two things at once. Distant shouts of outrage, and, much closer at hand, light feet pattering on the pavement. He drew into the shadow at the side of the road and waited.

The two boys came round the corner, running easily, and laughing. When Petrella stepped out, the laughter ceased. Then the boys spun around, and started to run the other way.

Petrella ran after them. He saw at once that he could not catch both, and concentrated on the younger and slower boy. After a hundred yards he judged himself to be in distance, and jumped forward in a tackle. It was high by the standards of Twickenham, but it was effective, and they went down, the boy underneath. As they fell, something dropped from the boy's pocket and slid, ringing and spinning, across the pavement.

"Of course you've got to charge him," said Haxtell later that night. "It's true Codlin can't really identify him, but the boy had a gun on him, and he was running away from the scene of the crime. Who is he, by the way?"

"His name's Christopher Connolly. His father's a shunter at the goods depot. I've left them together for a bit, to see if the old man can talk some sense into him."

"Good idea," said Haxtell. "Can we get anything on the gun?"

"It's an air-pistol. Therefore no registration number. And foreign. Newish. And a pretty high-powered job. If it's been stolen we might have it on the lists."

"Check it," said Haxtell. "What about his pockets?"

"Nothing except this." Petrella pushed across a scrap of

paper. It had pencilled on it, in capital letters: WILL. BE AT USUAL PLACE 8 TONIGHT.

"What do you make of it?" said Haxtell.

"It depends," said Petrella cautiously, "if you think the dot after the first word is a full stop or just an accident."

Haxtell tried it both ways. "You mean it could be a plain statement: 'I will be at the usual place at eight o'clock tonight.' Or it could be an order, addressed to someone called Will."

"Yes. And Codlin did say that he thought he heard the bigger boy address the smaller one as Will."

"Is Connolly's name William?"

"No, sir. It's Christopher George. Known to his friends as Chris."

"What does he say about the paper?"

"Says I planted it on him. And the gun, of course."

"I often wonder," said Haxtell, "where the police keep all the guns they're supposed to plant on criminals. What about the other boy?"

"He says there was no other boy. He says he was alone, and had been alone, all the evening."

"I see." Haxtell stared thoughtfully out of the window. He had a sharp nose for trouble.

"One bright spot," he said at last. "Codlin always marked his notes. Ever since he caught an assistant trying to dip into his till. He puts a letter C in indelible pencil on the back."

"That might be a help if we can catch the other boy," agreed Petrella. He added, "Haven't I heard that name Codlin before? Something about a dog."

"He tied his dog up," said Haxtell. "A nice old spaniel. And beat him with a golf club. Fined forty shillings. It was before your time."

"I must have read about it somewhere," said Petrella.

"And if you think," blared Haxtell, "that that's any reason for not catching these – these young bandits – then I dare you to say it."

"Why, certainly not," said Petrella hastily.

"This is the third hold-up in a fortnight. The third that's been reported to us. All with guns – or what looked like guns. Now we've caught one of them. We've *got* to get the names of the other boys out of him. For their sake as much as anything. Before someone really gets hurt."

"I expect the boy'll talk," said Petrella.

Haxtell nodded. Given time, boys usually talked.

But Christopher Connolly was an exception. For he said nothing, and continued to say nothing.

The next thing that happened, happened to old Mrs. Lightly, who lived alone in a tiny cottage above the waterworks. Her husband had been caretaker, and she had retained the cottage by grace of the management, as long as she paid the rent of ten shillings a week. Lately she had been getting irregular in her payments, and she was now under notice to quit.

The evening after the capture of Connolly, just after dark, she heard a noise down in her front hall. She was a spirited old lady, and she came right out, carrying a candle to see what it was all about.

On the patched linoleum lay a fat envelope. Mrs. Lightly picked it up gingerly and carried it back to the sitting-room. She got very few letters, and, in any case, the last post had come and gone many hours earlier.

On the envelope, in pencilled capital letters, were the words: EIGHT WEEKS' RENT FROM SOME FRIENDS.

Mrs. Lightly set the candle down on the table, and with fingers that trembled tore open the flap. A little wad of notes slid out. She counted them. Two pound notes and four ten-shilling notes. There was no shadow of doubt about it. It was four pounds. And that was eight weeks' rent.

Or, looked at in another way, suppose it was seven weeks' rent. That would have the advantage of leaving ten shillings over for a little celebration. The whole thing was clearly a miracle; and miracles are things which the devout are commanded to commemorate. Mrs. Lightly placed the notes in the big black bag, folded the envelope carefully away behind a china dog on the mantelshelf, and got her best black hat out of the cupboard.

On the same evening, shortly after Mrs. Lightly left her cottage, four boys were sitting in the basement changing-room of the old sports pavilion. A storm lantern, standing on a locker, shed a circle of clear white light around it, leaving the serious faces of the boys in shadow. The windows were covered on the inside with cardboard and brown paper.

"I don't like it, Rob," the black-haired boy was saying. He was evidently repeating an old argument.

155

"What's wrong with it?" said the tall boy. He had a curiously gentle voice.

"Old Cator's what's wrong with it. He's a holy terror."

"He's a crook," said the fat boy.

The small boy said nothing. His eyes turned from one to the other as they spoke, but when no one was speaking they rested on the tall boy, full of trust and love.

"Isn't it crooks we're out to fix?" said the tall boy. "Isn't that right, Busty?"

"That's right," said the fat boy.

The black-haired boy said, "Hell, yes. But not just any crooks. Cator's got a night-watchman. And he's a tough, too. As likely as not, they both carry guns."

The tall boy said, "Are you afraid?"

"Of course I'm not afraid."

"Then what are we arguing about? There's four of us. And we've got two guns. There's two of them. When we pull the job, maybe only one'll be there. This is something we've *got* to do. We need the money."

"Another thing," said the black-haired boy. "Suppose we don't give quite so much away this time."

"You mean, keep some for ourselves?"

"That's right."

"What for?"

"I could think of ways to use it," said the black-haired boy, with a laugh. He looked round, but neither of the others had laughed with him. "All right," he said. "All right. I know the rules. Let's get this planned out."

"This is how it is, then," said the tall boy. "I reckon we'll have to wait about a week . . ." He demonstrated, on sheets of paper, with a pencil, and the four heads came close together, casting long shadows in the lamplight

Next morning Petrella reported to Chief Inspector Haxtell the minor events of the night. There was a complaint from the railway that some boys had broken a hole in the fence below the sports pavilion.

"Apart from that," said Petrella, "a beautiful calm seems to have fallen on Highside. Oh – apart from Mrs. Lightly."

"Mrs. Lightly?"

"Old Lightly's widow. The one who lives in the cottage next to the waterworks."

"Was that the one there was a bit in the papers about how she couldn't pay her rent?"

"That's right," said Petrella. "Only she got hold of some money, and that's what the drinking was about. It was a celebration. She seems to have drunk her way steadily along the High Street. Mostly gin, but a certain amount of stout to help it down. She finished by busting a shop window with an empty bottle."

"Where'd she got the money from?"

"That's the odd thing. She was flat broke. Faced with eviction, and no one very sympathetic, because they knew that as soon as she got any money she'd drink it up. Then an angel dropped in, with four quid in an envelope."

"An angel?"

"That's what she says. A disembodied spirit. It popped an envelope through the letter-box with four ten-shilling notes and two pounds in it."

"How much of it was left when you picked her up?"

"About two pounds ten," said Petrella.

"I don't see anything odd in all that," said Haxtell. "Some crackpot reads in the papers that the old girl's short of money and how her landlord's persecuting her, and he makes her an anonymous donation, which she promptly spends on getting plastered."

"Yes, sir," said Petrella. He added gently, "I've seen the notes she *didn't* spend. They're all marked on the back with a C in indelible pencil."

"They're *what*?"

"That's right, sir."

"It's mad."

"It's a bit odd, certainly," said Petrella. Something, a note almost of smugness in his voice, made the Superintendent look up. "Have you got some line on this?"

"I think I might be able to trace those notes back to the boy who's been running this show."

"Then don't waste any time talking about it," said Haxtell. "We need results, and we need 'em quickly. We've got to get some results." He added, with apparent inconsequence, "I'm seeing Barstow this afternoon."

Petrella's hopes, such as they were, derived from the

envelope, which he had duly recovered from behind the china dog on Mrs. Lightly's mantelshelf. The name and address had been cut out, but two valuable pieces of information had been left behind. The first was the name Strangeway's printed in the top left-hand corner. The second was the postmark, the date on which was still legible.

Petrella knew Strangeway's. It was a shop that sold cameras and photographic equipment, and he guessed that its daily output of letters would not be large. There was a chance, of course, that the envelope had been picked up casually. But equally, there was a chance that it had not.

Happily, the manager of Strangeway's was a methodical man. He consulted his day-book, and produced for Petrella a list of names and addresses. "I think," he said, "that those would be all the firm's letters that went out that day. They would be bills or receipts. I may have written one or two private letters, but I'd have no record of them."

"But they wouldn't be in your firm's envelopes."

"They might be. If they went to suppliers."

"I'll try these first," said Petrella.

There were a couple of dozen names on the list. Most of the addresses were in Highside or Helenwood.

It was no use inventing any very elaborate story. He was too well known locally to pretend to be an insurance salesman. He decided on a simple lie.

To the grey-haired old lady who opened the door to him at the first address he said, "We're checking the election register. The lists are getting out of date. Have you any children in the house who might come of age in the next five years?"

"There's Jimmy," said the woman.

"Who's Jimmy?"

She explained about Jimmy. He was a real terror. Aged about nineteen. Just as Petrella was getting interested in Jimmy she added that he'd been in Canada for a year.

Petrella took down copious details about Jimmy. It all took time, but if you were going to deal in lies, it was as well to act them out.

That was the beginning of a long day's work. Early in the evening he came to No. 11 Parham Crescent. The house was no different from a million others of the brick boxes that encrust the surface of London's northern heights.

The door was opened by a gentleman in shirtsleeves, who agreed that his name was Brazier and admitted to the possession of a sixteen-and-a-half-year-old boy called Robert.

"Robert Brazier?"

"Robert Humphreys. He's my sister's son. She's been dead two years. He lives here – *when* he's home."

Petrella picked up the lead with the skill of long experience. Was Robert often away from home?

Mr. Brazier obliged with a discourse on modern youth. Boys nowadays, Petrella gathered, were very unlike what boys used to be when he – Mr. Brazier – had been young. They lacked reverence for their elders, thought they knew all the answers, and preferred to go their own ways. "Sometimes I don't see him all day. Sometimes two days running. He could be out all night for all I know. It's not right – Mr. – um . . . "

Petrella agreed that it wasn't right. Mr. Brazier suffered from such acute halitosis that listening to him was an ordeal. However, he elicited some details. One of them was the name of the South London school that Robert had left eighteen months before.

Petrella did some telephoning, and the following morning he caught a bus and trundled down to Southwark to have a word with Mr. Wetherall, the headmaster of the South Borough Secondary School for Boys. Mr. Wetherall was a small, spare man with a beaky nose and he had been wrestling for quarter of a century with the tough precocious youths who live south of the river. The history of his struggles was grooved into his leathery face. He cheerfully took time off to consider Petrella's problems; all the more so when he discovered what was wanted.

"Robert Humphreys," he said. "I had a bet with my wife that I'd hear that name before long."

"Now you've won it, sir."

"Yes," said Mr. Wetherall. He gazed reflectively round his tiny, overcrowded study, then said, "This is a big school, you know. And I've been here, with one short break, for more than ten years. Two or three complete generations – maybe two thousand boys. And out of all that two thousand I could count on the fingers of one hand – without using the thumb — the ones who I'd call natural leaders. And of those few I'm not sure I wouldn't put Robert Humphreys first."

Mr. Wetherall added, "I'll tell you a story about him. While he was here, we were planning to convert a building into a gymnasium. I'd got all the governors on my side except the chairman, Colonel Bond. He was opposed to spending the money, and until I'd won him over, I couldn't move. One day the Colonel disappeared. He's a bachelor who spends most of his time at his club. No one was unduly worried. He missed a couple of governors' meetings, which was unusual. Then I got a letter. From the Colonel. It simply said that he had been thinking things over, and had decided that we ought to go ahead with our gym. He himself wouldn't be able to attend meetings for some time, as his health had given way."

Petrella goggled at him. "Are you telling me — ?" he said.

"That's right," said Mr. Wetherall calmly. "The boys had kidnapped him. Robert organised the whole thing. They picked him up in a lorry, and kept him in a loft, over an old stable. Guarded him, fed him, looked after him. And when they'd induced him to write that letter, they let him out."

"How did they disguise themselves?"

"They made no attempt to disguise themselves. They calculated, and rightly, that if the Colonel made a fuss people would never stop laughing at him. The Colonel had worked the sum out too, and got the same answer. He never said a word about it. In fact, it was Humphreys who told me. It was then I made my confident prediction. Downing Street or the Old Bailey."

"I'm afraid it may be the Old Bailey," said Petrella, unhappily.

"It was an even chance," said Mr. Wetherall. "He was devoted to his mother. If she hadn't died, I believe there's hardly any limit to what he might have done. He's with an uncle now. Not a very attractive man."

"I've met him," said Petrella. As he was going he said, "Did you get your gym?"

"I'll show you it as we go," said Mr. Wetherall. "One of the finest in South London."

It took another whole day for Petrella to finish his enquiries, but now that the clue was in his hand, it was not difficult to find the heart of the maze. It had been a day of blazing heat; by nine o'clock that night when he faced Haxtell, hardly a breath was moving.

"There are four of them," he said. "Five with Chris Connolly, the one we caught. First, there's a boy called Robert Humphreys. His first lieutenant's Brian Baker, known as Busty."

"A fat boy," said Haxtell. "Rather a good footballer. His father's a pro."

"Correct. The third one is Les Miller."

"Sergeant Miller's boy?"

"I'm afraid so, sir."

The two men looked at each other.

"Go on," said Haxtell grimly.

"The fourth, and much the youngest, is one of the Harrington boys. The one they call Winkle. His real name's Eric, or Ricky. There seems to be no doubt that the air-guns they've been using were stolen from a shop in Southwark, which is, incidentally, where Humphreys went to school."

"And Humphreys is the leader?"

"I don't think there's any doubt about that at all, sir. In fact, the whole thing is a rather elaborate game made up by him."

"A game," said Haxtell, pulling out a handkerchief and wiping the sweat from his forehead.

"Of Robin Hood. That's why they used those names. Fat Brian was Friar Tuck, red-headed Chris was Will Scarlet, Les was the Miller's son. And Ricky was Allen-a-Dale. Robert, of course, was Robin. I believe that historically — "

"I'm not interested in history. And you can dress it up what way you like. It doesn't alter the fact that they're gangsters."

"There were two points about them," said Petrella. "I'm not suggesting it's any sort of mitigation. But they really did adhere to the ideas of their originals. They didn't rob old women or girls – and they're usually the number-one target for juvenile delinquents."

Haxtell grunted.

"They chose people they thought needed robbing." Petrella caught the look in his superior's eye and hurried on. "And they didn't spend the money on themselves. They gave it away. All of it, as far as I can make out. To people they thought needed it. More like the real Robin Hood than the synthetic version. Hollywood's muddled it up for us. You hear the kids saying, 'Feared by the bad. Loved by the good.' But that wasn't really the way of it. Robin Hood didn't rob people because they were bad. He assumed they were bad, because they were rich. He was an early Communist."

Petrella stopped, aware that he had outrun discretion.

"Go on," said Haxtell grimly.

"Of course, he's got idealised now," Petrella concluded defiantly. "But I should think the authorities thought *he* was a pretty fair nuisance – when he was actually operating – wouldn't you?"

"And you suggest, perhaps, that we allow them to continue their altruistic work of redistributing the wealth of North London?"

"Oh no, sir. We've got to stop them."

"Why, if they're doing so much good?"

"Before they get hurt. As you said yourself."

Haxtell was spared the necessity of answering by a clatter of feet in the corridor and a resounding knock at the door. It was Detective Sergeant Miller, and he had his son with him.

"Good evening, Miller," said Haxtell. "I was half expecting you."

"I've brought my boy along," said Sergeant Miller. He was white with fury. "He's got something he's going to tell you."

The boy had been crying, but was calm enough now. "It's Humphreys and the others," he said. "They're going to do Cator's Garage tonight. I wouldn't agree to it. So they turned me out of the band. So I told Dad."

Just so, thought Petrella, had all great dynasties fallen. He was aware of a prickling sensation, a crawling of the skin, not entirely accounted for by the onrush of events. He looked out of the window and saw that a storm had crept up on them. Even as he watched, the first thread of lightning flicked out and in, like an adder's tongue, among the banked black clouds.

Les Miller was demonstrating something on the table.

"They've found a way in round the back. They get across the canal on the old broken bridge, climb the bank, and get in a window of an outhouse, which leads into the garage.

162

There's a watchman, but they reckon they can rush him from behind, and get his keys off him. Cator keeps a lot of money in the garage."

Petrella said, "I expect that's right, sir. We've had our eyes on that gentleman for some time. If he's in the hot-car racket he'd have no use for cheques or a bank account."

"We'd better warn Cator," said Haxtell, "and get a squad car round there quick. What time's the operation due to start?"

Before the boy could answer, the telephone sounded. Haxtell picked off the receiver, listened a moment, and said, "Don't do anything. We'll be right round," and to the others, "It has started. That was the watchman. He's knocked one boy out cold."

As Petrella ran for the car the skies opened, and he was wet to the skin before he reached it.

Outside Cator's Garage, a rambling conglomeration of buildings backing on the canal, they skidded to a halt, nearly ramming a big green tourer coming from the opposite direction. Herbert Cator jumped out, pounded up the cinder-path ahead of them, and thumped on the door.

The man who opened the door looked like a boxer gone badly to seed. The right side of his face was covered with blood, from a badly torn ear and a scalp wound. He was holding a long steel stoke-raker in one hand. "Glad you've got here," said the man. "Three of the little bastards. I got one of 'em."

He jerked his head towards the corner where fat Friar Tuck lay on his face, on the oil-dank floor.

"Where are the others?" said Haxtell.

"In there." He pointed to the heavy door that led through to the main workshop. "Don't you worry. They won't get out of there in a hurry. The windows are all barred."

Haxtell walked across, slipped the bolt. and threw the door open.

It was a big room, two storeys tall. The floor space jammed with cars in every stage of dismemberment. The top a clutter of hoisting and lifting tackle, dim above the big overhead lights.

"Come out of there, both of you."

"The big one's got a gun," said the man. "He nearly shot my ear off."

163

"Keep away then," said Haxtell. He turned back again, and said, in a booming voice, "Come on, Humphreys. And you, Harrington. The place is surrounded."

As if in defiant answer came a sudden, deafening crash of thunder. And then all the lights went out.

"Damnation," said Haxtell. Over his shoulder to Petrella and Miller he said, "Bring all the torches we've got in the car. And the spotlight, if the flex is long enough — "

Cator said, "Hold it a moment. Something's alight." A golden-white sheet of flame shot up from the back of the room. Cator said thickly, "They've set fire to the garage, the devils."

In the sudden light Petrella saw the boys. They were crouching together, on an overhead latticework gantry. Cator saw them, too. His hand went down, and came up. There was the roar of a gun, once, twice, before anyone could get at him. Then Petrella was moving.

The light showed him the iron ladder that led upwards. He flung himself at it and went up it. Then along the narrow balcony. When he reached the place where he had seen them, the boys had gone. He stood for a moment. Already the heat was becoming painful. Then, ahead of him, he saw the door to the roof. It was swinging open.

As he reached it, the whole interior of the room went up behind him in a hot white belch of flame.

Out on the roof he found the boys. Ricky Harrington was on his knees, beside Humphreys. The flames, pouring through the opening, lit the scene with cruel light.

Petrella knelt down beside him. One look was enough.

"He's dead, ent he?" said Ricky, in a curiously composed voice.

"Yes," said Petrella. "And unless the fire engine comes damned quick, he's going to have company in the next world."

The boy said, "I don't want no one to rescue me." He ran to the side of the building, vaulted the low coping, and disappeared. Petrella hurled himself after him.

He was just in time to see the miracle. Uncaring what happened to him, Ricky had landed with a soft splash in the waters of the North Side Canal.

If he can do it, I can, thought Petrella. Roast or drown.

He jumped. The world turned slowly in one complete fiery circle, and then his mouth was full of water.

He rose to the surface, spitting. There was no sign of the boy. Petrella tried to think. They had jumped from the same spot. There was no current. He must be there. Must be within a few yards.

He took a deep breath, turned over, and duck-dived. His fingers scrabbled across filth, broken crockery, and the sharper edges of cans. When he could bear it no longer he came up.

At the third attempt his fingers touched clothing. He slithered for a foothold in the mud, and pulled. The small body came with him, unresisting.

A minute later, he had it on the flat towpath. He was on the far side of the river, but even so he had to stagger twenty yards and turn the corner of the wall to escape the searing blast of the heat.

Then he dumped his burden and started to work, savagely, intently fighting for the life under his hands.

It was five minutes before Ricky stirred. Then he rolled onto his side, and was sick.

"What's happened?" he said.

"You're all right," said Petrella. "We'll look after you now."

"Not me, him." Then he seemed to remember, and sat still.

In the sudden silence Petrella heard a distant and plaintive bugle note. He knew that it was only the hooter from the goods depot, but for a moment it had sounded like a horn being blown in a lonely glade; blown for the followers who would not come.

The Coulman Handicap

THE door of No. 35 Bond Road opened and a thick-set, middle-aged woman came out. She wore a long grey coat with a collar of alpaca wool buttoned to the neck, a light grey hat well forward on her head, and mid-grey gloves on her hands. Her sensible shoes, her stockings, and the large, fabric-covered suitcase, which she carried in her right hand, were brown.

She paused for a moment on the step. Women of her age are often near-sighted, but there was nothing in her attitude to suggest this. She had bold, brown, somewhat protuberant eyes, set far apart in her strong face. They were not unlike the eyes of an intelligent horse.

She looked carefully to left and to right. Bond Road was never a bustling thoroughfare. At twelve o'clock on that bright morning of early April it was almost empty. A roadman, sweeping the gutter; a grocer's delivery boy, pushing his bicycle, nose down in a comic; the postman, on his mid-morning round. All of them were well known to her. She waited to see if the postman had brought her anything, and then set off up the pavement.

In the front parlour of No. 34, a lace curtain parted one inch and closed again. The man sitting on a chair in the bow window reached for the telephone which stood by his hand and dialled.

He heard a click as the receiver was lifted at the other end and said, "She's off. Going west." Then he replaced the receiver and lit himself a cigarette. The stubs in the tray beside the telephone suggested that he had been waiting for some time.

At that moment no fewer than twenty-four people, in one way or another, were concentrating their attention on Bond Road and on Mrs. Coulman, who lived at No. 35.

"It's a carrier service," said Superintendent Palance of No. 1 District, who was in charge of the joint operation, "and it's got to be stopped." Jimmy Palance was known throughout the Metropolitan Police Force as a fine organiser, a

166

teetotaller, a man entirely lacking in any sense of humour, who worked with a Pawnbrokers' List and the Holy Bible side by side on his tidy desk.

"The first problem of a thief who steals valuable and identifiable jewellery is to get rid of it. What does he do with it?"

"Flogs it?" suggested Chief Inspector Haxtell of Y Division.

"No fence'll touch it," said Chief Inspector Farmer of X Division. "Not while the heat's on."

"Then he hides it," said Haxtell. "In a safe deposit, or a bank. Crooks do have bank accounts, you know."

"Or a cloakroom, or a left-luggage office."

"Or with a friend, or at an accommodation address."

"Or sealed up in a tin, under the third tree from the corner."

"No doubt," said Superintendent Palance, raising his heavy black eyebrows, "there are a great number of possible hiding-places. I myself have listed twenty-seven distinct types. There may be more. The difficulty is that by the time the thief wishes to recover his loot. he is as often as not himself under observation."

Neither Haxtell nor Farmer questioned this statement. They knew well enough that it was true. A complicated system of informers almost always gave them the name of the perpetrator of any big and successful burglary. "All we then have to arrange is to watch the thief. If he goes near the stuff we will be able to lay hands on the man himself, and his cache, and his receiver."

"True," said Haxtell. "So what does he do?"

"He gets in touch with Mrs. Coulman. And informs her where he has placed the stuff. Gives her the key, or cloakroom ticket, and leaves the rest to her. It is not even necessary to give her the name of the receiver. She knows them all, and gets the best prices. She gets paid in cash, keeps a third, and hands over two-thirds to the author of the crime."

"Just like a literary agent," said Farmer, who had once written a short story.

"Sounds quite a woman," said Haxtell.

"She has curious antecedents," said Palance. "She is German. And I believe, although I've not been able to check it, that she and her brothers were in the German Resistance."

167

"The fact that she's alive proves she was clever," agreed Haxtell. "Now, I gather you want quite a few men for this. Tell us how you plan to tackle it."

"It's going to be a complicated job," said Palance. "But here is the outline . . ."

At the end of the street, after turning into the main road, Mrs. Coulman had a choice of transport. She could take a bus going south, or could cross the street and take a bus going north. Or she could walk two hundred yards down the hill to one underground station, or an equal distance up it to another. Or she could take a taxi. She was a thick-set woman of ample Teutonic build; and experience, gained in the last month of observation, had suggested that she would not walk very far, and would be more likely to walk downhill than up.

Near each bus stop a man and girl were talking. Opposite the underground a pair of workmen sat, drinking endless cups of tea. In a side street two taxis waited, a driving glove over the meter indicating that they were not for hire. A small tradesman's van, parked in a cul-de-sac, acted as mobile headquarters to this part of the operation. It was backed halfway into a private garage, chosen because it was on the telephone.

Mrs. Coulman proceeded placidly to the far end of Bond Road, waited for a gap in the traffic, crossed the main road, and turned up a side road beyond it.

An outburst of intense activity followed.

"Still going west," said the controller in the van. "Making for Highside Park. Details one to eight, switch in that direction. Number one car straight up Loudon Road and stop. Number two car parallel. Details nine and ten, cover Highside Tube Station and the bus stops at the top of the hill."

Mrs. Coulman emerged, panting slightly, from the side road which gave onto the top of Highside Hill, paused, and caused consternation in the ranks of her pursuers by turning round and walking back the way she had come.

Control had just worked out the necessary orders to jerk the machine into reverse when it was seen that Mrs. Coulman had retraced her steps to admire a flowering shrub in a front garden she had passed. Looking carefully about her to see that no one was watching, she nipped off a small spray and put it in her buttonhole. Then she turned back towards Highside Hill and made, without further check, for the tube station.

Details number nine and ten were Detective Sergeants Petrella and Wynne. They were waiting inside the station, at the head of the emergency stairs, and were already equipped with all-day tickets. When Mrs. Coulman reached the station entrance, therefore, she found it deserted. She bought a ticket for Euston and took the lift. A young man in corduroys and a raincoat, and an older one in flannel trousers, a windcheater and a club scarf, were already on the platform, waiting for the train. They got into the coaches on either side of her.

Above their heads the machine jerked abruptly into top gear. A word was exchanged with the booking-office clerk and two taxis sped towards Euston.

Mrs. Coulman, however, had disconcertingly changed her mind. Euston, Warren Street, Goodge Street, Tottenham Court Road – station after station came and went and still she sat on. Her seat had been chosen to command the exits of her own and the two neighbouring carriages. She seemed to take a close interest in the people who got on and off. But if she noticed that the men who had come from Highside were still with her, she gave no sign.

It was nearly half an hour later when she quitted the train at Clapham Common Station and made for the moving staircase, looking neither to right nor to left.

Petrella had time for a quick word with Wynne. "It's my belief the old bitch has rumbled us," he said. "Get on the blower and bring the rest of the gang down here, as quickly as possible. Meanwhile, I'll do my best to keep on her tail."

This proved easy. Mrs. Coulman walked down the street without so much as a backward glance, and disappeared into the saloon bar of The Admiral Keppel public house. Petrella made a detour of the place to ensure that it had no back entrance, and settled down to watch. It could hardly have been better situated for his purpose. The doors of its saloon and public bar opened side by side on to the same strip of pavement. Opposite them stood a sandwich bar, with a telephone.

"I don't think we ought to crowd the old girl," said

169

Petrella into the telephone. "It's my impression she's got eyes in the back of her head. If you could send someone – not Wynne, she's seen too much of him already this morning – and put a man at either end of the street, so that *we* don't have to follow her immediately as she goes — "

The voice at the other end approved these arrangements. Time passed. Petrella saw Detective Constable Mote ambling down the pavement, and he flagged him in.

"She's been there a long time," he said. "It must be nearly closing time."

"Sure she hasn't come out?" said Mote.

Petrella looked at his little book. "Two business men," he said. "One youth with a girlfriend, aged about seventeen and skinny. One sailor with a kitbag. That's the score to date."

The door of the public bar opened and three men came out and stood talking to the landlord, who seemed to know them. The men went off down the road together, the landlord disappeared inside, and they heard the sound of bolts being shut.

"Hey," said Petrella. "What's all this?"

"It's all right. There's still someone in the saloon bar," said Mote. "I can see the shadow on the glass. Seems to be knocking her drink back."

"Slip across and have a look," said Petrella.

Mote crossed the road lower down and strolled up past the ground-glass window of the saloon bar.

"It's a woman," he reported. "Sitting in the corner, drinking. I think the landlord's trying to turn her out."

As he spoke the door was flung open and the last of the customers appeared. She was the same shape as Mrs. Coulman, but she seemed to have changed her hat and coat, and to have done something to her face, which was now a mottled red.

She stood on the pavement for a moment, while the landlord bolted the door behind her. Then she ploughed off, straight and strong up the street, dipping very slightly as she progressed.

A thin woman coming out of a shop with a basket full of groceries was nearly run down. She saved herself by a quick sidestep, and said, in reproof, "Carnchew look where you're goin'?"

The massive woman halted, wheeled, and hit the thin

woman in the eye. It was a beautiful, co-ordinated, unconscious movement, as full of grace and power as a backhand
passing-shot by a tennis champion at the top of her form.

The thin woman went down, but was up again in a flash.
She was no quitter. She kicked her opponent hard on the
ankle. A uniformed policeman appeared, closely followed by
Sergeant Gwilliam, who had been waiting round the corner
and felt that it was time to intervene. The massive woman,
thus beset, back-heeled at her first assailant, aimed a
swinging blow with a carrier-bag full of bottles at the
constable, missed him, and hit Sergeant Gwilliam.

Some hours later Superintendent Palance said coldly, to
Chief Inspector Haxtell, "I take it that Sergeant Petrella is a
reliable officer."

"I have always found him so," said Haxtell, equally coldly.

"This woman, to whom he seems, at some point, to have
transferred his attention, is certainly not Mrs. Coulman."

"Apparently not," said Haxtell. "In fact she is a well-
known local character called Big Bertha. She is also believed
to hold the woman's drinking records for both draught and
bottled beer south of the Thames."

"Indeed?" Superintendent Palance considered the information carefully. "There is no possibility, I suppose, that she
and Mrs. Coulman are leading a double life?"

"You mean," said Haxtell, "that the same woman is
sometimes the respectable Mrs. Coulman of Bond Road,
Highside, and sometimes the alcoholic Bertha of Clapham?
It's an attractive idea, but I'm afraid it won't wash. Bertha's
prison record alone makes it an impossibility. During the
month you've been watching Mrs. Coulman, Bertha has,
I'm afraid, appeared no less than four times in the Southwark
Magistrates Court."

"In that case," said Palance reasonably, "since the lady
under observation was Mrs. Coulman when she started,
Sergeant Petrella must have slipped up at some point."

"I agree," said Haxtell. "But where?"

"That is for him to explain."

"It's a stark impossibility," said Petrella, later that day. "I
know it was Mrs. Coulman when she went into the pub.
There's no back entrance. I mean that, literally. It's a sort of
penthouse, built onto the front of the block. The landlord
himself has to come out of one of the bar doors when he

leaves. And our local people say he's perfectly reliable. They've got nothing against him at all."

"Could she have done a quick-change act? Is there a ladies' lavatory, or some place like that?"

"Yes. There's a lavatory. And she could have gone into it, and changed into other clothes which she had ready in her suitcase. It's all right as a theory. It's when you try to turn it into fact that it gets difficult. I saw nine people coming out of that pub. The first two were business types from the saloon bar. The landlord didn't know them, but they seemed to know each other. And anyway they just dropped in for a whisky and out again. Then there was a boy and girl in the public bar. They held hands most of the time and didn't weigh much more than nine stone nothing a piece."

"None of them sounds very likely," agreed Haxtell. "And the three workmen were local characters, or so I gather. That leaves the woman and the sailor."

"Right," said Petrella. "And since we know that the woman wasn't Mrs. Coulman, it leaves the sailor. He was broadly the right size and shape and weight, and he was the only one carrying anything. Thinking it over, one can see that's significant. He had a kitbag over his shoulder."

"Just how is a suitcase turned into a kitbag?"

"That part wouldn't be too difficult. The suitcase could easily be a sham. A fabric cover round a collapsible frame, which would fold up to almost nothing and go inside the kitbag with the wig and hat and coat and rest of the stuff."

"Where did the kitbag come from? Oh, I see. She would have had it inside the suitcase. One wave of the wand and a large woman with a large suitcase turns into a medium-sized sailor with a kitbag."

"Right," said Petrella. "And there's only one drawback. The sailor was a man, not a woman at all."

"You're sure?"

"Absolutely and completely sure," said Petrella. "He crossed the road and passed within a few feet of me. He was wearing bell-bottomed trousers and a dark blue sweater. There are certain anatomical differences, you know. And Mrs. Coulman was a very womanly woman."

"A queenly figure," agreed Haxtell. "Yes, I see what you mean."

"It's not only that," said Petrella. "A woman might get

away with being dressed as a man on the stage. Or seen from a distance, or from behind. But not in broad daylight, face to face in the street. A man's hair grows in quite a different way, and his ears are bigger, and — "

"All right," said Haxtell. "I'll take your word for it." He paused and added, "Palance thinks you fell asleep on the job, and Mrs. Coulman slipped out when you weren't looking."

"I know," said Petrella. An awkward silence ensued.

Petrella said, "Will they keep up the watch?"

"I should they'd lay off her a bit," said Haxtell. "It's an expensive job, immobilising a couple of dozen men. And a dinosaur would be suspicious after yesterday's performance. I should think they'd let her run for a bit. There's no reason you shouldn't keep your eyes open, though – unofficially."

Petrella devoted what time he could spare in the next three months to his self-appointed task. His landlady's married sister had a house in Bond Road, so he spent a lot of time in her front parlour and, after dark, prowling around No. 35, the end house on the other side of the road. He also made friends with the booking-clerks at Highside station and Pond End station; and spent an interesting afternoon in the German Section of the Foreign Office.

"One thing's clear enough," he said to Haxtell. "When she's on the job, she starts on the underground. Taxis and buses are too easy to follow. If you go by underground, the pursuit has got to come down with you. Or guard the exit of every underground station in London simultaneously, which is a stark impossibility. Anyway, I know that's what she does. She's been seen three times leaving Highside station, carrying that trick suitcase. She books to any old station. She's only got to pay the difference at the other end. She's a bit more cautious, too, after that last fiasco. She won't get onto the train if there's any other passenger she can't account for on the platform. Sometimes she's let three or four trains go past."

Haxtell reflected on all this, and said, "It seems a pretty watertight system to me. How do you suggest we break in on it?"

"Well, I think we've got to take a chance," said Petrella. "In theory it'd be safer with a lot of people, but actually, I don't think it would work at all. That kind can always spot organised opposition. There's just a chance, if you'd let two

173

or three of us try it, next time we get word that she's likely to be busy — "

"We'll see," said Haxtell.

Three nights after these words were spoken, on a Saturday, the redoubtable twin brothers, Jack and Sidney Ponting, made entry into Messrs. Alfreys' West End establishment by forcing the skylight of an adjacent building, picking three separate locks, cutting their way through an eighteen-inch brick wall, and blowing the lock neatly out of the door of the new Alfrey strong room. When the staff arrived on Monday they found a mess of brickwork and twisted steel. The losses included sixty-four large rough diamonds deposited by a Greek ship-owner. They were to have formed the nuptial head-dress of his South American bride.

"It's a Ponting job," said Superintendent Palance. "It's got their registered trade mark all over it. Get after them quick. They're probably hiding up."

But the Pontings were not hiding. They were at home, and in bed. They raised no objection to a search of their premises.

"It's irregular," said Sidney. "But what have we got to hide?"

"You boys have got your job to do," said Jack. "Get it finished, and we can get on with our breakfast."

Palance came up to see Haxtell.

"They certainly did it. They most certainly did it. Equally certainly they've dumped the diamonds. And none of them has reached a receiver yet, I'm sure of that. And the Pontings use Mrs. Coulman."

"Yes," said Haxtell. "Well, we must hope to do better this time."

"Are you set on trying it on your own?"

Palance was senior to Haxtell. And he was longer in service, and older in experience. Haxtell thought of these things, and paused. He was well aware of the responsibility he was shouldering, and which he could so easily evade. Then he said, "I really think the only way is to try it ourselves, quietly."

"All right," said Palance. He didn't add, "And on your own head be it." He was never a man to waste words.

Four days followed, during which Petrella attended to his

other duties as well as he could by day, and prowled round the curtilage of No. 35 Bond Road by night. Four days in which Sergeant Gwilliam, and Detective Constables Wilmot and Mote were never out of reach of a telephone; and Haxtell sweated.

On the fifth night Petrella gave the signal: Tomorrow's the day. And at eleven o'clock next morning, sure enough, the front door opened and Mrs. Coulman peered forth. She was wearing her travelling coat and hat, and grasped in her muscular right hand was the fabric-covered suitcase.

She walked ponderously down the road. However acute her suspicions may have been, there was nothing for them to feed on. For it is a fact that at that moment no one was watching her at all.

Ten minutes later she was purchasing a ticket at Highside Station. The entrance to the station was deserted. She waited placidly for the lift.

The lift and Sergeant Gwilliam arrived simultaneously. He was dressed as a workman, and he seemed to be in a hurry. He bought a ticket to the Elephant and Castle and got into the lift beside Mrs. Coulman. In silence, and avoiding each other's eye, they descended to platform level. In silence they waited for the train.

When the train arrived, Sergeant Gwilliam hesitated. He seemed to have an eye on Mrs. Coulman's movements. They approached the train simultaneously. At the very last moment Mrs. Coulman stopped. Sergeant Gwilliam went on, the doors closed, and the train disappeared bearing the Sergeant with it.

Mrs. Coulman returned to her seat on the platform and waited placidly. By the time the next train arrived, the only other occupants of the platform were three schoolgirls. Mrs. Coulman got into the train, followed by the schoolgirls. Two stations later the schoolgirls got off. Mrs. Coulman, from her customary seat beside the door, watched them go.

Thereafter, as the train ran south, she observed a succession of people getting on and off. There were three people she did not see. Petrella, with Mote and Wilmot, had entered the train at the station before her. Sergeant Gwilliam's planned diversion had given them plenty of time to get there. Petrella was in the first and the other two were in the last carriages of the train.

It was at Balham that Mrs. Coulman finally emerged. Two women with shopping-bags, who had joined her carriage at Leicester Square, went with her. Also a commercial traveller with samples, whom she had watched join the next carriage at the Oval.

Petrella, Mote, and Wilmot all saw her go, but it was no part of their plan to follow her, so they sat tight.

At the next stop, all three of them raced for the moving stairs, hurled themselves into the street, and found a taxi.

"I'm off duty," said the taxi-driver.

"Now you're on again," said Petrella, and showed him his warrant card. "Get us back to Balham Station, as quick as you can."

The taxi-driver blinked, but complied. Petrella had his eye on his watch.

"She's had four minutes' start," he said, as they bundled out. "You know what to do. Take every pub in your sector. And get a move on."

The three men separated. There is no lack of public houses in that part of South London, but Petrella calculated that if they worked outwards from the station, taking a sector each, they could cover most of them quite quickly. It was the riskiest part of the scheme, but he could think of no way to avoid it.

He himself found her.

She was sitting quietly in the corner of the saloon bar of The Gatehouse, a big, newish establishment at the junction of the High Street and Trinity Road.

There was no convenient snack bar this time; there was very little cover at all. The best he could find was a trolley-bus shelter. If he stood behind it, it did at least screen him from the door.

The minutes passed, and added up to a quarter of an hour. Then to half an hour. During that time two people had gone in, and three had come out, but none of them had aroused Petrella's interest. He knew, more or less, what he was looking for.

At last the door opened and a man emerged. He was a thick, well set-up man, dressed in a close-fitting flannel suit which was tight enough across the shoulders and round the chest to exhibit his athletic frame. And he was carrying a canvas bag, of a type that athletes use to hold their sports gear.

He turned left, and swung off down the pavement with an unmistakable, aggressive masculine stride, a mature bull of the human herd, confident of his strength and purpose.

Petrella let him have the length of the street, and then trotted after him. This was where he had to be very careful. What he mostly needed was help. The chase swung back past the underground and there he spotted Wilmot and signalled him across.

"In the grey flannel suit, carrying a bag," he said. "See him? Then get right after him, and remember, he's got eyes in the back of his head."

Wilmot grinned all over his guttersnipe face. He was imaginatively dressed in a teddy-boy suit and he fitted into the South London streets as easily as a rabbit into a warren.

"Doanchew worry," he said, "I won't lose him."

Petrella fell back until he was a hundred yards behind Wilmot. He kept his eyes open for Mote. The more of them the merrier. There was a long, hard chase ahead.

He noticed Wilmot signalling.

"Gone in there," said Wilmot.

"Where?"

"Small shop. Bit of the way up the side street."

Petrella considered. "Walk past," he said. "Take a note of the name and number on the shop. Go straight on, out of sight, to the other end. If he goes that way, you can pick him up. If he comes back I'll take him."

Ten minutes went by. Petrella thought anxiously about back exits. But you couldn't guard against everything.

Then the man reappeared. He was carrying the same bag, yet it looked different. Less bulky in shape but, by the swing of it, heavier.

He's dumped the hat and coat and the remains of the suitcase at that accommodation address, thought Petrella. Even if we lose him, we know one of the Ponting hide-outs. But we mustn't lose him. That bag's got several thousand pounds' worth of stolen jewellery in it now.

Would it be best to arrest him, and give up any chance of tracing the receiver? The temptation was almost overmastering. Only one thing stopped him. His quarry was moving

177

with much greater freedom, as if convinced that there was no danger. Near the end of the run he would get cautious again. For the moment there was nothing to do but follow.

The man plunged back in the underground; emerged at Waterloo; joined the queue at the Suburban Booking-Office. Petrella kept well clear for he owned a ticket which enabled him to travel anywhere on the railway.

Waterloo was a station whose layout he knew well. By positioning himself at the central bookstall, he could watch all three exits. His quarry had bought, and was eating, a meat pie. Petrella was quite unconscious of hunger. His eyes were riveted on the little bag, swinging heavily from the man's large fist. Once he put it down, but it was only to get out more money to buy an orange, which he peeled and ate neatly, depositing the remains in one of the refuse bins. Then he picked up the bag again and made for his train.

It was the electric line for Staines and Windsor. He went through the barrier, and walked slowly up the train. There were very few passengers about, and it must have been near enough empty. He walked along the platform, and climbed into a carriage at the far end.

Some instinct restrained Petrella. There were still five minutes before the train left. He waited. Three minutes later the man emerged from the carriage, walked very slowly back down the train, glancing into each carriage as he passed, and got into the carriage nearest to the barrier. The guard blew his whistle.

Two girls who had been sauntering towards the barrier broke into a run – Petrella ran with them. They pushed through the gate. The guard blew his whistle again; they jerked open the door of the nearest carriage and tumbled in together.

"We nearly left that too late," said one of the girls. Her friend agreed with her. Petrella thought that they couldn't have timed it better. But he didn't say so. He was prepared to agree with everything they said. It was the quickest way he knew of getting on with people.

The girls were prepared to enjoy his company too. The dark vivacious one was called Beryl and the quieter mousy one was Doreen. They lived at Staines.

"Where are you getting out?" asked Beryl. "Or is that a secret?"

"I haven't made up my mind yet," said Petrella.

Beryl said he was a case. Doreen agreed.

The train ambled through dim, forgotten places like Feltham and Ashford. No one got out and no one got in. Petrella heard about a dance, and what had gone on afterwards in the car park. He said he was sorry he didn't live at Staines. It sounded quite a place.

"It's all right in summer," said Doreen. "It's a dump in winter. Here we are."

The train drew up.

"Sure you won't change your mind?" said Beryl.

"Perhaps I will, at that," said Petrella. Out of the corner of his eye he saw that his man had got out and was making his way along the platform.

"You'd better hurry up then. They'll take you on to Windsor."

"That'd never do," said Petrella. "I forgot to warn her that I was coming."

"Who?" said Doreen.

"The Queen."

His man was safely past the ticket collector now.

"Come on," said Beryl. They went past the collector together. "Wouldn't you like some tea? There's a good place in the High Street."

"There's nothing I'd like better, but I think I see my uncle waving to me."

The girls stared at him. Petrella manoeuvred himself across the open yard, keeping the girls between him and his quarry. The man had set off up the road without, apparently, so much as a backward glance, but Petrella knew that the most difficult part of the chase was at hand.

"I don't see your uncle," said Beryl.

"There he is. Sitting in that taxi."

"That's just the taxi-driver. I don't believe he's your uncle at all."

"Certainly he is. How are you keeping, uncle?"

"Very fit, thank you," said the taxi-driver, a middle-aged man with a brown bald head.

"There you are," said Petrella. "I'll have to say goodbye now. We've got a lot to talk about. Family business."

The girls hesitated, and then withdrew, baffled.

"You a policeman?" said the taxi-driver. "A detective or something?"

"As a matter of fact, I am."

"Following that man in the light suit? I thought as much. Very pretty, the way you got behind those girls. As good as a book."

His quarry was now halfway up the long, straight, empty road, which leads from Staines Station to the riverside. He had stopped to light a cigarette, and in stopping he half turned.

"Keep behind my cab," said the driver. "That's right, well down. He's getting nervous. I'd say he's not far from wherever it is he's going to. Good as a book, isn't it? Do you read detective stories?"

The man was walking on again now. He was a full three hundred yards away.

"I don't want to lose him," said Petrella. "Not now. I've come a long way with him."

"You leave it to me," said the cab-driver. "I've been driving round here for forty years. There isn't a footpath I don't know blindfold. Just watch which way he turns at the end."

"Turning right," said Petrella.

"All aboard." The taxi shot out of the station yard, and the driver turned round in his seat to say, "Might be making for the High Street, but if he wanted the High Street, why not take a bus from the other platform? Ten to one he's for the ferry."

"I say, look out for that dog," said Petrella.

The driver slewed back in his seat. Said, "Effie Muggridge's poodle. Asking for trouble," and accelerated. The dog shot to safety with a squeal of rage.

"Got to do this bit carefully," said the driver as they reached the corner. "Keep right down. Don't show so much as the tip of your nose, now."

Petrella obeyed. The taxi rounded the corner, and over it, in a wave, flowed the unmistakable smell of the river on a hot day – weed and water and tar and boat varnish.

"He's in the ferry," said the driver. "Got his back to you. You can come up for air now."

Petrella saw that a ferry punt ran from the steps beside a public house. There were three passengers on her, standing cheek by jowl, and the ferryman was untying and pushing out. He realised how hopeless he would have been on his own.

"What do we do?" he said.

"Over the road bridge and back down the other side. Plenty of time, if we hurry."

"What were we doing just now?"

The driver chuckled throatily. Petrella held his breath and counted ten, slowly. Then they were crossing Staines Bridge.

"Not much traffic at the moment," said the driver. "You ought to see it at weekends." They did a skid turn to the left, and drew up in the yard of another riverside inn.

"There's two things he could do," said the driver. "Walk up the towpath to the bridge. There's no way off it. Or he could come down the path – you see the stile? – the one that comes out there. I'll watch the stile. You go through that gate and down the garden – I know the man who owns it. He won't mind. You can see the towpath from his summer-house. If you hear my horn, come back quick."

With a feeling that some power stronger than himself had taken charge, Petrella opened a gate and walked down a well-kept garden, full of pinks and roses and stone dwarfs with pointed hats. At the bottom was a summer-house. In the summer-house he found a small girl reading a book.

"Are you coming to tea?" she said.

"I'm not sure," said Petrella. "I might be going to the cinema."

"You'll have to hurry then. The big film starts in five minutes."

Behind him a hooter sounded off.

"I'll run then," said Petrella. He scooted back up the garden. The girl never raised her eyes from her book.

"Just come out," said the taxi-driver. "Going nicely. We'll give him twenty yards. Can't afford too much leeway here. Tricky navigation."

He drove slowly towards the turning, and stopped just short of it.

"Better hop out and look," he said. "But be careful. He's stopped twice already to blow his nose. We're getting pretty warm."

Petrella inched up to the corner, and poked his head round

the wall. The man was going away from him, walking along the pavement, but slowly. It was an area of bungalows, some on the road, some on the river bank, with a network of private ways between.

The taxi-driver had got out, and was breathing down the back of his neck.

"Got to take a chance," he said. "If we follow him, he'll spot us for sure. I'll stay here. If he turns right, I'll mark it. If he turns left he's for Riverside Drive. You nip down that path, and you can cut him off."

Petrella took the path. It ran between high hedges of dusty bramble and thorn; hot and sweet-smelling in the sun. It was the dead middle of the afternoon, with hardly a dog stirring. Petrella broke into a jog trot, then slowed for the road ahead.

As he reached the corner, he heard footsteps on the pavement. Their beat was unmistakable. It was his man, and he was walking straight towards him.

Petrella looked round for cover and saw none. He thought for a moment of diving into the shallow ditch, but realised that he would merely be attracting attention. The footsteps had stopped. Petrella held his breath. He heard the click of a latch. Feet on flagstones. The sudden purring of an electric bell.

The chase was over.

"I'm not saying," said Palance, "that it wasn't a success. It was a success. Yes."

Haxtell said nothing. He knew just how Palance was feeling and sympathised with him.

"We've got back the Alfrey diamonds, and we've got our hands on that man at Staines. An insurance broker, of all things, and quite unsuspected. Judging from what we found in the false bottom of a punt in his boat-house he's been receiving stolen goods for years. And we've stopped up one of the Ponting middlemen at that tobacconist's in Balham. A little more pressure and we may shop the Pontings, too."

"Quite," said Haxtell sympathetically.

"All the same, it was a mad way to do it. You can't get over that, Haxtell. How long have you known that Coulman was a man?"

"We realised that as soon as we started to think about it,"

said Haxtell. "It was obviously impossible for a real, middle-aged buxom woman to turn into a convincing man. But, conversely, it was easy enough for a man dressed as a woman, padded and powdered and wigged, to whip it all off and turn back quickly into his own self."

"Then do you mean to say," said Palance, "that the Mrs. Coulman my men were watching for a month – doing her shopping, gossiping, hanging out her washing, having tea with the vicar – was really a man all the time?"

"Certainly not," said Haxtell. Observing symptoms of apoplexy, he said, "That *was* Mrs. Coulman. She had a brother – two, actually. One was killed by the Nazis. The other one got over to England. Whenever she had a big job on hand, her brother would come along at night. The house she lived in was at the end of the row. There was a way in at the side. He could slip in late at night without anyone seeing him. Next day he'd dress up in his sister's coat and hat and go out and do the job. She stayed quietly at home."

"When you realised this," said Palance, "wouldn't it have been better to do the job properly? You could have had a hundred men if necessary."

"It wouldn't have worked. Not a chance. You can't beat a methodical man like Coulman by being more methodical. He'll outdo you every time. The underground, the change of clothes, the careful train check before he starred for Staines, the long straight road, and the ferry. What you want with a man like that is luck – and imagination."

"Yes, but — " said Palance.

"Method, ingenuity, system," said Haxtell. "You'll never beat a German at his own game. Look at the Gestapo. They tried for five years and even they couldn't pull it off. The one thing they lacked was imagination. Perhaps it was a good thing. A little imagination, and they might have caused a lot more bother."

He sounded pleased, and had every reason to be. His own promotion to Superintendent had just come through.

The Sark Lane Mission

"You're wanted down at Central," said Gwilliam. "They want to have a little chat with you about your pension."

"My pension?" said Detective Sergeant Petrella. Being nearer twenty than thirty, pensions were not a thing which entered much into his thoughts. "You're sure it's not my holiday? I've been promised a holiday for eighteen months."

"Last month I saw the pensions officer," said Gwilliam, "he said to me, 'Sergeant Gwilliam, it's a dangerous job you're doing.' It was the time I was after that Catford dog-track shower and I said, 'You're right, there, my boy.' 'Do you realise, Sergeant,' he said to me, 'that every year for the past ten years one hundred and ninety policemen have left the force with collapsed arches? And this year we may pass the two hundred mark. We shall have to raise your insurance contributions.'"

Petrella went most of the way down to Westminster by bus. It was a beautiful morning, with spring breaking through all round. Having some time in hand he got off the bus at Piccadilly, walked down St. James's, and cut across the corner of the park.

It was a spring which was overdue. They had had a dismal winter. In the three years he had been in Y Division, up at Highside, he could not remember anything like it. The devil seemed to have got among the pleasant people of North London. First, an outbreak of really nasty hooliganism; led, as he suspected, by two boys of good family, but he hadn't been able to pin it on them. Then the silly business of the schoolgirl shop-lifting gang. Then the far from silly, the dangerous and tragic matter of Cora Wynne.

Wynne was the oldest by several years of the Highside detectives, having come to them from the Palestine police. He was a quiet but well-liked man, and he had one daughter, Cora, who was seventeen. Six months before, Cora had gone. She had not disappeared; she had departed, leaving a note behind her saying that she wanted to live her own life.

"Whatever that means," Wynne had said to Superintendent Haxtell.

"Let her run," Haxtell had replied. "She'll come back." He was right. She came back at the end of the fifth month, in time to die. She was full of cocaine, and pregnant.

Petrella shook his head angrily as he thought about it. He stopped to look at the crocuses which were thick in the grass. A starved-looking sparrow was trying to bolt a piece of bread almost as large as itself. A pigeon sailed smoothly down and removed it. Petrella walked on, up the steps into King Charles Street, across Whitehall, and under the arch into New Scotland Yard.

He was directed to the office that dealt with pensions, allotted a wooden chair, and told to wait. At eleven o'clock a messenger brought in a filing tray with six cups of tea on it, and disappeared through a swing door in the partition. Since the tray was empty when he returned, Petrella deduced that there must be at least six people devoting attention to the pensions of the Metropolitan Police and he hoped that one of them would soon find time to devote some attention to him.

He became aware that the messenger had halted opposite him.

"You Sergeant Pirelli?" he said.

"That's right," said Petrella. He had long ago given up correcting people about it.

"CID, Y Division?"

"Ten out of ten."

"Whassat?"

"I said you're quite right."

"I'll tell 'em you're here," said the messenger.

Five minutes later a cheerful-looking girl arrived and said, "Sergeant Petrella? Would you come with me, please?"

His opinion of the Pensions Section became a good deal more favourable. Any department that employed a girl with legs like that must have some good in it.

So engrossed was he in this speculation that it did not, at first, occur to him to ask where they were going. When they reached, and pushed through a certain swing door on the first floor, he stopped her.

"You've got it wrong," he said. "This is where the top brass work. If we don't look out we shall be busting in on the Assistant Commissioner."

"That's right," said the girl. She knocked on one of the doors on the south side of the corridor; opened it without waiting for an answer; said, "I have Sergeant Petrella here for you," and stood aside.

He advanced dazedly into the room. He had been there once before, and he knew that the grey-haired man behind the desk was Assistant Commissioner Romer, of the CID; a man who, unlike some of his predecessors, had not come to his office through the soft byways of the legal department, but had risen from the bottom-most rung of the ladder, making enemies at every step, until finally he had found himself at the top; when, there being no one left to fight, he had proved himself a departmental head of exceptional ability.

In a chair beside the window he noted Superintendent Costorphine, who specialised in all matters connected with narcotics. He had worked for him on two previous occasions and had admired him, although he could not love him.

Romer said, in a very friendly voice, "Sit down, will you, Sergeant. This is going to take some time. You know Costorphine, don't you? I'm sorry about this cloak-and-dagger stuff, but you'll understand better when I explain what it's about, and what we're going to ask you to do. And when I say 'ask' I mean just that. Nothing that's said this morning is anything approaching an order. It's a suggestion. If you turn it down, no one's going to think any the worse of you. In fact, Costorphine and myself will be the only people who will even know about it."

Assuming a cheerfulness which he was far from feeling, Petrella said, "You tell me what you want me to do, sir, then I can tell you if I want to run away."

Romer nodded at Costorphine, who said in his schoolmasterly voice, "Almost a year ago, we noted a new source of entry of cocaine into this country. Small packets of it were taken from distributors *inside* the country. It was never found in large quantities, and we never found how it got in.

"Analysis showed it to be Egyptian in origin. It also showed quite apppreciable deposits of copper. It is obviously not there as the result of any part of the process of manufacture, and it is reasonable to suppose that it came there during some stage in shipment or entry.

"Once the source had been identified, we analysed every

186

sample we laid hands on, and it became clear" — Costorphine paused fractionally, not for effect, he was a man who had no use for effects, but because he wished to get certain figures clear in his own head — "that rather over half of the total intake of illicit cocaine coming into this country was coming under this head. And that the supply was increasing."

"And along with it," said Romer, "were increasing, at a rate of geometrical progression, most of the unpleasant elements of criminal activity with which we have to deal. Particularly among juveniles. I've had some figures from America which made my hair stand on end. We're not quite as bad as them yet, but we're learning."

Petrella could have said, "There's no need to tell me. I knew Cora Wynne when she was a nice, friendly schoolgirl of fourteen, and I saw her just before she died." But he kept quiet.

Romer went on, "I suppose if youth thinks it may be blown to smithereens inside five or ten years by some impersonal force pressing a button, it's predisposed to experiment. I don't know. Anyway, you'll understand why we thought it worth bringing down a busy detective sergeant from Y Division and wasting his morning for him.

"Now, I'm going to give you some facts. We'll start, as our investigators started about nine months ago, with a gentleman called Batson. Mr. Batson is on the board of the Consort Line, a company which owns and runs three small cargo steamers: the *Albert Consort,* the *William Consort,* and the *Edward Consort*: steamers which run between various Mediterranean ports, Bordeaux, and London."

When Romer said, "Bordeaux," Petrella looked up at Costorphine, who nodded.

"Bordeaux, but not the racket you're thinking of," he said. "We've checked that."

"Batson," went on Romer, "is not only on the board of the Consort Line. It has been suggested that he *is* the board. But one thing about him is quite certain. Whatever his connection with this matter he, personally, takes no active part. He neither carries the stuff nor has any direct contact with the distributors. But I think that, at the end of the day, the profit goes to him.

"That being so, we looked carefully at his friends, and the one who caught our eye was Captain Cree. Ex-captain now,

187

since he has retired from the services of the Consort Line, and lives in considerable affluence in a house at Greenwich. He maintains a financial interest in the *Consorts* through his friend, Mr. Batson, and acts as chandler and shore agent for them – finds them crews and cargoes, and buys their stores.

"All of which might add up, in cash, to a nice house at Greenwich, but wouldn't really account for" — Romer ticked them off on his fingers — "two personal motor cars, with a chauffeur body-servant to look after the same, a diesel-engined tender called *Clarissa* and based on Wapping, with a full-time crew of three and, in addition to all these, a large number of charitable and philanthropic enterprises, chiefly among seamen and boys in the dockside area."

"He sounds perfectly terrible," said Petrella.

"Such a statement, made outside these four walls," said Romer, "would involve you in very heavy damages for defamation. Captain Cree is a respectable, and a respected, citizen. One of his fondest interests is the Sark Lane Mission."

"The Sark Lane — "

"The name is familiar to you? It should be. The Mission was one of the first in Dockland, and it was founded by your old school."

"Of course. I remember now. We used to have a voluntary subscription of five shillings taken off us on the first day of every term. I don't think anyone took any further interest in it."

"I should imagine that one of the troubles of the Sark Lane Mission is that people have not taken enough interest in it. The Missioner for the last twenty-five years has been a Mr. Jacobson. A very good man, in his way and, in his early years, energetic and successful. Jacobson finally retired last month, at the age of seventy-five.

"I should imagine that for the last ten years his appearances at the Mission have been perfunctory. The place has really been kept going by an old, ex-naval man called Batchelor – and by the regular munificence of Captain Cree."

"I see," said Petrella. He felt that there must be something more to it than that.

"The appointment of the Missioner lies with the School Governors, but they act on the recommendation of the Bishop of London. Sometimes the post is filled by a clergyman. Sometimes not. On this occasion, the recommended candidate was the Reverend Freebone."

"Philip Freebone!"

"The present incumbent of the Church of St. Peter and St. Paul, Highside. You know him, I believe?"

"Very well indeed. He started up at Highside as curate, and when the incumbent died he was left in charge. I can't imagine anyone who would do the job better."

"I can," said Romer.

When he had got over the shock, Petrella did not pretend not to understand him.

"I don't think I could get away with it, sir," he said. "Not for any length of time. There'd be a hundred things I'd do wrong."

"I'm not suggesting that you should pose as a clergyman. You could go as Mr. Freebone. You've had some experience with youth clubs, I believe."

"For a few months before I joined the police, yes. I wasn't very successful."

"It may have been the wrong sort of club. I have a feeling you're going to be very successful in this one."

"Has Freebone been told?"

"He knows that he's got the job. He hasn't been told of the intended – er – rearrangement."

"I think you may have some difficulty there. Phil's one of the most obstinate people I know."

"I will have a word with his Bishop."

"I am afraid clergyman do not always do what their Bishops tell them these days," remarked Costorphine.

"This isn't a job on which we can afford to make a second mistake," continued Romer.

Petrella looked up.

"We got a man into the Consort Line about six months ago. It took some doing but we managed it in the end, without, as far as we know, arousing any suspicions. He was engaged as an ordinary seaman, under the name of Mills. He made voyages on all three of the ships, and gave us very full but absolutely negative reports. He was on his way home a fortnight ago in the *Albert Consort*, and was reported as having deserted ship at Marseilles."

"And hasn't been seen since?"

"He's been seen," said Romer. "The French police found

him in the foothills behind Marseilles two days ago. What was left of him. He'd been tortured before he was killed."

"I see," said Petrella.

"I'm telling you this so that, if you go in at all, you go in with your eyes wide open. This is an international crowd, who are calculating their profits in millions. And who must be responsible, directly, and indirectly, for hundreds of deaths a year. A single life is not of great importance."

"No," said Petrella. "I can quite see that . . ."

A fortnight later the new Missioner came to the Sark Lane Mission. This was a rambling, two-storey, yellow brick building in the style associated, through the East End, with temperance and good works.

The street doors opened into a small lobby, in which a notice said, in startling black letters, WIPE YOUR FEET. Someone had crossed out FEET in pencil and hopefully substituted a different part of the body. On the left of the lobby was a reception office, which was empty.

Beyond, you went straight into the main Mission room, which rose the full two-storv height of the building and looked like a drill hall, half-heartedly decorated for a dance. Dispirited red and white streamers hung from the iron cross-bars which spanned the roof. A poster on the far wall bore the message, in cotton-wool letters, "How will you spend Eternity?"

At the far end of the hall three boys were throwing darts into a board. Superficially they all looked alike, with their white town faces, their thick dark hair, and their general air of having been alive a lot longer than anyone else.

When, later, Mr. Freebone got to know them, he realised that there were differences. The smallest and fattest was a lazy but competent boy called Ben. The next in height and age was Colin, a dull boy of fifteen, who came to life only on the football field; but for football he had a remarkable talent, a talent which was already attracting the scouts from the big clubs, and was one day to put his name in the headlines. The oldest and tallest of the boys was called Humphrey, and he had a long, solemn face with a nose which started straight and turned to the right at the last moment, and a mouth like a crocodile's. It was not difficult to see that he was the leader of the three.

None of them took the slightest notice of Mr. Freebone, as he padded across the scarred plank flooring to watch them.

In the end he said, "You're making an awful mess of that, aren't you?" He addressed this remark to the fat boy. "If you want fifteen and end on a double it's a waste of time going for one."

The boy gaped at him. Mr. Freebone took the darts from him, and threw them. First a single three; then, at the second attempt, a double six.

"There you are, Ben," said the tall boy. "I told you to go for three." He transferred his gaze to Mr. Freebone. "You want Batchy?" he said.

"Batchy?" said Mr. Freebone. "Now who, or what, would that be?"

"Batchy's Batchelor."

This was even more difficult, but in the end he made it out. "You mean the caretaker. Is his name Batchelor?"

"'Sright. You want him, you'll find him in his room."

He jerked his head towards the door at the far end of the building.

"Making himself a nice cupper," said Ben. "I once counted up how many cuppers Batchy drinks in a day. Guess how many? Seventeen."

"I'll be having a word with him soon, I expect," said Mr. Freebone. "Just for the moment I'm more interested in you. I'd better introduce myself. My name's Freebone. I'm the new Missioner."

"What's happened to old Jake?" said Ben. "I thought we hadden seen him round for a bit. He dead?"

"Now that's not nice, Ben," said the tall boy. "You don't say, 'Is he dead?' Not when you're talking to a clergyman. You say, 'Has he gone before?'"

"Clergyman or not," said Mr. Freebone, "I shouldn't use a ghastly expression like that. If I meant dead, I'd say dead. And Mr. Jacobson's not dead anyway. He's retired. And I've got his job. Now I've told you all about me, let's hear about you. First, what are your names?"

The boys regarded him warily. The man-to-man approach was not new to them. In their brief lives they had already met

191

plenty of hearty young men who had expressed a desire to lead them onwards and upwards to better things.

In the end it was Humphrey who spoke. "I'm Humphrey," he said. "The thin one's Colin. The fat one's Ben. You like to partner Ben we'll play 301 up, double in, double out, for a bob a side."

"Middle for diddle," said Mr. Freebone.

At the end of the third game, at which point Mr. Freebone and Ben were each richer by three shillings, Humphrey announced without rancour that he was skinned and would have to go home and get some more money. The others decided to pack it up, too.

"I hope we'll see you here this evening," said the new Missioner genially, and went in search of the resident caretaker, Batchelor, whom he found, as predicted, brewing tea in his den at the back of the hall.

He greeted the new Missioner amiably enough.

"You got lodgings?" he said. "Mr. Jacobson lived up at Greenwich and came down every day. Most days, that is."

"I'm going to do better than that," said Mr. Freebone. "I'm going to live here."

"*Live* here?"

"Why not? I'm told there are two rooms up there."

"Well, there *are* two rooms at the back. Gotter nice view of the factory. It's a long time since anyone lived in 'em."

"Here's someone going to start," said Mr. Freebone.

"There's a pile r junk in 'em."

"If you'll lend me a hand, we'll move all the junk into one of the rooms for a start. I've got a camp bed with my luggage."

Batchelor gaped at him.

"You going to sleep here *tonight?*" he said.

"I'm going to sleep here tonight and every night," said Mr. Freebone happily. "I'm going to sleep here and eat here and live here, just as long as they'll have me."

The next week was a busy one.

As soon as Batchelor saw that the new Missioner was set in his intention and immovable in his madness, he made the best of it, and turned to and lent a hand.

Mr. Freebone scrubbed, and Batchelor scrubbed. Windows

192

were opened which had not been opened in living memory. Paint and distemper arrived by the gallon.

Almost everyone fancies himself as a decorator, and as soon as the boys grasped that an ambitious programme of interior decoration was on foot, they threw themselves into it with zeal. One purchased a pot of yellow paint, and painted, before he could be stopped, the entire outside of the porch.

Another borrowed a machine from his employer without his employer's knowledge, and buffed up the planks of the main room so hard there was soon very little floor left. Another fell off the roof and broke his leg.

Thus was inaugurated Mr. Freebone's Mission at Sark Lane; a Mission which, in retrospect, grew into one of the oral traditions of the East End, until almost anything would be believed if it was prefaced with the words, "When ol' Freebone was at Sark Lane."

It was not, as his charges were quick to remark, that he was a particularly pious man; although the East End is one of the few places where saintliness is esteemed at its true worth. Nor that he interested himself, as other excellent Missioners had done, in the home life and commercial prospects of the boys in his care. It was simply that he lived in, with, and for the Mission. That, and a certain light-hearted ingenuity, allied to a curious thoroughness in the carrying out of his wilder plans.

The story will some day be told more fully of his Easter Scout camp; a camp joined, on the first night, by three strange boys whose names had certainly not been on the original roll, and who turned out to be runaways from a Borstal institution – to whose comforts they hastily returned after experiencing, for a night and a day, the vigorous hospitality of the Sark Lane Scout Troop.

Nor would anyone who took part in it lightly forget the Great Scavenger Hunt which culminated in the simultaneous arrival at the Mission of a well-known receiver of stolen goods and the Flying Squad; or the Summer Endurance Test in the course of which a group of contestants set out to swim the Thames in full clothes, and ended up at a debutante's Steamer Party. In which connection Humphrey claimed to be one of the few people who has danced, dripping wet, with a royal personage.

Captain Cree turned up about a month after Mr. Freebone's arrival. The first intimation that he had a visitor was a hearty burst of bass laughter from the club room. Poking his head round the door he saw a big, heavy figure, the upper half encased in a double-breasted blue jacket with brass buttons, the lower half in chalk-striped flannel trousers. The face that slewed round as he approached had been tanned by the weather to a deep russet, and then transformed to a deeper red by some more cultivated alchemy.

"Mussen shock the parson," said Captain Cree genially.

"Just showing the boys some pictures the Captain of the *William* picked up at Port Said on his last trip. You're Freebone, arnchew? I'm pleased to meet you."

He pushed out a big red hand, grasped Mr. Freebone's and shook it heartily.

"I've heard a lot about you," said Mr. Freebone.

"Nothing to my credit, I bet," said Captain Cree, with a wink at the boys.

"I know that you're a very generous donor to the Mission," said Mr. Freebone, "and you're very welcome to come and go here as you like."

Captain Cree looked surprised. It had perhaps not occurred to him that he needed anyone's permission to come and go as he liked. He said, "Well, I call that handsome. I got a bit of stuff for you outside. The *William* picked it up for me in Alex. I've got it outside in the station wagon. You two nip out, and give my monkeys a hail, and we'll get it stowed."

Humphrey and Ben departed, and returned escorting two sailors, dressed in blue jerseys, with the word *Clarissa* in red stitching straggling across the front.

"Dump 'em in there, David," said Captain Cree to the young black-haired sailor. "There's a half gross of plimsolls, some running vests, a couple of footballs, and two pairs of foils. You put them down, Humphrey. I'm giving 'em to the Mission, not to you. Where'd you like 'em stowed?"

"In the back room, for the moment, I think," said Mr. Freebone. "Hey – Batchelor."

"Old Batchy still alive?" said Captain Cree. "I thought he'd have drunk himself to death long ago. How are you, Batchy?"

"Fine, Captain Cree, fine, thank you," said the old man, executing a sketchy naval salute.

"If you've finished stewing up tea for yourself, you might give a hand to get these things under hatches. You leave 'em out here a moment longer, they'll be gone. I know these boys."

When the Captain had departed, Mr. Freebone had a word with Humphrey and Ben who were now his first and second lieutenants in most club activities.

"He's given us a crate of stuff," said Humphrey.

"Crates and crates," agreed Ben. "Footballs, jerseys, dart boards. Once he brought us a couple of what's-its – those bamboo things – you know, with steel tips. You throw 'em."

"Javelins?"

"That's right. *They* didn't last long. Old Jake took 'em away after Colin threw one at young Arthur Whaley."

"Who were the sailors?"

"The big one, he's Ron Blanden. He used to be a boy round here. The other one's David," Ben explained. "He'd be off one of the ships. Old Cree gets boys for his ships from round here, and when they've done a trip or two, maybe he gives 'em a job on the *Clarissa*. That's his own boat."

"I see," said Mr. Freebone.

"He offered to take me on, soon as I'm old enough," said Humphrey.

"Are you going to say yes?"

Humphrey's long face creased into a grin. "Not me," he said. "I'm keeping my feet dry. Besides, he's a crook."

"He's what?"

"A crook."

"He can't just be *a* crook," said Mr. Freebone patiently. "He must be some sort of crook. What does he do?"

"I dunno," said Humphrey. "But it sticks out he's a crook, or he wouldn't have so much money. Eh, Ben?"

Ben agreed this was correct. He usually agreed with Humphrey.

Later that night Mr. Freebone and Batchelor sorted out the new gifts. The foils were really nice pairs, complete with masks and gauntlets. Mr. Freebone, who was himself something of a swordsman, took them up to his own room to examine them at leisure. The gym shoes were a good brand, with thick rubber soles. They should be very useful. Boys, in those parts, wore gym shoes almost all day.

"We usually wash out the vests and things," said Batchelor.

195

"You know what foreigners are like."

Mr. Freebone approved the precaution. He said he knew what foreigners were like. Batchelor said he would wash them through next time he had a boil-up in his copper.

A fortnight later – that was, in the last week of May – the officer on the monitored telephone in the basement at New Scotland Yard received a call. The call came at six o'clock in the evening, precisely, and the caller announced himself as Magnus.

The officer said, "Count five slowly, please. Then start talking." He put out his hand and pressed down the switch. The tape recorder whirred softly as the man at the other end spoke. Later that evening Romer came down to the Yard and listened to the play-back. The voice came, thin and resonant, but clear.

"Magnus here. This is my first report. I've settled into my new job. I feel little real doubt that what we suspect is correct but it's difficult to see just how the trick is pulled.

"The *Clarissa* meets all incoming *Consorts*. She takes out miscellaneous stores, and usually fetches back a load of gear for the Mission. It must be the best-equipped outfit in London. The customs experts give the stuff the magic-eye treatment before it's put on the *Clarissa,* and I've managed to look through most of it myself. Once it's in the Mission it's handed straight over to the boys, so it's a bit difficult to see how it could be used as a hiding-place.

"Cocaine's not bulky, I know, but I gather the quantities we're looking for are quite considerable. I have a feeling this line in sports goods might be a big red herring. Something to take our eye off the real job.

"Carter, the mate of the *Clarissa*, is, I think, an ex-convict. His real name is Coster, and he's been down a number of times for larceny and aggravated assault. He carries a gun. Nothing known about the crew.

"Captain Cree" – here the tape gave a rasping scratch – "Sorry. That was me clearing my throat. As I was saying, Captain Cree's a smart operator. I should think he makes a good bit on the side out of his chandlering, but not nearly enough to account for the style he lives in. You'd imagine a man like him would keep a little woman tucked away somewhere, wouldn't you? But I never heard any whisper about the fair sex. A pity. We might get a woman to talk. That's all for now."

The weather was hot and dry that summer, and through July and August increasing supplies of illicit cocaine continued to dribble into London as water through a rotten sluice-gate; and the casualty figures and the crime graphs climbed, hand in hand with the mercury in the thermometer. Superintendent Costorphine's face grew so long and so bleak that Romer took to avoiding him. For all the comfort he could give him was that things would probably get worse before they got better.

At Sark Lane Mr. Freebone was working an eighteen-hour day. Added to his other preoccupations was an outbreak of skin disease. The boys could not be prevented from bathing in the filthy reaches and inlets of the Thames below Tower Bridge.

When he could spare a minute from his routine work he seemed to cultivate the company of the crew of the *Clarissa*. Carter was surly and unapproachable, but the boys were pleasant enough. Ron Blanden was a burly, fair-haired young man of twenty. He had ideas beyond the river, and talked of leaving the *Clarissa* and joining the Merchant Navy.

David, the young black-haired one, seemed to be a natural idler, with few ideas beyond taking life easy, picking up as much money as he could, and dressing in his smartest clothes on his evenings off. He once told Mr. Freebone that he came from Scotland, but his eyes and hair suggested something more Mediterranean in origin. There was a theory that he had been in bad trouble once, in his early youth, and was now living it down.

Mr. Freebone had no difficulty, in time, in extracting the whole of the candid Ron Blanden's life story, but David, though friendly, kept his distance. All he would say – and this was a matter of record – was that he had made one trip on the *Albert Consort* that April, and had then been offered a job by Captain Cree which he had accepted.

"I don't like that David," said Batchelor one evening.

"Oh, why?" said Mr. Freebone.

"He's a bad sort of boy," said Batchelor. "I've caught him snooping round this place once or twice lately. Fiddling round with the sports kit. I soon sent him packing."

"Hmm," said Mr. Freebone. He changed the subject somewhat abruptly. "By the way, Batchelor, there's something I've been meaning to ask you. How much do we pay you?"

"Four pounds a week, and keep."

"And what does Captain Cree add to that?"

The old man stirred in his chair, and blinked. "Who said he added anything?"

"I heard it."

"He pays me a pound or two, now and then. Nothing regular. I do jobs for him. Anything wrong with that?"

Magnus had fallen into the routine of reporting at the appointed hour on every second Wednesday. Towards the end of September his message was brief, and contained a request. "Could you check up on the old boy who acts as caretaker at the Mission? He calls himself Batchelor and claims to be ex-RN. I don't believe that's his real name and I don't believe he was ever in the Navy. Let me know through the usual channels and urgently."

Costorphine said to Romer, "Something's brewing down there. My contacts all tell me the same story. The suppliers are expecting a big autumn run."

Romer made a small, helpless gesture. "And are we going to be able to stop it?" he asked.

"We can always hope," said Costorphine. "I'll find out about that man Batchelor. Jacobson will know something about him. He took him on, I believe . . ."

It was a week later that Humphrey said to Mr. Freebone, apropos of nothing that had gone before, "He's a character, that David, all right."

"What's he up to now?" said Mr. Freebone, between gasps, for he was busy blowing up a batch of new footballs.

"Wanted to cut me in on a snide racket."

Mr. Freebone stopped what he was doing, put the football down, and said, "Come on. Let's have it."

"David told me he can get hold of plenty of fivers. Good-looking jobs, he said. The *Clarissa* picks 'em up from the Dutch and German boats. He had some story they were a lot the Gestapo had printed during the war. Is that right?"

"I believe they did," said Mr. Freebone. "But they'd be the old white sort."

"That's right. That's why he wanted help passing 'em. If he turned up with a lot of 'em, it'd look suspicious. But if some of us boys helped him . . . "

In a rage, Mr. Freebone sought out Captain Cree, who listened to him with surprising patience.

"Half those lads are crooks," he said, when the Missioner had finished. "You can't stop it."

"I'm not going to have your crew corrupting my boys," said Mr. Freebone. "And I look to you to help me stop it."

"What do you want me to do? Sack David?"

Mr. Freebone said, "I don't know that that'd do a lot of good. But he's not to come near the Mission."

"I'll sort him out," said the Captain. He added, "You know, what you want's a holiday. You've had a basinful of us since you came, and you haven't had a day off in six months that I can see."

"As a matter of fact," said Mr. Freebone, "I was thinking of taking a long weekend soon."

"You do that," said the Captain. "Tell me when you're going, and I'll keep an eye on the place for you myself."

He sounded almost paternal . . .

"This is report number thirteen," said the tape-recorded voice of Magnus. "I hope that doesn't make it unlucky. I had a narrow escape the other day, but managed to ride the Captain off. I'm bound to say that, in my view, things are coming to a head. Just how it's going to break I don't know, but some sort of job is being planned for next weekend. Cree and Carter have been thick as thieves about it.

"Talking about thieves, I was glad to hear that my hunch about Batchelor was correct, and that he had been inside. There's something about an old lag that never washes off. It was interesting, too, that he worked at one time in a chemist's shop, and had done a bit of dispensing in his youth. All he dispenses openly now are cups of vile tea. That's all for now. I hope to be on the air again in a fortnight's time with some real news for you."

Costorphine said, "That ties in with what I've heard. A big consignment, quite soon."

"We'd better put the cover plan into operation," said Romer.

"You've got two police boats on call. Whistle them up now."

"A police launch would be a bit out-gunned by *Clarissa*. I've arranged a tie-up with the Navy. There's a launch standing by at Greenwich. We can have her up when we want her. Only we can't keep her hanging about for long – she's too conspicuous."

"I've got an uneasy feeling about this," said Romer. "They're not fools, the people we're dealing with. They wouldn't walk into anything obvious."

"Do you think Petrella — "

"You've got to admit he's been lucky," said Romer. "It was luck that the job was going, and luck that we managed to get it for him. And he's done very well, too. But luck can't last for ever. It only needs one person to recognise him – one criminal he's ever had to deal with, and he must have had hundreds through his hands in the last few years."

"He'll be all right," said Costorphine. "He's a smart lad."

"I'm superstitious," said Romer. "I don't mean about things like black cats and ladders. I mean about making bargains with fortune. You remember when we were talking about this thing in here, way back in March, I said something about a single life not being important. It might be true; but I wish I hadn't said it, all the same."

Costorphine confided to his wife, that night, "It's the first time I've ever seen the old man jumpy. Things must be bad. Perhaps the politicians are after him."

That Saturday night there were about two dozen boys in the club room of the Mission; and it says a lot for the enthusiasm engendered by Mr. Freebone that there was anyone there at all, for if ever there was a night for fireside and television this was it. The wind had started to get up with the dusk, and was now blowing in great angry gusts, driving the rain in front of it.

At half past four Captain Cree, faithful to his promise, had come up to keep an eye on things in the Missioner's absence. There had been nothing much for him to do, and he had departed for the dock where *Clarissa* lay. Now, through the dark and the rain, he drove his big station wagon carefully back, once more, through the empty streets, and man-oeuvred it into the unlighted cul-de-sac beside the Mission Hall.

Carter, a big, unlovely lump of a man, was sitting beside him, smoking one of an endless chain of cigarettes. This time Captain Cree did not trouble with the front entrance. There was a small side door, which gave on to a dark lobby. Out of the lobby, bare wooden stairs ran up to Mr. Freebone's bedroom; on the far side a door opened through to Batchelor's sanctum.

Captain Cree stood in the dark, empty lobby, his head bent. He was listening. Anyone glimpsing his good-natured red face at that particular moment might have been shocked by the expression on it.

At the end of a full minute he relaxed, went back to the street door, and signalled to Carter. The back of the station wagon was opened, and the first of four big bales was lifted out and humped indoors. The bolt of the outer door was shot.

Batchelor was waiting for them. Everything about him showed that he, too, knew that some crisis was impending.

"You locked the door?" said Captain Cree. He jerked his head at the door which led into the Mission Hall.

"Of course I locked it," said Batchelor. "We don't want a crowd of boys in here. How many have you got, for Chrissake?"

"Four," said Carter. He was the coolest of the three.

"We'll do 'em all now," said Captain Cree. "It'll take a bit of time, but we won't get a better chance than this. When's *he* coming back?" An upward jerk of his head indicated that he was talking about the occupant of the back attic.

"Sunday midday, he said. Unless he changed his mind."

"He'd better not change it," said Carter.

He helped Batchelor to strip the thick brown-paper wrapping from one of the bales. As the covering came away the contents could be seen to be woollens, half a gross of thick woollen vests. In the second there was half a gross of long pants. Grey socks in the third. Gloves and balaclava helmets and scarves in the fourth.

Carter waddled across to the enormous gas-operated copper in the corner, and lifted the lid. A fire had been lit under it earlier in the afternoon, and was now glowing red; the copper was full of clean hot water.

What followed would have interested Superintendent Costorphine intensely. He would have realised how it is possible to bring cocaine into the country under the noses of the smartest customs officials; and he would have appreciated just why those samples might contain minute traces of copper.

The three men worked as a team, with the skill born of long practice. Carter dumped the woollens by handfuls in the copper. Captain Cree took them out, and wrung each one carefully into a curious contraption which Batchelor had pulled from a cupboard. Basically this was a funnel, with a drip tray underneath. But between funnel and tray was a fine linen gauze filter. And as the moisture was wrung from each garment, a greyish sediment formed on the filter.

When the filter was so full that it was in danger of becoming clogged the Captain called a halt. From a suitcase he extracted an outsize vacuum flask, and into it, with the greatest possible care, he deposited the grey sediment.

It took them over an hour to go through the first three packages. During this time the water in the copper had itself been emptied and filtered, and the copper refilled. Twice, during this time, a boy had rattled on the door that led into the hall, and Batchelor had shouted back that he was busy.

"Tip the last lot in," said the Captain, "and be quick about it." They were all three sweating. "We don't want anyone bursting in on us now."

He had never handled such a quantity before. The third flask was in use. Two were already full. He had his back to the door leading to the lobby, and they none of them heard or saw it open.

"What on earth are you all up to?" said Mr. Freebone.

The three men swung round in one ugly, savage movement. The plastic cap of the flask fell from Captain Cree's hand and rolled across the floor.

"What is it – washing day?"

There was a silence of paralysis as he walked across the room, and peered down into the flask. "And what's this stuff?"

"What – where have you come from?" said Captain Cree hoarsely.

"I've been up in my room, writing," said Mr. Freebone. "I changed my mind, and came back. Do I have to ask your permission?" He extended one finger, touched the grey powder in the flask, and carried his finger to his lips.

Then Carter hit him. It was a savage blow, delivered from behind, with a leather-covered sap, a blow which Mr. Freebone neither saw nor heard.

They stared at him.

"You killed him?" said Batchelor.

"Don't be a damned fool," said Carter. He looked at Captain Cree. The same thought was in both their minds.

"We shall want some cord," he said. "Have you got any?"

"I don't know — "

"Go on. Get it."

It took five minutes to truss up Mr. Freebone. He was showing no signs of life, even while they manhandled him out and dumped him in the back of the station wagon.

Captain Cree seemed to have recovered his composure.

"You stay here and watch him," he said to Carter.

"Are we going to gag him?"

"I think that would be a mistake," said the Captain. "Leave too many traces." They looked at each other again. The thought was as clear now as if it had been spoken. "If he opens his mouth, hit him again."

Carter nodded, and the Captain disappeared into the building. In half an hour the job was finished, and he came out carrying a suitcase.

"Not a blink," said Carter.

The Captain placed the suitcase carefully in the back of the car, where it rested on the crumpled body of Mr. Freebone. Then he climbed into the driving seat, backed the car out, and started on the half-mile drive to Pagett's Wharf, where the *Clarissa* lay.

The wind, risen almost to gale force, was flogging the empty streets with its lash, part rain, part hail, as the big car nosed its way slowly across the cobbles of the wharf.

Captain Cree turned off the lights and climbed out, followed by Carter. Twenty yards away, in the howling wilderness of darkness, a single riding light showed where the *Clarissa* bumped at her moorings. At their feet the river slid past, cold and black.

The Captain said into Carter's ear, "We'll take the cords off him first. I put 'em on over his clothes so they won't have left much mark. If he's found, what's to show he didn't slip, and knock his head going in?"

"*If* he's found," said Carter.

Back at the Mission, Batchelor was facing a mutiny.

"What've you been up to, locked in here all evening?" said Humphrey. "That was the Captain's car in the alley, wasn't it?"

"That's right," said Ben.

"And what've you done with Mr. Freebone?"

"He ent here," said Batchelor. "And you can get out of my room too, all of you."

"Where is he?"

"He went away for the weekend. He'll be back tomorrow."

As soon as he had said this, Batchelor realised his mistake. "Don't be soft," said Humphrey. "He came back after tea. We saw him. Pop upstairs, Ben, and see if he's in his room."

"You've got no right — " said Batchelor. But they were past taking any notice of what he said.

"And what were you doing with all those clothes?" He pointed at the sodden pile in the corner. "Is this washing night, or something?"

Batchelor was saved answering by the reappearance of Ben. "He's been there," he said. "The light's on. And there's a letter on the table he was finishing writing. *And* his raincoat's there."

"He wouldn't go without a coat," said Humphrey. "Not on a night like this. He's been took."

Here Batchelor made his second mistake. He broke for the door. Several pairs of hands caught him, and threw him back ungently into the chair. For the moment, after the scuffle, there was silence and stillness.

Then Humphrey said, "I guess they were up to something. And I guess Mr. Freebone came back when he wasn't expected. And I guess the Captain and Carter and that lot have picked him up."

"So that's all you can do, guess," said Batchelor viciously. But the fear in his voice could be felt.

"All right," said Humphrey calmly. "Maybe I'm wrong. You tell us." Batchelor stared at him. Humphrey said, "Is that water hot, Ben?"

Ben dipped the top of his finger in, and took it out again quickly.

Humphrey said, "Either you talk, or we hold your head down in that."

It took six of them to get him halfway across the floor. Batchelor stopped cursing and started to scream. When his nose was six inches away from the water he talked.

"Pagett's Wharf," said Humphrey. "All right. We'll lock him up in here. If he's lying to us, we'll come back and finish him off afterwards."

"How do we get there?" said one of the boys.

"Night like this," said Humphrey, "the quickest way to get anywhere's to run."

The pack streamed out into the howling darkness.

In the big foredeck cabin of the *Clarissa*, Captain Cree was giving some final instructions to Carter when he heard the shout. Carter jumped across to the cabin door and pulled it open.

"Who's out there?" said the Captain.

"Ron's on deck," said Carter. "David's ashore some-where."

"Who was that shouted?"

"It sounded like Ron," said Carter.

This was as far as he got. The next moment a wave of boys seemed to rise out of the darkness. Carter had time to shout before something hit him, and he went down.

The attack passed into the cabin. Captain Cree got his hand to a gun, but had no time to fire it. Humphrey, swinging an iron bar which he had picked up on deck, broke Cree's arm with a vicious side swipe. The gun dropped from his fingers. "Pull him in," said Humphrey. "Both of them."

Captain Cree, his right arm swinging loosely in front of him, his red face mottled with white, held himself up with his sound hand on the table.

Carter lay on the floor at his feet, and Ben kicked him, as hard and as thoughtlessly as you might kick a football. The boys had tasted violence and victory that night, and it had made them drunker than any strong drink.

"There's one thing can keep you alive," said Humphrey. "And that's Mr. Freebone. Where is he?"

For a count of ten there was silence. The Captain's mouth worked, but no sound came out of it.

Almost gently Humphrey said, "So you dropped him in the river. He's going to have three for company. Right?"

That was right. That was the way things were done in the land of violence and hot blood. Humphrey swung his iron bar delicately.

"You can't," said the Captain. "You can't do it. I'll tell you everything. I'll do what you like. There's a hundred thousand pounds' worth of cocaine in that suitcase. It's yours, for the taking."

"We'll pour it in after you," said Humphrey. "It'll be useful where you're going."

"You can't do it — "

"Who's stopping us?"

"I am," said a voice from behind them. The third member of the *Clarissa*'s crew, David, stepped through the door into the cabin.

He was drenched with rain, dishevelled, and out of breath from running; but there was something about him which held all their eyes.

"How — "

"It'll save a lot of time and trouble," said David, "if I tell you that I'm a police officer. My name, not that it matters, is Petrella. I'm a sergeant in the plain-clothes branch, and I'm taking these three men into custody."

"But," said Humphrey, "they've killed Mr. Freebone."

"They meant to kill him," said Petrella. "No doubt of it. But there've been two police launches lying off this wharf ever since dusk, and one of them picked him up. He's at Leman Street Police Station, and from what he's told me, we've got more than enough to send both these men away for life. So don't let's spoil a good thing now."

There was a bump at the side of the boat as the River Police tender hitched on alongside. The first man in the cabin was Superintendent Costorphine, looking like a bedraggled crow. He pounced on the suitcase.

"Three months' supply for London," said Petrella. "It'll need a bit more drying-out, but it's all there . . ."

Later, Petrella found Philip Freebone propped up on pillows in St. George's Hospital, where he had been taken, under protest, and deposited for the night.

"There's nothing wrong with me," he said. "I'd just as

soon be back in my bed at the Mission. There's a lot to do. I shall have to find a replacement for Batchelor."

"Are you going on with that job?"

Freebone looked surprised. "Of course I am," he said. "I've enjoyed it. I knew I should. That's why I wouldn't let you do it."

"The trouble is," said Petrella, "that you've set yourself too high a standard. The boys will never have another night like tonight as long as they live. Do you realise that if I hadn't turned up, they really were going to knock Captain Cree off and put him and Carter over the side?"

"Yes, I expect they would." Freebone thought about it, and added, "It's rather a compliment, really, isn't it? What are you going to do now, Patrick?"

"Take a holiday," said Detective Sergeant Petrella. "A good, long holiday."

Paris in Summer

"WELL," said Superintendent Haxtell, "I must say, I think you've earned it."

"Thank you, sir," said Detective Sergeant Petrella, whose mind was several hundred miles away from the dreary mid-summer dustiness of Crown Road Police Station. It was ranging free, in Seville, under the orange trees. In his ears no longer sounded the grinding throb of traffic, as it panted up Highside Hill. He was sitting on the patio of the Villa Hernandez, listening to the chorus of the cicadas at sunset.

"It's a long time since you had a holiday."

"Eighteen months since I had a proper one," said Petrella.

"You'll be going abroad?"

"I'm planning to spend most of it with my father, in Spain. On the way out I'm putting in a couple of days with my mother's great aunt in Paris."

"Somehow," said Haxtell, "I have never associated Paris with anyone's great-aunt."

"She's a marvellous old lady. She's eighty-two. And she lives in a flat overlooking the Avenue Victor Hugo, and spends her time with other old ladies and gentlemen, deploring modern youth and sipping abricotine."

Haxtell looked curiously at his subordinate. "You speak French, don't you?" he said. "Proper French, I mean. Not just 'plume de ma tante' stuff."

"I speak French better than Spanish," said Petrella. "Although I was born in Spain. We all moved to Bordeaux when I was six. That's a good age for picking up a language, because you don't forget it again easily."

"Well, behave yourself," said Haxtell. He wondered if he ought to tell Petrella that his promotion to Inspector was now practically on the plate. In fact, the only reason that it had not come through was that the person who could sign the most important documents was himself on holiday. He decided against it. If there was any hitch, it would have been better to have said nothing. When the news came through it would excuse all delays.

"Paris, eh?" said Sergeant Gwilliam, after lunch that day. "You want to watch your step."

"I shall be staying," said Petrella, "with my great-aunt. Aged eighty-two."

"Well, mind you don't keep the old lady out of bed," said Gwilliam.

Detective Constable Wilmot was the youngest of the not-very-aged detective staff of Highside, and rather a protégé of Petrella. As they were all packing up to go home that evening Wilmot took him aside and said, "When you're in Paris, do you think you could give someone a letter for me?"

Petrella managed not to look surprised. "Yes, I could easily do that," he said.

"It's a girl," said Wilmot, blushing. "Perhaps I'd better explain about it."

"No reason to, if you don't want to."

"There's nothing to it, really. I've been writing to her. She's been writing to me. Pen pals. It started with something I seen in a magazine. I asked once or twice for a photograph, only she never sent me one."

"I see," said Petrella. "So you'd like me to deliver your

next letter by hand, take a good look at her, and see if she's worth writing to."

"Thassit," said Wilmot. He had a great respect for Petrella's acumen. "If she turns out to be some old bag with dropped arches, I won't bother to write any more, see. But if she's a fizzer – well, that's different."

Petrella was on the point of saying that as long as she wrote interesting letters he couldn't see that it mattered much what she looked like, when he realised that he would be being priggish. So he simply said, "Write her name and address down and I'll see what I can do. If she's terrific, I might take her on myself."

Wilmot grinned and scribbled something on a piece of paper, which Petrella put into his wallet and forgot all about in the excitement and pleasure of organising his departure.

His father, who was a believer in the comfort and dignity of travel, had sent him the money for his fare, and Petrella had booked a sleeper on the night ferry from Victoria. This is a very pleasant way to go to France. He climbed into his berth, and was asleep before the train was clear of the London suburbs. After that he woke twice. First, when the train stopped at Folkestone, and in the sudden stillness he heard the rattling of the chains and bolts as the carriages were locked to the ship; and some hours after that, to the gentle pitching of the summer–calm Channel. The next time he opened his eyes, fruit trees were flashing past the window, and the sleeping–car attendant, who seemed to have been transmogrified into a Frenchman, was telling him that breakfast was served.

It was when he stepped out of the Gare du Nord, and the summer heat of Paris hit him in the face, that he remembered Wilmot's letter.

Having no intention of imposing himself upon his elderly relative earlier than he need, he had deposited his bag in the *consigne*, intending to spend the day picking up his acquaintance with Paris where he had left it off some three years before.

Paris was like that. Not a woman, demanding constant attention, but a man, whose friendship you could enjoy, abandon, and take up again without the least hard feeling, exactly where you had dropped it.

He would have his midday meal at the Ruban Bleu, in a side street of the Place de l'Opéra; and his evening meal at the Beaux Arts, behind the Quai des Augustins. Between times, he would stroll slowly due west from the Petit Carousel right down to the Bois, and then back again by the Avenue Victor Hugo, where he would tantalise himself by imagining the things he would buy if he were a very rich man.

First, though, for Wilmot's girlfriend.

He read the name and address. Mlle. Natalie Arture, 97 Rue Antoine, 18. He turned the pages of the street guide. There was only one Rue Antoine in the Eighteenth Arrondissement, and that, fortunately, was quite near the Gare du Nord. It was shown as a small, rather crooked street, running north from the Place de la Goutte d'Or.

Turn left at the end of the station. Then right, straight on for about two hundred yards, then right again. His nose glued to his street map Petrella took very little note of his surroundings. He crossed the Place de la Goutte d'Or. It seemed curiously empty for nine o'clock on a fine summer morning. There were two cafés in the Place, but neither of them had its sun awnings lowered or its chairs and tables out. The hush was sabbatical.

Petrella located the Rue Antoine. It was even more crooked than the plan had suggested; a canyon of a street; tall, uninteresting houses rising to the sky on either side; the *pavé* chipped and dirty; no pavement, but a runnel of what he hoped was only water down the middle of the street.

For a moment he hesitated. As in all Paris streets, the numbering started at the point nearest the river; which meant that No. 97 would be a good way down this unsavoury-looking trap. Then it seemed to him that he was being unduly squeamish. Having got so far, it was silly not to complete his task.

It was the silence that was unnerving. The street itself was quite empty; the few shops that he passed were closed and barred; all windows giving on the street were shuttered. Halfway along he came to a place, round a sharp bend, where the cobble-stones which formed the *pavé* had been hacked up and removed. It afforded no obstacle to a pedestrian who could jump it, if nimble enough, or climb down into the shallow ditch and up on the other side. But nothing on wheels could have got past.

It was in his mind that he had seen something like it before, and then he remembered: the streets in the Moorish quarter in Seville had been so broken, to prevent motorists straying where they should not, but that had been during the plague epidemic.

The memory brought him up all standing. Then he reflected that what he was thinking was nonsense. There would have been police, officials, notices warning pedestrians; all the apparatus of a cordon sanitaire. He was letting his imagination run away with him.

No. 97 turned out to be a leather-worker's shop. The sign above the shop said, ANGRIFFE FRÈRES. It was bolted and barred, like all the rest.

Petrella rang the bell. Then he knocked a couple of times on the door. He wondered where Mlle. Arture would fit into the house of a Monsieur Angriffe and his brothers. He wondered if any of the Angriffe family were at home. He wondered if anyone lived in the street at all.

Suddenly, quietly, and without any sound of bolts or locks, the door opened, and a man looked out. He was middle-aged, his skin was the colour of milky coffee, and he had black hair and a pair of brownish eyes, rimmed in yellow. He looked at Petrella, and said nothing at all.

Petrella said, "Mademoiselle Natalie — "

The man opened the door six inches. "You are a day late," he said, "but come in."

Petrella stepped over the threshold, and followed the man down the empty hall and into a kitchen at the end. He got the impression, as he went past, that the front rooms were all empty, but the kitchen was crowded. There were two women working at the stove, and another in front of the sink. A child was asleep in a cot in the corner, being rocked by an older girl. A boy of perhaps twelve, with bright mischievous eyes in a monkey face, squatted under the table. None of them seemed, at first sight, to be a very probable correspondent of Detective Constable Wilmot, of Y Division, Highside.

"Mademoiselle Natalie — " said Petrella again.

"Business," said the man. "Let us stick to business. Business before pleasure. If you will wait a moment."

He opened what looked like the door of a cupboard, and disappeared up a flight of steps. The occupants of the room stared at him in undisguised astonishment. There was nothing hostile about their interest. Indeed, he fancied he read, in the bright eyes of the boy, a sort of admiration.

The man of the house reappeared. He was holding a thick canvas envelope, a little larger than an ordinary registered envelope. Its shape indicated that it contained something more solid than paper.

He handed it to Petrella and said, "Will you tell your principal that this must terminate the matter. I think he will understand."

"I fear — " began Petrella. Then changed his mind abruptly. If something had gone wrong, if the whole of his errand was a mistake, the important thing was to get out of the house. The long, blind street was a trap. Apologies and excuses would come better from outside it.

Something more seemed to be expected of him. He put his hand into his pocket and pulled out Wilmot's letter. It was a long and conscientious piece of night-school French, and it contained, as Petrella knew, two photographs of Wilmot, one in plain clothes, and one in uniform. He wondered just what the Angriffe family would make of them.

"For Mademoiselle Natalie," he said, and handed the thick envelope to the man, who held out his hand and took it. The tips of his fingers paused on the envelope, and Petrella knew that he was trying to detect whether there was money in it, and if so, how much.

"Remember," he said, putting as much authority into his voice as he could muster, "that is for Mademoiselle. In person. You understand? In person."

"Yes, yes," said the man hastily.

"Now I must go," said Petrella. For a moment the man looked as if he would have liked to say something more. Then he changed his mind, moved to the door, and opened it.

As soon as the house door had shut behind him, Petrella started to walk very quickly. He wanted to run, and go on running until he was in front of the Gare du Nord, in sight of a gendarme. He had gone fifty yards when he heard the pattering of steps.

Looking over his shoulder he saw that it was the boy. On the slippery *pavé* his bare feet were making twice the speed of Petrella's iron-tipped shoes. There was no question – he would be caught before he reached the end of the street.

He thought it better to stop, and face about.

"Monsieur," said the boy, in nervous, sibilant French. "There has been a great mistake. Will you please hand back the envelope?"

"Not to you," said Petrella, "and not here. When I have seen what is in it, then perhaps."

"It would be better," said the boy.

"That is not for you to say."

Petrella half turned to go. He saw the knife out of the corner of his eye. It came up, in a silver stream, from the ground, clenched in the boy's small tight fist. Petrella jumped back, slipped, heard the edge of the blade make a noise like "shurr" as it went through the thick tweed of his jacket, and then was running for his life.

When he reached the Place de la Goutte d'Or, he realised that the boy had not followed him. Just the one, quick, upward knife-swing of the professional killer, the swing that puts the knife in under the ribs and into the heart; and then no more. He looked down at his coat and saw that it was cut cleanly, from below the side pocket to the second button. Six roads led from the Place. He guessed that any of the three southern ones would serve him. He plunged into the nearest and started down it.

At first he thought that the sound was a ringing in the ears. Then, when he stopped, he could hear it quite clearly. It was a fluting whistle. It came from the street ahead, or from the rooftop above him. From anywhere and from everywhere. Then, breaking the silence, the sound of a lorry coughing into life.

He had delayed too long. The sound came from in front. The pursuit was ahead of him.

To his left, a gap showed in the houses, fronted by a high, boarded fence. He could reach the top. It seemed clear of nails, barbed wire, and other sharp obstacles, so he pulled himself up and dropped into the open space behind. It was some sort of builder's yard.

213

He picked his way between the stacks of tiles, bricks, and pipes to the wall at the far end. The coping was out of his reach, but there was a ladder lying under one of the sheds. He stood this up against the wall, saw that there was an asphalted courtyard within dropping distance below him, straddled the wall long enough to kick down the ladder behind him and dropped.

He guessed from the white lines on the asphalt that he was in a school playground, surrounded on three sides by buildings. As he stood, uncertain, one of the doors ahead of him opened and thirty or forty children ran out. They were boys, some white, some coffee-coloured. When they caught sight of him, they stopped and stared.

Petrella walked up to the largest boy, and said, "I wish to see your master."

The boy gaped at him. Petrella realised that, apart from his sudden appearance in the playground, his torn coat and his black hands must call for some explanation.

"I have had an accident," he said shortly.

"Perhaps I can help?" A stout man, with gold-rimmed glasses and a thick beard, was standing in the doorway.

"Might I have a word with you?" said Petrella.

"It would seem called for," agreed the man.

"In private."

"Very well. If you will follow."

They went into a small classroom.

"I observed your entrance," said the man. "My name, by the way, is Cleroux. If you do not wish to mention yours, I will not insist. I imagine that you are in some sort of trouble."

"I'm glad," said Petrella, "that you do not ask for explanations, for there is practically nothing I could explain."

"You speak French well," said Monsieur Cleroux. "But I think you are a foreigner. English, perhaps. It is the clothes more than the accent."

"Yes, English."

"I shall ask nothing. I have my school. We have all sorts of boys, as you see. I take no part in politics."

"If I could have a quick wash," said Petrella, "and get back to the more public part of the city, I should be for ever in your debt."

"Wash, certainly," said Monsieur Cleroux. "As for the

rest, you could not leave now by the front gate. It would not even be advisable for you to come to the window. From what I observe in the road, I assure you that it is so."

"I'll take your word for it," said Petrella. "Which way can I go?"

"We have an arrangement. In case of fire. You go through a window on the first floor, across the roof, and into the factory next door. We should only use it, you understand, in an emergency. Once you are in the factory, it should be possible for you to walk out without question – if you looked a little more presentable. There is a wash-basin next door."

While Petrella was cleaning his face and hands and combing his hair, Monsieur Cleroux stood behind him. He seemed suddenly nervous. "I wonder," he said, "it seems impertinent. But I wonder if you could help me."

"Of course."

"It is just that we have had arguments in the school – as to the proper word. Is it right, in England, to call the man who collects the tickets on a bus an inspector or a collector?"

Petrella explained, as best he could, the respective functions of a ticket inspector, a ticket collector, and a conductor. Monsieur Cleroux thanked him profusely.

Five minutes later, one hand in his side pocket to hold together the slit in the jacket, he was walking out of the Works Entrance of the Frambouillet Motor Accessories Factory. So far as he knew, his departure aroused no interest.

He strolled through three or four streets, going south, towards the centre of the town. At the first opportunity he went into a shop and bought himself a light, pastel linen sun jacket of a type much worn by young men about Paris that summer. The shopkeeper obligingly parcelled up his tweed jacket for him into a neat brown paper package. Petrella bought himself some sun glasses as well, and then, his mind more easy, strolled down the Rue d'Hauteville and into the Boulevard Poissonière where he picked himself a crowded café.

Most of the patrons were sitting out on the pavement under the striped awning. He went into the interior, which was nearly empty, and pleasantly cool. He settled at a table in the corner, where he could not be overlooked, took the bulky envelope from his inner pocket, and slipped the point of a table knife under the flap. For a moment, the stout manilla resisted. Then it gave with a rasping jerk, and a fold of tissue paper shot out and hit the table; and out from the folds of the tissue paper slid a little snake.

It was made of gold, and had tiny, crimson eyes. Petrella had seen snakes of a similar type before, but they had been made of larger links and were comparatively crude. This was a piece of magic, made of two or three hundred tiny interleaved plates, none of them loose, yet all of them moving freely, fitted into each other with miraculous perfection, so that the whole thin body rippled with venomous life. What it must be worth, he could not begin to imagine.

"Pretty thing," said a voice. "Buy it for your girl?" A waiter had come up. He was a big blond boy with the look of a German.

"That's right," said Petrella. He picked up the snake by its tail and slid it back into the envelope.

"I bought mine a hairclip last week," said the waiter. "It cost me three weeks' pay. The proprietor here is a pig. He pays nothing."

Petrella ordered a *fine*, drank it down quickly, and left a tip almost large enough to buy the waiter's young lady a second hairclip.

Then he went out into the street. At the door of the café, he paused for a quick look. All seemed in order. Twenty yards away, on the other side of the road, was parked an old, ivy-green Renault saloon, which had not been there when he went in. Nothing suspicious about that. Plenty of Renaults in Paris.

He crossed the road, and made for the gardens of the Palais Royal. He wanted time to think.

He was fairly clear now what had happened. He had gone to the wrong address. What he had said had been construed as a password, and he had been entrusted, by some part of the Algerian terrorist organisation, with a very valuable piece of property, probably stolen, and designed to be sold for their funds.

So much was clear.

What was far less clear was what he was going to do next.

216

He could go to the police. And tell them what? At best, be held for endless questioning. If the snake had been less valuable or less attractive, he might have pushed it down behind a seat in the Métro and left it.

In the end, he went out, bought a stamped envelope, addressed it to his great-aunt, and slipped the snake into it. He added a note, asking her to place the snake in her own bank for safekeeping, and added that he had changed his plans, and was leaving for Spain that night by the ten o'clock train.

When he had posted the envelope he felt better. A good lunch at the Ruban Bleu completed the cure. In the afternoon he walked out to the Bois de Boulogne, went off the path into a clearing in the bushes, lay on his back, and went to sleep.

He was woken by a soft thud in his stomach. He came straight out of sleep and up on his feet, ready for anything.

Standing a few paces away, staring at him, was a small girl. It was her ball which had hit him. His sudden movement had frightened the child, and she started to cry.

"There, there," said Petrella. "Do not be alarmed."

A stout lady, dressed, despite the heat of the afternoon, in a sealskin coat, arrived upon the scene, panting. She swept up the girl, like a baby seal, into her flippers and glowered at Petrella.

"I alarmed her, I am afraid," he said. "I woke up."

"Chérie does not cry because a man wakes up," said the lady. "What did you do to her?"

For the second time that day Petrella's discretion got the better of his valour. He walked rapidly off into the bushes, but not so rapidly that he did not hear the lady say, "There are men of a certain type who should not be allowed to enjoy their liberty."

He got back to the Place de la Concorde by early dusk, and chose himself a restaurant for his evening meal. His train went at ten. The change of plan would mean abandoning his reserved sleeper, but a night in a first-class railway carriage was not a great ordeal.

He had his baggage to collect from the Gare du Nord. If he allowed an hour, that should be ample. He ordered his meal with care and ate it with deep satisfaction.

It was while he was drinking his coffee and turning the

pages of his *Paris Soir* that his eye was caught by the
announcement in the Stop Press. The print was smudgy, but
the meaning was clear enough.

"Just after midday today, a party of Algerian terrorists
forced a letter-box in the Boulevard Poissonière. The affair
was elaborately organised. A heavy lorry was backed up to
the box, a grapnel inserted, and the front of the box ripped
out. The contents were collected and removed. An armed
party kept watch to prevent interference. By the time the
police arrived, those guilty of this outrage had taken
themselves off. The precise object of this latest manoeuvre of
the terrorists is not known."

Petrella felt suddenly cold.

It was not the fact that the snake was now back with its
original owners. This was rough justice. It was the thought
that, since they had known precisely which box to open, they
could never have lost sight of him for a moment.

He got up and walked to the window.

Twenty yards up the street, on the other side of the road,
was parked an ivy-green Renault saloon.

Now that danger was at his elbow, Petrella's mind worked
with clarity. Get hold of the police? Impossible, now, to
explain why he had not handed the snake over to them at
once. Get out of the restaurant and keep moving until his
train left? Their organisation was clearly better, far better,
than he had imagined. But once he was in the street, surely he
could use the cover of darkness to slip them for the few vital
hours.

He took out enough money to cover his meal, with a
generous tip, and pushed it under the plate. Then he got up,
purposely leaving his hat and paper in full view on the chair
beside him, and strolled towards the vestibule.

"Have you a telephone?" he said to the girl behind the
desk. She pointed to the far end of the hall. He walked
towards it. To the left was a side door, bolted. To the right, a
flight of stairs. At the end, a telephone booth.

At the last moment, he darted to his right, up the stairs.
The girl in the desk, who had evidently been watching, called
out after him, but he took no notice.

At the top of the stairs a corridor presented itself, closed doors on both sides. Footsteps were coming up the stairs behind him. He picked a door on the right-hand side, and went in. It was a bedroom, unoccupied, and almost unfurnished. There was a bolt on the inside of the door, and this he shot.

The only window in the room opened on to a very narrow, flat open space, ahead of which was darkness of perhaps six feet in width, and uncertain depth. Not knowing what lay below made it curiously difficult to jump.

It was a rattling on the handle of the door which launched him. He shot upwards and outwards and landed, on hands and knees, on the roof opposite. Here the going was fairly easy. He walked cautiously to the far end, lowered himself onto a sort of penthouse which stuck out into the back alley behind the restaurant, and dropped from that to the pavement.

As he picked himself up he realised the futility of his manoeuvre. His opponents were all round the building. Ten yards up the alleyway a cigarette glowed; and he heard, once again, the twittering whistle.

He turned and ran. The alley forked, and he went left at random. It was damnably dark, and in ten paces he realised that he was in a cul-de-sac. Next moment something hit him in the back, and three figures jumped at him, and he went down. He hit out blindly and went on hitting, long after he knew that it was useless.

A cloth was round his mouth, his left arm was already pinned. Strong, cruel hands were feeling for his other hand, for his nostrils, for his eyes.

Then a very bright light came on and, with explosive suddenness, a machine pistol opened fire, the bullets thudding into the wall behind them.

Like bees unclustering from a swarm at the first whiff of smoke, his assailants left him. The last to go slid his hand down, but Petrella saw the knife and had enough strength left to wrench his head back out of reach. He felt the point, like the touch of a white-hot wire, slide down the back of his head, and lodge against the collar-bone with an agonising jolt.

Then the man was gone. Petrella lay quite flat and still on the cobbles, under the bright light now centred upon him.

At no point did he completely lose consciousness. He

knew that he was being picked up, none too gently. He realised that he was being placed in the car, to which the bright light was in some way attached. And when he finally opened his eyes and sat up, it was no surprise to him to find himself sprawled in a chair in the back room of a Bureau de Police.

It was a surprise, however, to find that he recognised the man who was looking down at him.

"Commissaire," he said. "Commissaire Michel, of Bordeaux."

"Formerly of Bordeaux, now of Paris. And your name is Petrella. You are, or were, a member of the British police."

"I still am," said Petrella. "What's left of me."

"You are very lucky," said the Commissaire, "that the damage is not greater. Perhaps you would care to explain why you are tackling, single-handed and, as far as I know, unaccredited, the Algerian terrorist organisation or, perhaps I should say, private army."

"I'm on holiday," said Petrella.

"I see," said the Commissaire. "A vigorous commencement to your vacation. I would suggest that you drink this – and tell us exactly what you have been up to."

Petrella drank the proffered wine thirstily; then he talked.

Commissaire Michel said, "I re-name you The Cat. You have nine lives. How you came alive out of the Rue Antoine I cannot say. Would you mind letting me see the paper on which your compatriot wrote the young lady's address."

Petrella took out the piece of paper from his pocket and Commissaire Michel, after one glance at it, said, "It is, of course, not the Rue Antoine you wanted, but the Rue St. Antoine, in the Fourth Arrondissement. A very different street, in a very different type of district."

"And the snake?"

"As you suppose. A gift for the terrorist funds. It would, eventually, have been sold for its true value in the Rue St. Honoré – after it had passed through three or four pairs of hands. Perhaps you gave some password. Or seeing you were alone and unarmed, in a quarter where an armed patrol will penetrate only if another armed patrol is covering it – they jumped to conclusions. A messenger to take charge of the snake was expected. You arrived. Therefore you *were* the messenger. A not uncommon form of reasoning."

"They'd got it back. What were they worrying about?"

"Your crime did not lie in taking the snake. It was that you could recognise the man who had given it to you."

"I see," said Petrella. "You haven't got some more of that wine, have you? By the way, how was it that you happened to be on the spot so conveniently? I haven't really thanked you for that yet."

"We observed that the organisation was in pursuit of someone. Therefore we watched them. Can you use your arm?"

"I don't think there's anything broken."

"You understand that the man who used the knife was trying to blind you? To blind you, or mark the front of your face so deeply that you would be recognisable if you came to Paris again."

"No," said Petrella. "I didn't understand."

He realised that there was a lot that he did not understand, and would probably never understand about the secretive bitter warfare into the fringes of which he had trespassed.

"I have made arrangements," said the Commissaire, "for you to be taken by ambulance to the station. You will be put into a special sleeper, and two 'male nurses' will travel with you as far as the Spanish frontier."

He saw the look on Petrella's face, and began to laugh.

"Cheer up," he said. "Memories are not long. It would be well, I think, if you were to stay out of Paris for six months. You have an aged relative in Paris. I will arrange that she is informed – very discreetly."

"You won't shock *her*," said Petrella. "She's got no more nerves than a bull-terrier. What I was wondering – it's a great impertinence. But might one of your subordinates be able to take a letter to the Rue St. Antoine? Mademoiselle Arture will perhaps be expecting a communication."

"Of course," said the Commissaire. "In an affair of the heart, no effort must be spared."

It was two weeks later and Petrella was lying back in a long wicker chair on the verandah of the Villa Hernandez, listening to the cracked bell of the monastery on the hill, and waiting for his evening drink. When the man brought it to him, there was a letter beside it on the tray. And the envelope bore a French stamp.

It was from Commissaire Michel. It concluded, "So I dispatched one of my own men, Agent Crozier, to the Rue St. Antoine. I should judge that Mademoiselle Arture is a lady of uncommon attractions since Crozier has repeated his visit three times in the past week. I should suggest that perhaps your friend should visit Paris in person, or he may find that Mademoiselle Natalie prefers a French policeman in the flesh to an English one on paper."

He was still laughing when his father stepped on to the verandah.

"Paris is such a wonderful place," he said.